D1706722

Sea without Shores

by

Norm Gibbons

Copyright @ 2016 by Norm Gibbons

First Edition – March 2016

ISBN
978-0-9949188-1-9 (Hardcover)
978-0-9949188-0-2 (Paperback)
978-0-9949188-2-6 (eBook)

All rights reserved.

No part of this publication may be reproduced in any form, or by any means, electronic or mechanical, including photocopying, recording, or any information browsing, storage, or retrieval system, without permission in writing from the publisher.

This is a work of fiction. Names, characters, places and incidents either are the product of the author's imagination or are used fictitiously. Any resemblance to actual persons, living or dead, events or locales is entirely coincidental.

Produced by:
Salmonberry Publishing
Box 85
Mansons Landing, BC, Canada
V0P 1K0

www.salmonberry.ca

Printed by Friesens in Canada

FSC
www.fsc.org
MIX
Paper from
responsible sources
FSC® C016245

ALSO BY NORM GIBBONS

Voyage of the Arrogant

To Michael and Lisa

"I picked up a star whose tube feet ventured timidly among my fingers while, like a true star, it cried soundlessly for life. I saw it with an unaccustomed clarity and cast far out. With it I flung myself as forfeit, for the first time, into some unknown dimension of existence. From Darwin's tangled bank of unceasing struggle, selfishness and death had arisen, incomprehensibly, the thrower who loved not man, but life.... Somewhere, my thoughts persisted, there is a hurler of stars, and he walks, because he chooses, always in desolation, but not in defeat."

The Star Thrower, **Loren Eiseley**

FOREWORD

March 14, 2014

Sirs and Madam:
At your request:

Our department was commissioned by the Refuge Cove Land and Housing Cooperative Association located at Refuge Cove on West Redonda Island to make comment on a hand written document recently discovered in the uncatalogued archives of the Cortes Island Museum on Cortes Island. As you may not know, these islands are adjacent to each other, serve as the gateway to Desolation Sound Marine Park, and form part of a small archipelago at the northern tip of the Strait of Georgia on the west coast of British Columbia, Canada. Both organizations, until recently, were unknown to me.

Specifically, I was asked to make a determination on the text: whether or not the document is historically <u>accurate</u>. The budget given allowed for only a cursory examination, and the reasons for making this determination were not explained by the client.

The manuscript is contained within seventeen Key-Tab Exercise Books, informally referred to as "scribblers." They are numbered one through sixteen, the last two scribblers both assigned the number sixteen and burdened with an inordinate collection of doodles. Included, along with the scribblers, are five, unfinished, pencil sketches by an unknown artist.

After some searching, we learned that the trademark "Keystone," though now defunct, was once owned by S&L Limited, and that these exercise books were manufactured during the early 1970's. Since the time period in the "scribblers" begins September 1974 and ends November 1975, and are the approximate manufacture dates of the Keystone Key-Tabs, we are given to understand that the textual content was written at, or close to, the moments when the said events unfolded.

Strangely titled, *Sea without Shores,* on the cover of Scribbler One, the document is allegedly narrated by a Mr. Adam Wilkes, who casts himself as a self-educated recluse, jilted lover, investigative reporter, raging alcoholic, and worshipper of sunrises, though not sunsets. No authorial name is affixed in the manuscript; therefore we are unable to comment on whether the alleged narrator and/or author are one and the same. The setting occurs in the Desolation Sound region and centres in Refuge Cove. Using charts and tide tables for references, including one perfectly delightful site visit, it seems that the narrator and/or author was quite familiar with the area. However, positioning (even the existence) of certain buildings, specific points of land, questionable businesses, and exact locations of reefs were, by my reckoning, well off target. Due to these inconsistencies, and his bumptious claim to local knowledge, we harbour grave doubts that the narrator and/or author was in fact a resident in the small Refuge Cove community.

A search of tax rolls, electoral lists, post box numbers, bank records from no longer existing financial institutions, criminal records, and personal interviews on both Cortes and West Redonda Islands reveals that no Adam Wilkes ever existed. In interviews with former residents of Refuge Cove – few live there now - no person remembers Mr. Wilkes. Nor do they recognize the names of any of the characters in the document. Nor do they remember any of the events that allegedly took place within the community, although one resident, who wishes to preserve her anonymity, vaguely remembers a "bearbeque," as briefly mentioned in Scribbler One. Another resident, who took an inordinate interest in the manuscript, but read only a few chapters due to legibility issues, wondered how the writer could actually know what people dream, and asked, rather perceptively, "Was the writer psychic?"

Though one can never be sure about such things, when a researcher like myself encounters a *Sea without Shores*, a man who flies, pens that write by themselves, and dogs and trees that speak, then one is inclined to conclude that the document in question seems the workings of a chaotic and confused mind. To be generous, the "scribblers" might be viewed as the earliest of drafts. Perhaps, an edited version exists. We would therefore recommend further searches into the uncatalogued archives of the museum.

Returning to the specific request in our commission, with few reservations, the manuscript is historically <u>inaccurate</u>.

We trust this information satisfies your inquiry.

Regards and best wishes,

Dr. Edward E. Edwards, Professor Emeritus,
Humber School of Creative & Performing Arts
Toronto, Ontario
Canada

Table of Contents

The Refuge Cove Community

James and Nicole Mason – *Storekeepers*
Children: Wade (11) Tara (9) Dog: Angel

Peter and Laura Baxter – *Seafarmer and School Teacher*
Child: Charlotte (7)

Liam and Kathleen Black – *Salal Pickers*
Child: Sarah (9) Cat: Felix-the-Cat

Jack and Vivian Smith – *Shellfish Pickers*
Children: Twins, Mary and Elizabeth (9) Cat: Winifred

Brad and Jim Jenzen – *Sons of Captain Perry Jenzen (deceased) of the Arrogant*

Maddie Archer – *Logging Camp, Lewis Channel, Aunt to Jenzen Brothers*

Adam Wilkes – *Recluse, storyteller, contemporary of Captain Perry Jenzen*

Alice – *Widow, Elder*

MacLeod – *Bachelor, Elder*
Dog: Son of Moocho

Jeremy – *Log Salvager*
Dog: Moocho

Sylvia – *Widow, Witch*

Heinrik – *Entrepreneur*
Dog: Pemah

Sebastian – *Seafarm caretaker, birdman*
Dog: De Gaulle

Calvin – *Handyman*

Carver – *MacLeod's nephew, newcomer*

Bruce Harris – *Bachelor, Resident of Savary Island*
Dog: Buster

Duende – *No man's dog, Every man's dog*

~ 1 ~

Subterfuge

"Dogs do speak, but only to those who know how to listen."

My Name is Red, **Orhan Pamuk**

ADAM WROTE: *"I have always been of an inferior race."* The recluse closed his daily journal and looked out the cabin window.

Dawn fog slowly tumbled from the lagoon and over the still waters of Refuge Cove. He watched the fog drift across Lewis Channel and careen against the opposing shore of Cortes Island, where it broke into lesser lumps of mist and ether.

He sipped his tea.

Soon the sun crested the hills behind The Refuge and bathed the small community in modest warmth and fall light.

A blue fibreglass canoe sliced over the water approaching the northern shore where Adam lived. Wade paddled from the stern, and two dogs, Duende and Angel, jostled for lookout at the bow. As the boat glided closer, Duende curled his upper lip and nipped at Angel's ear, but she refused to concede her pre-eminent position.

In anticipation, Adam walked down to the beach and took up his position on a surf-tumbled log. He heard Wade's words drifting across the water, "Settle down up there." Though a boy, the dogs heed him, knowing they can push their eagerness only so far.

Adam waved to the boy. By way of response, Wade interrupted his rhythm and lifted the paddle. Angel – an unadulterated Labrador - shuddered and whined, hardly able to contain her excitement, and Duende nipped at her ear again.

The canoe bow gently crunched on the pebbled shore, and the sea gave the tiniest licks at the land. "No," the boy warned the dogs, "not yet." Wade maneuvered the boat so that it rested broadside to the shoreline. He gave the "OK," and Angel exploded from the bow. Within seconds she greeted the recluse with enough slather, tail whips, and wet paws to convince, not only him, but also the ocean, bluffs, and trees that he was the most beloved personage on the planet. By way of contrast, Duende vacated the bow with the dignity of a pompous arsehole, careful not to get one claw of one pad of one paw wet. The mutt scooted down the beach feigning an interest in harassing two seagulls.

The boy reached under the center thwart. "Dad asked me to bring your supplies."

"Lucky guy. You get an extra recess."

"Our second this morning."

"I thought as much when I saw the girls dancing on the dock."

Adam held the gunnel to avoid a mishap, and Wade stepped out of the canoe carrying a heavy cardboard box. They sat on the log while Angel sniffed the contents. Inside, Adam found seven mickeys of scotch, a can of Vogue tobacco, matches, cigarette papers, two squat bottles of indigo ink, page size blotters, twelve Key-Tab scribblers, an old weekend edition of the Vancouver Sun, and a large bundle of Heinrik's venison jerky. Then he saw a small parcel from the Parker pen company addressed to Mr. Adam Wilkes, General Delivery, Refuge Cove, British Columbia, Canada.

"Will you start to write now, Mr. Wilkes?" Wade asked.

"No excuses, I guess."

The boy pointed at the scribblers, "Dad got you the fat ones."

"Just as I ordered," said Adam, as he thumbed through the blank pages.

"Everyone says you've got tons of stories."

"That's all they leave you with."

He gave the boy a jerky, tore off a piece for Angel, and another for Duende, who had now decided to join the party.

"Will the stories be about here or Cortes?" Wade asked.

"Whatever pops into my head."

"Tara says you know everything about everything."

"A slight exaggeration."

"She wants you to remember as far back as you can."

"Tell your sister the stories won't be about remembering."

Wade didn't quite understand that last comment, and the aspiring storyteller didn't care to continue the discussion, as he had no desire to capture the past in a Reader's Digest genre. The stories he had in mind would be more in the style of investigative journalism, but with a touch of invention for those times when certainties became illusive. In other words, and in heroic fashion too, much like the cub, Washington Post reporters, Bob Woodward and Carl Bernstein, who broke the Watergate scandal, Adam would use the pen rather than the sword to plumb the depths for truth, or whatever else might hide down there.

Wade took a drawing from inside his jacket and handed it to Adam. "This is for your calendar."

Adam looked at the drawing and immediately recognized the *L.O.Larson*, a tug that pulled out of Teakerne Arm.

"She's low in the water."

"Dad fuelled her yesterday and put 3108 gallons in the bow tank."

"That trimmed her nicely."

"The *L.O.* will be good for September."

"September's a busy month for pulling booms. I'll paste it over a stupid prairie wheat field."

The solitary man had often imagined that the boy knew how

to draw even before he saw his first boat. He suspected that this creative aptitude came from Wade's mother, Nicole, whose watercolours – primarily local flora and fauna – were remarkably accurate and beautiful. He feared though, that this skill, more likely the sensitivity accompanying his rare gift, would leave him vulnerable in the flight through life.

"By December," Wade boasted, "you'll have the best boats on the coast."

"What ship will October be?"

"Maddie's *Tom Forge.*"

"The *Forge* has special meaning for me."

"How come?"

"You'll have to wait for the stories now won't you."

Wade looked back at the dock and said, "The girls stopped twirling. I better go."

He and Angel climbed into the canoe, and Adam helped them shove off. Apparently, Duende wanted to extend his visit. As they pulled away, Adam commented, "When I watch you shoot baskets in front of the freight shed, I see the ball bounce before I hear it."

"That's because sound goes way slower than light."

HIS KITCHEN nook consisted of a wrap-around wooden bench and Arborite table. The chrome legs looked indestructible and ugly. His altered calendar hung on an easily accessible patch of wall where the story fabricator could make his daily entries: sunless days, moonless nights, temperature readings, boat traffic, bird sightings, reminders, clever witticisms, and on and on.

He took down the calendar. The August drawing that Wade had given him a month ago revealed the self-dumping log barge, *Island Forester*, which Adam had crewed on for many years. He flipped to September, opened his bottle of Lepage's paste, and brushed the glue over the prairie wheat field. He positioned the *L.O. Larson* over top and pressed it down. He scribbled a note in the September 1 square: *white raven, Maddie's Forge.*

His Key-Tabs waited in a neat pile aligned with the corner of the table. The new fountain pen, recently filled despite shaky hands, had been christened, Parker. The indigo inkbottles, now known as Indiga One and Indiga Two, anticipated their glee in consigning truth to immortality. As added insurance, his page-size blotters guaranteed that the edges of truth would remain crisp and clear.

He still used older forms of technological advancement, ill at ease with the ballpoint pen and the wasteful notion of one-time use. The smooth quiet glide upset him too. To be sure, the raucous scratch of a nib across a page confirmed progress, much like a baptism to an entirely new emotion, which could dilate the eye, so that for an instant only, the writer clearly witnessed the daemons shaking Time's hours and minutes before falling off the planet. And would not a pause to refill Parker with Indiga's juices allow the writer to re-consider headway, the opportunity to lance the sprouting of boils and blisters from past transgressions?

Already he had started the undertaking by numbering his scribblers one through twelve, not a prodigious beginning, but a beginning nonetheless. Twelve months for those who believed that time was worth counting. Twelve steps (Adam – firmly planted on step one) for those who kept alive a history with intoxication. Twelve disciples for those who lusted after magical tongues of fire and their many voices. A jury of twelve for those who held steadfast faith in justice. And twelve Stations of the Cross (mistake, there're fourteen) for those who loved to suffer. If he became flamboyant, which certainly seemed a possibility, James stocked more ink and scribblers in his general store.

The aspiring, pen-pusher kept his writing paraphernalia close at hand in the event that a change in the weather, a strange boat entering the harbour, a community member failing to conceal their innermost desire, or a bolt of lightning splaying his toes, might provoke inspiration. His favourite spot at the table faced the window. Often, Duende sat on a cushion beside him. Through the gap on Centre Island, man and dog could see the small community of Seaford on Cortes Island where Adam had been born. From their shared perspective, the pair saw all of The Refuge and could watch the boat traffic in Lewis Channel too.

They drank their tea, or scotch, Adam from his chosen cup, and Duende from his best-loved saucer, which the man's best friend easily reached with his elastic tongue. If ever sloppy, the diligent dog mopped the splashes from the table and licked the drips hanging from his chops. Adam never had to concern himself with the waste of precious liquids.

To be clear, the alpha male was not Adam's dog. Rather, everyman's dog. Or, no man's dog. The decision always Duende's. The pooch arrived, or departed, when least expected. He approached during beautiful sunsets, as Adam brushed his remaining teeth, or when he concentrated on splitting the thinnest sticks of dry, cedar kindling, but rarely when the scriber held a pen. Often the dog went AWOL on days when Adam felt particularly alone. He doubted that Duende fully comprehended that stark emotion of abandonment, or why, even without a pressing need for the long journey into desolation, humans were attracted to that forsaken place.

Unquestionably, his sole companion was the quintessence of the agreeable canine. Two hands high. Hazel-brown eyes. Broad head. Well-sprung ribs. Short, coarse, black hair – a little too oily for Adam's liking – but waterproof nonetheless. The beast bore the countenance of a saint, though that was a deception, which the mutt often used to his advantage. He was a good swimmer with webbed paws, but only when other means of locomotion were lacking. He wore proudly and honourably a small, white heraldic over his chest, displayed with the aplomb of a retired general. His muzzle showed as grizzled grey, suggesting inevitable decline, yet even so, Duende remained agile on the trails and frisky when he and Adam roughhoused. If excited, the Heinz 57 produced long strings of drool - wet, messy, and socially unacceptable.

Adam thought of Duende (his patronymic during seriously introspective moments) as the mendicant on the move. Doo-Doo (the name he hated most) held low regard for the other dogs in the bay, though he had a grudging tolerance for Angel. Canines in The Refuge could be counted on one hand: Duende, Angel, Moocho, Son of Moocho and De Gaulle. Oh dear, another mistake, we forgot Pemah so two hands were required. Felines outnumbered community members by a factor of ten to one, and they shall remain nameless except for a few pampered pets, such as Winifred and Felix-the-Cat. Seagulls persisted as Duende's greatest hate, one can presume because they - not he - enjoyed the freedom of flight.

Other non-humans lived in these backwaters too. One old, black bear (the community scourge). Honey bees (fireweed pollinators). A mangy, malnourished cougar (the cat culler). Eagles (overlords of the sky). Deer (tick ridden), mink (scarce, though a family lived under Alice's house), beaver (in the Lagoon, where they smacked their tails, woke the dead, and watched clandestine meetings of the living), rats (in the freight shed), flying squirrels (nearly extinct), flying ants (only on the first hot day of summer), boring flightless squirrels (chatter boxes), dexterous raccoons (nocturnal garbage eaters), common river otters (who spent most of their time in the sea just like their flippered and lush pelted cousins, eating crabs, urchins, perch, and banana peels), and a lone, omega wolf that howled into the darkening nights from the high bluffs overlooking The Refuge.

One never had to worry about stepping on Duende's messes, which was a constant worry in the summer with the appearance of rhinestoned, poofed, and yappy tourist dogs off the yachts - mostly poodles and Pomeranians. The other day, using his binoculars, Adam saw him smoothly release three, hard stools while straddling two sections of dock. Clean as a whistle. Three quiet splashes gratefully accepted by the sea. Without exception, the community conceded that a clean dog would always be welcome.

Duo (the children liked that name best) made daily rounds of the homes in The Refuge and spent the nights wherever a warm fire burned, and wherever scraps from a delicious dinner were served along with informing conversation. As well, he patrolled the docks and whined until the vessel owners invited him aboard for an aperitif and mouth watering hors d'oeuvres. The tugs coming in to refuel had become his favourites. The crews fed him packages of wieners, thick slices of bologna, and charred T-bone steaks until his hairless gut gathered splinters from the planks on the dock. They encouraged him to shake a paw, or roll over and play dead, but he always refused, though Adam now realized from experience that the little critter knew all these tricks and more.

A sailboat had abandoned him when a pup, and his owners never returned to reclaim their pet. One wonders, upon seeing the splendours in The Refuge, had Duende quickly decided in his juvenile, doggy way to reject the gypsy life, rather than stow on the next vessel leaving the harbour?

The hound began speaking to our solitary man a few months earlier – a rich, born-to-rule, baritone voice coming from one so small. The recluse didn't question this unusual phenomenon, though he perceptively chalked up the event to his hermitic existence. At the time of their first chat, Duende arrived riding on a wind, as in a fairy tale, or so Adam had hallucinated, but that fancy must be dispelled, and given over to the distortion of wisdom in a glass, which moments earlier, he had energetically emptied into his blood stream.

In any event, company was company.

When Adam thought back on the pleasant colloquies they'd shared over the last months, at the very least, he took delight in finally having someone to talk to: they engaged in highbrow, philosophical debates (unfortunately, the dog had no idea who the hell Heidegger and Nietzsche were); and then a whole week of psychological digressions on the verifiable sources of emotion (there again, the pooch had little to offer except to say, "Watch my tail."); and they spent a two-mickey, all-nighter bleating their confessions – the dog's, brief and without shame, and the hermit's, laughably long and more to do with regret than repentance. Unfortunately, no saviour appeared to grant absolution and dole out the necessary penance.

Strangely, on that debaucherous night, these bits of remorse edged their way to the surface when the man explained to the dog that the name, *Strait of Georgia,* was nothing more than British hubris insulting the ear, whereas he much preferred *Salish Sea,* which the indigenous folks promoted as a substitute. Despite that superlative alternative, our budding scribe had boasted a third option, *Sea without Shores.*

When Duende wisely asked, "A sea without shores, why such a breach in logic?" Adam gave a long-winded justification, not because he's a verbose son of a bastard, but simply because at the time, alcohol compelled his tongue to waggle in self-reproach and the guilt of a lifetime. "My own preference," he said, while rolling his fourteenth cigarette of the evening, "had its genesis in a moment of youthful bliss. The absurd notion arrived as I toppled out of my workboat and splashed into the sea, following an all night party, no longer aware that a brew of scotch, rye, vodka, and a dozen beers should manifest an extraordinary feeling of fear rather than the levity engulfing my soul. Given the circumstances, that this sudden prospect of danger should – but didn't – take sovereignty over all other emotions, second thoughts did raise serious objections. As I clawed at a cold December ocean, and as the vital juices rushed from my heart into my brain, the unorthodox thought gnawed, to be precise, at a spot in the left temporal lobe, where a state of curiosity could still magically blossom; that is to say, I wondered if I had chanced upon a *Sea without Shores.* Fortunately, before this dream of life ended, Captain Perry Jenzen grabbed me by the collar and hauled me - like a stubborn, tail-slapping, white-bellied, and eye-migrating halibut - into his fish boat. I never returned the favour."

"Who's this Captain you speak of?" the intrigued canine asked.

"You want to use the past tense my little pet. He was a good friend, who killed himself and others. "

IT MAY be due to Duende's influence that Adam has made a commitment to fill the scribblers with his fabrications. As Adam now looks for a favour from the dog, he asked the following question already knowing the answer.

A: I call you Duende, but others call you, Do, Duo, Doo-Doo, or Do-End. Which name do you prefer?

D: Duende.

A: Did you say, Duende?

D: I don't like repeating myself.

Adam threw the four-legger a chunk of jerky.

A: Fine. I thought as much. Nicknames can be endearing at times, but on other occasions, disrespectful. Don't you agree?

Adam threw him another jerky.

A: I plan a number of vignettes about life, death, and sex in The Refuge, perhaps a sojourn to Cortes Island and Desolation Sound on occasion, and find myself bereft of essential details. Would it behoove you to lend an assist?

No answer.

The soon-to-be scrawler on scribblers downed his scotch, and that lubricant induced a thought to whizz by: The mongrel enjoys my begging.

A: Seeing as you have access to all homes here, it would be easy to gather the information required. People would be completely unsuspecting, as they could never imagine that you understand the talk of humans.

Adam threw him another jerky.

A: I'm asking you in particular, because the other dogs in The Refuge have less than two brain cells to share between them, and that certainly is not the case for you, as I have come to realize during the challenging chinwags we've had over the last weeks and months.

D: You want me to spy.

A: That's not a pleasant way to put it, Duende.

D: It may not be pleasant, but I know the truth when I smell it. Is it not the case that you wish for me to scratch on the community's scabs and sores?

A: In a manner of speaking, yes, and I enjoy your use of metaphor, but more simply, all I want is for you to report any heart-to-heart of interest, although if you have access to their dreamworld that would be a bonus. At the very least, if I'm to fill these pages and give the needed exercise to Parker, I'll require a modest foundation of fact. You must assuredly grasp that the blanks in my imagination have taken on the properties of an empty universe.

Adam sipped on his scotch.

Doo-Doo jumped down from his cushion and looked up at Adam.

D: I'm not interested.

A: Just a few tidbits. Then the stories'll write themselves.

The dog trotted to the door and gave a few customary scratches. Adam opened the door and heaved his last jerky onto the welcome mat. The dog inhaled the treat and ran off with his flaccid tail signalling discontent.

A: Start with the bear. How come I hear rifle shots every night?

① Refuge —

Each time the Rasputin tape ended with "they shot him until he was dead, Oh, those Russians!" Jeremy raced for the re-wind button.

During those potentially painful moments of silence, as the community feared the ~~emotion~~ frenzied emotion might sputter and die, while the tape raced back to its beginning, "There was a certain man in Russia long ago," and never regain the heights of the previous moment, Carver came to the rescue - to the surprise of all - who knew every word in the long-story-song, and kept the passions ~~this~~ flowing during the hiatus, leading his followers with "Ra-Ra-Rasputin, Russia's greatest love machine~~s~~ it was a shame how he carried on." Then, the children answered, since they had ~~me~~ memorized the lyrics much quicker and ~~more~~ thoroughly than the adults: "Ra Ra Rasputin, There was a cat that really was gone," and the enthusiasm forced the adults to join the chorus ~~too~~, with Carver clapping his hands and ~~stomping~~ his feet, shouting another two lines, "most people looked at~~s~~ him with terror and Fear!"

~ 2 ~

Chair In The Sky

"It seemed to him that something, he didn't know what, was beginning; had already begun. It was like the last act on a set stage. It was the beginning of the end of something, he didn't know what except that he would not grieve."

The Bear, **William Faulkner**

Scribbler One:

HEINRIK ENCOUNTERED bear scat while he blazed a new trail to nowhere. In the dark of night, Laura and Peter heard "the thing" maul their compost pile for its newest treasure. The Smiths found their paint cans smashed open and the paint spilled over their back porch and down the rocks leaving a dilemma for Nature to reconcile blue moss with pink tree roots. Jeremy's outhouse got knocked down because of the off-stew he had thrown in the hole. "It" smashed through Sylvia's garden fence in two different places and left waste to six rows of late corn. She cursed the beast; nevertheless, her invocation only served to make him bolder. Calvin discovered his eight-hundred-foot plastic waterline chewed apart in fourteen places, and, as luck would have it, he was out of connectors and hose clamps. While on a recent outing with their teacher, Laura, the six school children heard grunting and groaning in a valley behind the old orchard. Not an apple remained on a tree. The salal gatherers refused to work in the bush, and even the shellfish pickers, now that the night tides had returned, felt skittish, hearing it wander the intertidal shores, clanking, pawing, and crunching clams, oysters, and crabs. Somebody had to stand up for the Wild and it sure looked like the bear got the job.

The storekeeper, James, went to the Black's cabin to feed Felix-the-Cat, because the couple, along with their daughter Sarah, had gone to visit their parents in Vancouver, and he, the busiest man in The Refuge, got stuck with the chore. Until the bear ransacked the Black's cabin, no one believed the animal would break into a home.

As James and the dogs approached, he saw one board from the front door clinging to the doorjamb. The others were scattered in splintery dismemberment over the porch floor. A twenty pound bucket of bulk peanut butter lay ravaged and squashed – the contents no more – except for the odd brown streak, which Felix-the-Cat licked clean, as James, Angel, and Duende entered the house.

Broken jars and ripped boxes were strewn across the kitchen and side-pantry floors. A fine dusting of whole-wheat flour covered the walls and ceilings, as if a diligent behemoth had gone over the surfaces with an extra-sized powder puff. Crushed tins lay punctured everywhere. Apparently, a large spike, teeth, or claws had stabbed repeatedly through each container, and then the contents sucked dry. Shards of plates and glasses covered the surfaces of the counters and cupboards. The bear had ripped the curtains from the windows, shattered windowpanes, and smeared strawberry jam over the stove and stove pipe. It had devoured an entire case of six-inch candles except for a few waxy stubs. Untouched, the braided garlic hung on a beam, but a mishmash of spices plugged the sink. Kerosene odour from broken lamps contaminated the air.

That afternoon the community turned out to clean and board up the cabin. They scrubbed and disinfected. They dug a hole behind the Black's home and buried the useless bits and pieces. Peter, from the seafarm, suggested that anything in need of repair should go to the store's workshop. A group of men hauled down broken drawers, tables, chairs, and window frames. They agreed to have a work bee to mend the damaged items at a later date. The widow, Sylvia, suggested that the women assemble next day at her house to sew curtains and wash the sheets and blankets. She volunteered to organize a collection of canned goods and dry staples for the Black's return.

James, Nicole, and the dogs walked home after the clean up. Nicole had hardly spoken a word all day, though she had worked hard with the others to bring back the cabin to a pristine condition. James' wife had barely spoken to him during the last few weeks.

As they tread the trails, in an effort to ferret out the reason for her "silent treatment," James recalled a recent quarrel about electricity, and wondered if that small tiff were the reason. She had requested, politely of course, that he install switches on the walls rather than have impractical and unsightly pull cords dangling from each bare bulb. Nicole had demonstrated how she needed to jump and grab the one in the living room. He remembered laughing. Then she requested that they run their own generator continuously, or, "here's a better thought," why not hook directly to the store's big generator so they could have a freezer, fridge, and electric heaters. She wanted the luxury of flicking a light switch anytime, hot water on demand, and heat from any source other than the old wood heater and stove. Nicole claimed the logs he used in building the house were far too dark, and that it seemed like night even during the day. "Living in this cave makes me crazy." His wife had asked for all the pleasures of modern conveniences, and didn't think these requests out of line.

James had explained in a nicer way that he had no intention of making the Arabs happy by burning unnecessary fuel in the generator, pull chains worked fine (he could lengthen the one that was too short, which he had done the next day), appliances weren't really necessary with the store's facilities right there, and colour was colour when it came to logs.

Only a few tears had trickled down her cheek on that occasion. But those were tears from the past.

Later that evening, after the couple put Wade and Tara to bed, they quarrelled again. Usually the husband and wife fought at night when they were sure the children slept, never in front of the community with its turned-up ear, and always following weeks of pent-up feelings and targeted silences.

Nicole started the fight. "I'm leaving with Tara and Wade."

Her voice woke James, who had been napping on the couch. He sat up quickly, as did Angel and Duende, who were sleeping in their favourite spot behind the wood heater.

As he considered various replies to her declaration of departure, Nicole got up from her chair and walked to the kitchen. He presumed to make tea. The making of tea would signal that the fight would last longer than the one over electricity. Similar rituals had evolved during their twelve years of marriage, and both parties respected the fragile arrangement. He still, however, could not forgive her for waking him from his snooze.

As she walked into the kitchen, he answered her threat to leave with a gush of one word questions, "When?" then louder "Where?" and then he shrieked "Why?"

He fought an urge to rise from his chair, rush into the kitchen, grab her by the shoulders, shake her like a rag doll, and shout through a spray of saliva only inches from her face. Perhaps if it had not been so late at night, when, as everyone knew, the powers of judgment and restraint were lessened, then his thoughts would have been more controlled. Alarmed at his outburst - that feelings had nearly become actions - James looked up at the loft to hear if he had woken the children with the rising crescendo in his voice. He assumed Nicole did the same. Angel gave a moan, as if she understood the new emotion stifling the air. Duende sniffed the air and moved to the kitchen doorway so that he might have a better view.

As the silence persisted in the kitchen, James took advantage of the quiet and guessed the answer to "When?" – that would be tomorrow. And the answer to "Where?" – that would be her parents in Victoria. He should have just asked, "Why?"

He reconstructed what had taken place so far and rationalized, I only raised my voice so that my wife might clearly hear.

James assumed that her threat to leave with Tara and Wade had not been blurted out, but rehearsed during the last weeks. Otherwise she would have said more; she would have spoken more extravagantly, giving a medley of reasons for her decision.

An incident had occurred two days earlier, and he connected it to their intended departure. He had passed by Alice's house on the boardwalk and overheard Nicole and Alice through the widow's kitchen window. Nicole said, "Life...my life...could have been..." and then something about "choices made," and Alice's reply, "Yes, yes, dear, it's ... for all women." The blanks in the conversation had bothered him. James felt embarrassed about his eavesdropping, but the more he had thought, the more he became angered that Nicole and Alice shared such an intimacy. As in a simple equation, the computation went: closeness to others necessarily lessened closeness to himself. A plus B equalled less C.

Now, faced with Nicole's ultimatum, James walked to the kitchen doorway. The water boiled on the Coleman burner, and Nicole watched it carefully. He knew nothing further would be said until the tea had steeped and been poured. He felt more at ease knowing that they would settle into an established pattern. He felt more at ease, because he was alert, or so he thought, to nuances missed earlier. James patted Duende on the head and scratched behind his ear.

Nicole had wandered into his life on a sunny summer day fourteen years ago. She had arrived with her parents on the *Saga,* and while they polished the brass on their fifty-five-foot, Chris-Craft yacht, she inhabited the fishing tackle section in the general store. The attractive woman filled the air with questions about whether or not to use a number four-and-a-half Tom Mack, or one of those "great big fives," maybe half brass and half chrome, or just straight chrome, "What do you think would be best?" Then she wanted to know how deep to troll, and should she use one of those "new fancy dodgers," and what size weight, "eight or ten ounce" or even heavier, what pound test line, how fast to troll, what would be the best reel to use – a shower of incessant questions. He had to come over from the cash register and ignore other customers, but she sighed so sweetly with each decision to make, and as her questions floated off her moist, red lips, his eyes fastened upon her pale white throat colouring quickly with cherry blotches, and lower down, he watched her chest heaving in fierce anticipation. Feeling obliged, James had to take her on the night bite after work and show her how to catch a salmon off Production Point.

During the winter they exchanged letters. For the first time, mail day became as important to him as it was to the rest of the community: her letters, entirely poetic (he attributed her expressive powers to a university education), on blue and scented paper, describing his world – trees, water, wind, and wild life – things he took for granted, in a way that caused him to stop and study intently what he saw, though the shopkeeper should have been replacing a rotten boardwalk or some other nonsense job. And Nicole enclosed little watercolours of wildflowers she had done herself. James didn't recognize the Latin names, but he did recognize the flowers. He had never before known an artist.

His letters, on scribbler sheets, had described problems with machines – rings, pistons, commutators, spark plug gaps, and head warp. Rarely was he able to express his own dreams and ambitions, but somehow he must have said enough to bring their destinies together. When the *Saga* headed home the following summer, Nicole stayed behind. Her parents thought she was only playing a temporary and rebellious game, which they called "a silly phase." When the lovers had married, James was certain their thirst for passion would never quench.

She poured the boiling water into the preheated teapot.

As the tea slowly steeped, she said, "Tomorrow!" then louder, "Parents!" and even louder, "Frightened!"

Those answers were out of keeping with James' expectations. She was not supposed to speak until they both huddled over their teacups. He had almost forgotten his questions. Her loud staccato mimic came back more terse, more mad, and more hurt than answers from previous fights.

James let time pass.

They both liked strong tea.

She put out cookies - a good sign. She gave a cookie to Duende and one to Angel, who had now come into the kitchen too. Nicole's movements seemed poky, but still deliberate. She grew more beautiful the longer James looked.

He reckoned that the presence of the bear had caused her to distort the very nature of The Refuge, as though it had somehow become a menacing place. He could see how she might think that worse things were possible. They sat down at the kitchen table, and Nicole poured the tea.

"A bear's not going to come into a house if it's occupied."

That's how he started, the beginning the hardest part. He told her everything he knew about bears and nature and wildlife. It occurred to him that if he could get rid of her fears, then he would be rid of his own. As James spoke, he saw that their fight would gradually settle into something gentle and familiar. She turned the gold band on her wedding finger. By telling her everything, and languishing in the details, and by recalling some of their best family memories, James found he could extend this moment of peace.

Their misunderstanding opened slowly like a magnolia blossom – white, sweet, and lime scented.

He said the bear would head for the mainland as soon as the salmon started up the rivers – "Any day now." He explained how frightened even he could get in the city – "It depends on what you're used to." He assured her many times that she had nothing to fear - "You're safe. The children are safe."

It took time for the petals to unfold.

She stirred and stirred her tea, and when he couldn't stand it any longer, he said, "You're stirring your hair in your tea."

She squeezed it dry.

A liquid pearl from the corner of her eye splashed on the table. He had seen this before, sadness and beauty woven into a fine tapestry.

The more he talked, the more she cried.

GEESE HONKED south in long trailing vees marking the change in season. Fall shadows lengthened. Eagles abandoned their nests and congregated at rivers for the great salmon feast. Alders and maples disrobed, leaving their limbs to hide the blue sky. Noisy, leaf-littered trails announced the footsteps of passers-by.

By now the bear should have made its way to the mainland and swum from island to island; it should not have been on West Redonda Island, and certainly not in The Refuge. While awaiting the salmon on their final journey, bears were supposed to be ripping grubs from old hemlock logs and working the late berries over-hanging the shaded riverbanks. Was not the time approaching to bask in a winter of animal stupor?

Following the "Black Attack," people heard rifle reports in the middle of the night, and, if they looked out their windows, saw flashlight beams slashing through the trees. Then the community members held impromptu meetings at dark scenes, only to learn that the beast got away one more time.

Soon the bear discovered the beehives.

"Mein Gott," Heinrik said a hundred times on that upsetting day.

The people called the hives, "Heinrik's Condos," and they loved "Herr Heinrik's Honey," the "3H" brand. His hives on the hill above James' house had been four-tiered upon the bear's arrival. Now the waxed frames lay scattered over a trampled and tortured moss. Contingents of upset bees made repair attempts. Portions of honeycomb lay about, the honey eaten. Drones, slow on assessing the nature of the dilemma, and unaware of the futility in their actions, guarded the bottom entrances to the tiers while the tops were open to the sky with workers coming and going freely. Opportunistic ants had located the debris, and the bee colony had to fight a rear-guard action.

James found the queen excluder. An immense bee-ball massed on it, and he presumed the queen safe. Heinrik spent the rest of the morning bringing new supplies and repairing the hives. He would have to feed them sugar water to overwinter too late in the season for the colony to recover from the tragedy. His dog, Pemah, yapped the entire day.

Heinrik conceived a plan of revenge with an assist from James. In the afternoon, they spiked a long ladder made from long poles and two-by-four rungs to an old fir snag near the hives. They fabricated and fastened a comfortable chair at the top. Though James had larger worries, he agreed to take the night shift, more from an inability to say no than his strong sense of community responsibility. Certainly, he held no conviction that the plan was sound.

Heinrik said the early shift, "a precaution only," would be James' since he was a family man. Shooting from the chair would be, "Easy." The beekeeper assured the storekeeper that the bear would not appear until after midnight, well after James' shift had ended.

Around the dinner table, James described the plan to his wife and children.

"It's almost certain the bear will return. Heinrik and I will take shifts. Shooting from the chair in the sky should be easy."

"That's a stupid plan, Dad," commented Tara.

He cited preparations and precautions they had taken and only partly reassured his family when he said his shift would finish at eleven o'clock, and then Heinrik would take the chair for the rest of the night. He emphasized that the bear stirred troubles after midnight, as everyone knew. He repeated "after midnight" three more times. Most likely his words had worn thin, diminished by over usage. Obediently, they ate their meal like monks in a monastery, steadfast in their oath of silence, broken only by the tinks of knives, forks, and spoons; the rustling of napkins, the occasional scrape of a chair leg on the floor when someone moved, and the loud tick-tick-tocking of the eight-day windup clock, which woke Angel and Duende on their mat behind the wood heater. The dogs cocked their ears and tilted their heads, trying to extract meaning from the remainder of time.

James skipped dessert and cleaned his 30-30 with the 4X scope. He experimented taping different flashlights in different ways to the barrel – bottom, sides, and top. He settled on the green "six-volter" and secured it to the barrel with windings of electrician's tape. He attached the flashlight in such a way that he could still see the metal sites beneath the scope. I've got options, he assured himself.

A week earlier, on a mail day, James had participated in a discussion in the store on how to rig a rifle for night use. Some said scopes were useless in the dark. The seafarmer, Peter, confirmed that point, by citing examples from his youthful hunting adventures. Others, who thought everyone had dispensed with the scope idea, said to mount the flashlight so that it shone on the metal sights, and forget about lighting the target. Jeremy, a log salvager with many opinions, and a reputation as a successful pitlamper, one of those people who perennially goes in the Out, and out the In, a man forever in motion, exhibiting migratory unrest during all four seasons, disagreed, and recommended the light be mounted to shine directly at an imagined target, no more than "thirty yards max."

James' rigging method ignored the advice given.

He put a new battery and bulb in his flashlight and tested the on-off switch. The flashlight made the gun feel heavy, clumsy, and off balance, not the light lever-action he was used to. As James made his preparations, Wade and Tara quietly started their homework. Nicole rattled the dishes in the kitchen.

Once, he said to her, "The whole community's under siege," perhaps forgetting her fears expressed from the day before, or perhaps regaining his sense of community responsibility. Nicole stared out the window over the kitchen sink with nothing to see except her own reflection against a blackening night. She coiled the ends of her hair with soapy fingers.

Later, he beseeched, "I can't do nothing."

That was when Nicole broke her silence.

"I know why you're doing this James – *you* think this is how *you* can stop us."

He didn't like the way she put emphasis on *you* – both times. He assumed the children were in on the plan. He read more into her flare-up than may have been necessary. Now it was evident, at least to him, an exit strategy had been working inside her head even before the bear made its appearance. His mind so completely distorted her outburst, that no matter what he did, or whatever happened, it was a foregone conclusion that nothing could stop her from leaving. This new perspective on his wife made him think of the bear as a precursor to a far greater menace, even though he had no idea what that might be.

James took extra ammunition and an extra flashlight. He dressed in layers of wool not wanting to be shivery, if, though extremely unlikely, he had to shoot. He laced his newly soled Kodiak boots, put four of Nicole's oatmeal, raisin, and carob cookies in his jacket breast pocket, and shoved a stick of Heinrik's father's special pepperoni sausage (deer and pig) in his hip pocket. James instructed Wade to make sure Angel and Duende didn't get out. Tara watched from the stairway to the loft. He gave his wife an aimless kiss and said, "I'm doing it not why you think."

And she replied, "You don't know what I think."

He patted the dogs on their heads and left. The hike to the beehive site took five minutes. He climbed the ladder to the chair in the sky with the same confidence of any man going off to work nightshift. The view would have been spectacular in the daylight.

The night cooled quickly, and the pale hives against the waning light looked helpless. James' fingers numbed, as he gripped the blued barrel of his rifle. He'd forgotten to bring gloves. He hung his gun over the arm of the chair and tucked his hands under his armpits.

He gazed at Venus above the mountains of Vancouver Island. He recognized Orion in the clear night sky. Stars winked on in each quadrant, and as he imagined, chirped like crickets and flashed like fireflies. He knew there would be a small moon and that it would crest the hill behind him, but only later in his shift. Looking out over his world, he saw what he knew: calm water, fog gathering along the eastern shore of Centre Island, and lights across the channel at Seaford and Squirrel Cove. A dull orange glow in the far sky told of the big town, Campbell River, where he and his family shopped every couple of months.

A tug rumbled in Lewis Channel pulling a log boom – probably the *L.O.Larson*, which he had filled with diesel three days earlier. The crew had played basketball on the dock with Wade and they had fed Angel and Duende three packets of wieners. The *L.O.* slipped behind the hills of Centre Island, but he could still see the weak light from the lanterns on the boom trailing a mile behind, hardly creeping along the water's surface, heading north, a flat boom on its way to Teakerne Arm for the sorters and bundlers. The boat made good time for a tug with a flat boom.

James ate the sausage and cookies. He stood on the top rung of the ladder and pissed onto the moss forty feet below.

The forest grew quiet. The birds had retired, except once he heard a double-hoot from a Great Horned owl. If there was an augury in that call, he didn't think to read it. Or know how.

A twig snapped – the nocturnal deer had started their search for the last soft greens before winter. He heard music from Calvin's cabin on the knoll a quarter mile away. James knew the Smiths were there for dinner; he heard their laughter occasionally, and thought they might even be dancing. Jeremy, on permanent anchor in the lee of Baby Oyster Isle, in the box he called a houseboat, had turned his generator on. It putted quietly. Only the *Storm Chaser*, his beefy salvage boat, was moored along side, so he didn't have company. James could barely make out the floatation on the longlines from the seafarm, where Peter's caretaker, Sebastian, burned a weak light inside his floathouse. Bradley and Jim Jenzen's rowboat sat beached below Adam's rundown shack, so they were having a visit. For a brief moment, James worried about old Wilkes and his screwed up life.

A satellite blinked on and off every few seconds, slowly making its way across the heavens. James heard the distant drone of a jumbo jet from a long Pacific flight beginning a descent for Vancouver International Airport, a hundred miles away. He saw a shooting star, more the memory of it, like a quick trailing flash. And then, trailing quickly another flash. He wanted to see stars raining from the heavens. He stared into that section of the universe to really witness a spectacle, but the night sky revealed nothing more. Recently, he had read about the thirty-three year cycle of the Leonid showers in a National Geographic magazine and imagined himself and his family wrapped in sleeping bags on their front porch watching a deluge of space debris burning through the atmosphere. He played with the conversation that he'd overheard between Nicole and Alice and filled the blanks with numerous possibilities. What was her problem? What was it about "her life?"

When he looked down at the hives, they no longer appeared pale and white, but grey, shapeless, and seemingly without edges, as they slowly melted into the coming darkness. Behind him, when he turned in the chair, he saw on the mossy bluffs below, where it was open and lighter, large boulders and clumps of salal. They might have been juniper bushes. Even though his eyesight had adjusted to the night, he still looked forward to the arrival of the small moon.

James let his memory drift. He recalled their tender moments together, those joyous occasions that no one but they knew, or would ever know. He compiled a mental list of their best times and resolved to remind her of these; perhaps one happy remembrance per day would be the perfect tonic. Happy wife, happy life. He considered climbing down the ladder and running down the hill to reassure Nicole that everything would be okay.

A noise blasted through the darkness, a smashing sound from

a scrub area to his right, a hundred yards distant, as if a bulldozer had flared to life. The animal racketed through salal and negotiated the forest without deviation – a straightforward demolition of the wilderness - no conscience, no thought for stealth, brazen confidence, and the master of its world. The noise rampaged by quickly and headed to the other beehive site above Alice's house.

Damn, it's not even close to eleven o'clock, thought James.

He took up his rifle.

The noise ceased. He calculated fifteen minutes had passed; time enough for condensation on his gun barrel to turn into a thin film of ice. The noise started again, not nearly so bold this time. He guessed the bear - behind him now, below him, somewhere near the base of the moss bluffs - had probably gone straight through his own back yard. Another twig snapped – not a deer this time – then a crunch noise on scarcely frozen moss. He turned his head to look down on the bluff. A new shape appeared on the hillside - dark, large, round, and motionless - not a juniper.

The small moon crested over a hill and partially lit the bluff. His concentration created interior silence: no hum of the *L.O. Larson*, no putt of Jeremy's generator, and no music from Calvin's tape deck. Then the shape moved to another ledge. James twisted in his chair and tried to look back and down, but his cramped leg screamed in agony.

James cursed that he had left his sign on the moss.

The bear snuffled and panted at the base of the fir tree, whiffed the piss, and gave a dry cough; then stood upright and clawed at the night. James had determined earlier that if by chance the bear came, he would wait until the animal engrossed itself in the hives before turning on the light. The bear jumped down onto a flat outcrop near the "condos" and made a "woof" sound when it landed. He saw a pale, lumbering blackness silhouetted against absolute blackness, and to the right of those images, the ghostly grey beehives.

It seemed the bear had satisfied itself that all was well; possibly the animal thought James had been and gone, or perhaps it wasn't astute enough to conceive of danger high in the tree. The bear relaxed, anticipated the sweet honey, and panted steadily. James pulled the butt of the rifle to his shoulder. The safety made a faint click. The bear didn't hear, or if it did, didn't care that a strange noise came from above. James took a deep breath and turned on the light. The bear had taken the lid off one hive and already removed two frames. Like an experienced apiarist, it took painstaking care.

The light didn't bother the animal either. And it didn't look up. In fact, the bear seemed grateful finally to see what it was doing – as if perhaps James was the moon.

He couldn't see the metal sights on his rifle foregrounded against the black coat of the bear so he looked through the scope. Momentarily, he congratulated himself for the options he had designed in his preparations. There was enough light to see the crosshairs in the scope but behind the crosshairs, he saw bristly fur, as though just inches from the bear. He ran the scope along the fur and realized he had been sighting on the rump, when the grey base of a bee "condo" jumped into view. He moved the scope back along what he thought might be the spine. He dissected the animal lengthwise until the crosshairs fell off the snout. James needed a perfect shot, between the front shoulders, over the spine, to shatter the lungs or explode the heart. He didn't want a wounded bear running around the community, frightening his family, chasing away his family, destroying his family, and messing with their perfect life.

Entirely content, the bear was licking wax and honey from a frame when James pulled the trigger. James didn't know why, but he switched the flashlight off. Maybe he thought turning the light off would restore the quiet.

His ears continued to hear the report of the rifle. The small moon found a small cloud so there wasn't enough light to see the next sequence of events. He heard a thump, a grunt, and a gurgling cough. The ladder and chair shook violently. He levered a new round into the chamber of his rifle. He had no time to switch the light on. James fired a second shot, where he assumed the rungs of the ladder would be, and the bear climbing towards him. He kept hearing the report of the second shot. He heard crunching over the frozen moss on the open bluff and a crash into a patch of salal, then quiet.

Sometime later, Calvin yelled from far off, "Did you get him?" He yelled back, "I think so." James still sat in the chair in the sky.

After a while, he saw lights igniting the tops of trees approaching from many directions. The community arrived in a volley: Heinrik, the Smith's with Calvin, the Black's who were back from Vancouver, Sylvia, then Jeremy, the new kid, Carver, Peter, the Jenzen brothers, a little pack of dogs, and finally Nicole without the children. The men carried guns. Everyone breathed hard.

"Doesn't your light work?" asked Jeremy.

After a pause, James said, "Oh," and switched it on.

"Come down from the tree," said Heinrik.

Heinrik and the others shone their lights on the ladder. James slung the rifle over his shoulder and started the climb down. His flashlight searched the sky randomly as he descended.

Heinrik called out, "Watch the rung!"

He did as he was told, skipping a broken rung with an extra long step.

"Where's the bear?" asked Nicole.

"Over the bluff."

Brad and Jim Jenzen moved to the edge of the bluff; divots of moss lay scattered here and there. Disoriented bees crawled everywhere. Brad searched with his light.

"Don't see nuffin," said Jim.

They inspected the ground for blood, bone fragments, tuffs of fur, pink and frothy lung tissue, but, as Jim had said, there was nothing to see. The dogs sniffed the ground but seemed reluctant to mount a chase.

Calvin said, "You said you got him."

"I said, I think I got him."

"We told you the scope would be useless," Heinrik scolded.

"You also said he wouldn't come 'til after midnight." James tried to shade his eyes from the lights.

They, one by one, cast their lights on the ground.

Heinrik asked, "What happened to the rung?" and all lights went for the mangled two-by-four. James looked at the rung too, and then down at his left foot.

"Maybe I shot my foot."

They took turns helping him home. Jim Jenzen helped the most though he was a miniature man. Whenever Nicole assisted, she gripped James' wrist so hard it made the pain in his foot slip away. During the descent to his home, the stars distracted him. They had increased in intensity as if enhanced by the crisp cold air. He wanted to comment on the spectacular sight but felt embarrassed about mentioning such an unimportant detail. When near his house, James said he couldn't be sure if he hit the bear. In fact, now he had doubts the bear had shown at all.

Once they were inside the house, Peter, who had a first-aid ticket, took James' boot off. The bullet had grazed the fleshy side of his foot above the small toe. Blood soaked his sock. He fell asleep on the couch while Peter dressed the wound. Wade and Tara watched from the stairs to the loft. People agreed to meet at daybreak to search for the bear; then they went home for the night.

As Heinrik left, he said to Nicole, "All we need is a wounded bear."

"Thanks to your damned bees and damned honey," she said.

When Jeremy left, he said, "I told him about that damned scope."

Nicole didn't bother getting James up to their bed in the loft, but covered him with their eider quilt. She propped his head with a better pillow and slept curled in his stuffed easy chair beside the couch.

He slept fretfully. Through the night he dreamed the same dream over and over. He saw a head rolling on the floor, unevenly thumping along, spinning occasionally, and powerless to keep a straight course, as it navigated across the great expanse of the room. There were holes in the head, and the brains had been sucked dry. The head reacted with aloofness – not horror, not grief, and not wonder.

During waking moments, he recalled the heroic fantasies that he had permitted himself through dinner, when his family refused to talk and the clock took charge of time. Typically, nothing worked out in the way he had imagined.

Realizing that he had performed badly, James dreaded facing the community in the morning, most of all Nicole. Secretly, he had hoped for a definitive outcome to the night in the chair in the sky. Regretfully, his family's departure now seemed more a possibility. His foot ached and throbbed when he woke at daybreak, but he said nothing.

Community members assembled at his house. More arrived than had been there during the night. Rubber boots and rifles littered the back porch. The people seemed tired, grumpy, and still frightened; no one talked except to inquire about James' foot. Jeremy arrived last, ready to tear the bear apart with his bare hands. Dutifully, Nicole served coffee. When Wade opened the backdoor to go to the outhouse, Angel and Duende raced by and headed for the bluffs.

Wade yelled, "Stay," but the dogs kept running – their hackles up, skirting alongside the bluff into the little valley, and giving strange whines and yelps no one had heard before. People grabbed their guns on the back porch, and in the panic, some got confused about whose gumboots were whose, as most boots were black with red trim. A few of the over zealous community members ran in their socks. James went too, in his slippers. Nicole couldn't stop him.

"Damn! If you could only see yourself," she yelled, but he couldn't hear her or see himself.

Angel froze ten feet from the bear, her front paw raised, hackles bristled even down her hind flanks, while the bear she pointed looked asleep, as innocent as any paschal lamb. Duende held back at a safer distance. When Heinrik arrived, he poked the black bulk with the barrel of his rifle.

"Dead," he said.

"Good dog, Angel," said Wade.

Then he turned and congratulated Duende, "You're a good dog too."

The bullet had entered between the front shoulder blades to the side of the spine, a tiny hole with only a few drops of blood clinging to the fur. No exit wound. Heinrik looked in the mouth and saw worn, broken, and missing teeth.

"An old bear."

He gutted it. Steam and an off odour rose from the cavity.

"Tck, tck, maybe we got it too late."

He showed round pieces of shattered lung tissue and said, "Lung shot."

"It gotsa be dead now," Jim observed.

Six men dragged the carcass back to James' house. The children got a day off school and watched the skinning and butchering. Laura tried to turn the event into an anatomy lesson. When skinned and hung from a tripod of poles, Peter and Laura's daughter, Charlotte, said, "It looks real, Mama," and everybody knew what she meant – how upsetting seeing the humanness, the manlikeness, and the nakedness, hanging there for the whole world to witness, now splayed open, bulked, muscled, headless, pawless, and dismembered.

Many averted their eyes unwilling to see a defrocked body.

James recalled the detached head from his dream and his reaction of aloofness, and, as though the failure of emotion in his dream were a prompt, he remained detached through the buzz of the day.

The children migrated up the hill to the chair in the sky. For the remainder of the afternoon, they re-enacted the scene from the night before. Wade took his dad's role, and the girls were happy to finally play with him. For once the basketball was silent. And for once, the girls were diverted from their dancing game on the dock. They limped from shooting their foot off and made a big deal out of climbing by the shot-up rung until Heinrik came and fixed it. They took turns role-playing the bear, sniffing the ground, pawing the sky, flopping with a thump, rattling the ladder, jumping up and faking a fall over the bluff, and thrashing in noisy clumps of salal. Laura supervised because of the height factor and to keep her students away from Heinrik, who was grumpy in a most bachelor-like fashion. He re-put his hives together, muttering low Germanic oaths while the children played.

Jeremy rubbed the hide (head and paws still attached) in rock salt and lugged it down to the store's walk-in freezer. He wanted the community to send it to a taxidermist so that they would have a memento of this important event. When he mentioned to Nicole that her family could have first dibs on the bear rug, she said, "I don't want first, second, third, or fourth dibs." Sylvia, a widow by occupation, and witch by night, washed down the carcass in a light solution of vinegar, but that didn't mitigate the ripe smell.

"It cooked itself," she said.

Each family took chunks of meat home to can in their pressure cookers despite the taint. James saved a hefty haunch, and hung it in the store cooler. Heinrik laid claim to the four-inch-thick, back fat for making lard. No one objected. Sebastian got the bladder and showed everyone how to make a tobacco pouch. He had only done this with pigs before, but pretty soon a smooth leathery pouch emerged from his persistent rubbing and crinkling. When he finished, Sebastian said, "Pigs make better pouches."

The dogs mauled the bones – Duende, Angel, Pemah, Moocho, Son of Mooch, and Sebastian's snooty and ailing De Gaulle, who could only gum the remains. Jeremy came up with the plan for a potluck dinner featuring a "bearbecue" for the following evening, which was Halloween. James, in an unexpected surge of enthusiasm - the thoughtless man - offered his place for the party without consulting Nicole.

That night they did not speak. He dreamed another strange dream. This time he hung as a lightning rod, naked, upside down, on a structure of poles in the eye of a vast solitude. Each time a bolt of lightning slashed through the night, the sweet metallic smell of ozone woke him.

JAMES ROSE early to prepare for the party. He pretended the pain in his foot belonged to a stranger's foot, and in that way hardly needed to limp. He built a new barbecue. It had to be big enough for the bear, but bigger still, because others would bring items for cooking, oysters for sure, and clams, maybe snapper and salmon if the new fellow, Carver, could perform his fishing tricks, and Sylvia might part with a harvest of fall mushrooms.

He found a rusted 45-gallon drum barrel in the creek bed and halved it lengthwise with his cutting torch. He welded the ends together and fabricated a stand with scraps of rebar. Physically, James felt better than the day before but the mood of aloofness lingered. Even though people kept appearing all day, loneliness crept in alongside that mood too. The two feelings competed and eventually blended into one, although there was no name for that hybrid emotion.

When he finished the welding job, he built a fire. He burned off the outside paint and the lube oil residue on the inside. He shovelled in a three-inch layer of sand and gravel, and then readied his achievement with a generous supply of fir bark. He retrieved a few grates from the burnt-out stoves in his "miscellany" shed behind the store. As James surveyed his creation, he thought the bearbecue ugly but functional; he had never thought of himself as an artist or designer, just someone who could make a new thing from junk.

Next, he cut the bear haunch into useable pieces and made a marinade to soak them in – olive oil, soy sauce, salt, pepper, garlic, and homemade red wine that had gone a trifle vinegary. He had hoped Nicole would volunteer to do the marinade, but she didn't, or wouldn't, so he remembered her recipe as best he could. For containers, he used four institution-size enamel pans, covered the meat with the spicy liquid, and weighted down everything with tight fitting boards and four big rocks.

Wade and Tara spent the day (Saturday, no school) constructing a giant burn pile in the backyard for the bonfire. Carver and a gaggle of girls came to help. With instructions from James, they put aside extra fuel for the bonfire by dragging debris from the forest, and then they made tables from sawhorses and old sheets of plywood. They put out tablecloths, dishes, and utensils. Another fine day – warm if you were in the sun, out of the wind, and wore a jacket. Maybe a scarf and gloves too.

Nicole warmed up slightly. She stayed out of James' way, sewing costumes on the treadle for the kids. She suggested bear suits, as she had a couple of moth-eaten, fur coats that could be altered for the occasion. They wanted to be rabbits.

When James asked her to show him how to make bearbecue sauce, Nicole said she'd do it herself, but to go and fetch honey from Heinrik, which he did right away. She did not seem to care that he had to go all that way on his shot up foot.

As the day wore on, his energy returned. He entertained a fuzzy notion of turning the lighting of the bonfire into a special ceremony. The official lighting would be a moment of recognition for this historic event in the life of their community. Nicole had once told him *ceremony* was the glue that held society together, and now he could see the need. James wanted a rite because they didn't have any, but more personally, he wanted it to be for them, and their children, and for their children's children, and on and on. Perhaps if his wife hadn't been a million miles away, she would have helped him sort out the words.

Before he knew it though, the over-eager children, spurred on by Carver, lit the fire. The fire raged quickly, so the local hero abandoned his vague idea about ceremony and the speech he had been rehearsing most of the afternoon.

THE MASON log home stood on a convergence of trails from around The Refuge. As the sun set behind Cortes Island, people arrived in a congestion, after tricking or treating at other houses along the old logging roads and trails. They were dressed in a flourish of costumes, except for Nicole who wasn't into the spirit yet. Heinrik arrived in lederhosen, high-laced hiking boots, and a sporty Tyrolean hat covered in Germanic hunting badges. James wore a pith helmet, which his deceased father had acquired from somewhere, and that was the extent of his costume. Calvin came as a short "Captain Pumpkin," wearing orange, stretchy leotards, stuffed with pillows, crimped at the neck, big black eyes for breasts, and a three-toothed mouth on the expansive stomach. Jeremy stumbled into the party already drunk and cross-dressed (socks for breasts and a sequined, black, velvet skirt over his jeans), as "Boomerella," with two rusted boom chains looped around his neck and shoulders, the long heavy links clinking over the ground. He'd been a boom man at Teakerne Arm before coming to The Refuge. As the chains clanked, he sounded and looked more like a mean ghost from a Christmas past than the beautiful maiden in search of a logger prince. He wore one caulk boot, unlaced, his other foot bare, and asked everyone as they arrived to admire what a perfect fit the boot was. Duende playfully attacked the tongue and laces. Sebastian had decked himself out in eagle feathers, and he flapped imaginary wings. Sylvia came as a witch. No surprise there. By chance, The Rutabaga Family, from the commune in Galley Bay, had turned up that day for their annual washing adventure in the store's laundromat, and on hearing of the party, they decided to overnight. Their psychedelic attire required little adaptation. The Smiths dressed as Siamese twins hip-wise joined, and they had a difficult time negotiating the trails. Their identical twin daughters, Mary and Elizabeth, materialized as identical but sexy clowns. The Blacks came as unexciting ghosts, and their daughter, Sarah, an unexciting sea hag. Jim Jenzen hauled a timber, making his tortured way up to Golgotha, and Brad whipped him with a bull kelp tail whenever his younger brother faltered. Jim and Brad's Aunt Maddie had arrived in the *Tom Forge,* and also decided to stay overnight, when she heard that there would be drinking. She looked and dressed like the cartoon character, Olive Oyl, so there was no need for her to worry about a costume change. Peter and Laura chose to be clowns, but Peter added zest and variation to his creation by placing a nasty crown (made from blackberry brambles) on his head. When approached, he asked for respect due, by having people call him, "the Clown of Thorns." Their daughter, Charlotte, nearly looked frightening as a Valkyrie. Even old MacLeod, who lived in a broken-down, marine ways, turned up as a blind man tapping over the paths with the cane he always used anyway. Carver wore a fake long nose, hair greased down and dyed purple. He had painted his face a bioluminescent blue.

When it seemed that the whole community had assembled, Wade wished out loud that Alice - almost the sole person in the bay that wasn't there, who lived below in her disintegrating home on the shore beside the store, who never went out of her house, though the women and children visited her often, and lived unendingly in the dark along with the blue glow of her 12/110 volt television, the only TV in the community - should be with them. "Why didn't we think of that?" said Jeremy, and soon a cohort of men ran down the hill, packed her up in a rusted wheelchair, bundled in blankets, happy, wearing her felt hat with a feather slanting out rakishly, and clutching her thermos of rye and water.

They pushed her close to the fire.

"I'm fine here," she said.

People adjusted Alice back and forth, as the fire roared up or died down, or as a breeze enveloped her in eye-watering smoke.

Mountains of food appeared, so much so that James worried the bear wouldn't get touched. A massive pot of clam chowder (the tomato-base kind, only the Blacks liked the milk-base kind), half-shell oysters with goat cheese, crumbles of gritty bacon and a garlic topping (Duende wished later that a little absinthe had been added), salmon, snapper, and still-flipping "rockies" (it seemed young Carver could think the fish into a boat). Heinrik carried a full box of pepperoni, which he usually hoarded, and everyone coveted. Peter brought his pet rock scallops that were the size of dinner plates, as he had been growing them in sea-cages for six years. Sylvia, in her witchy way, revealed a tempting succession of chanterelles and pines (she wouldn't say where she had found them), and goose green salad from the fifteen-foot intertidal mark. Of course, there were real salads (bean, green, tomato and onion, and potato), pickles (many kinds), steamed squash with almonds and maple syrup, zucchini casseroles (three kinds, though if eaten with one's eyes closed, they would have tasted identical), smoked salmon jerky left over from last year, tons of candy, marshmallows, and alcohol to fuel the bacchanal. Sebastian's creation was mashed potatoes (skins on, *sans* milk, and unmashable, as the tubers were under cooked). Jeremy supplied a major bucket of wiggling spot prawns and six Dungeness crabs. The Jenzen brothers brought ten bottles of cream soda, apparently their deceased father's favourite, as they had discovered in his logbook. The Rutabaga Family brought onions.

The bearbecue sauce made by Nicole tasted peppery, but sweet, sticky and delicious. James slathered it on everything; she had made gallons. Heinrik slipped James some of his father's slivovitz, but didn't share it around with anyone else. The sharing, more so than the alcohol, made James feel even better. As people approached the bearbecue, he said, "How do you like your bear, burnt or black?"

"Grizzly," said Jeremy.

People ate the bear any which way, and no one complained about the off-odour, or taste, that was not entirely concealed by Nicole's tangy sauce.

James overheard Jeremy commenting to Calvin, "Just cuz he got a perfect shot it don't mean he knew what he was doing."

And later he heard, "It was the second shot that got his foot."

He shied away from the male posturing, listened contentedly in the background, and tended the cooking. He definitely felt better and didn't care that they talked about him. Had not the crisis ended?

They played a game whereby the witch (Sylvia) invited blindfolded kids and the stoned Rutabagas to crawl into her house (a table with sheets draped over it). They had to feel her dead husband's brains (cold spaghetti), eyeballs (peeled grapes), fingers (wieners), and toes (cocktail sausages). Love Child, of the Galley Bay contingent, did not reappear for quite sometime, as she had stalled out while devouring the cocktail sausages.

Earlier, James had moved all their furniture against the walls thinking the party would migrate inside following the feast, and then they would dance until the cows came home. However, the kids rigged the music outside (Gary Glitter's, *Rock and Roll*, played continuously). The girls began their twirling routine around the fire, and soon started swiping socks from "Boomer-ella's" breasts so he switched personas and shed the boom chains and velvet skirt. He materialized, in his own mind at least, as a bear, and chased the children around the fire, stumbling mostly. The bonfire roared.

Everyone crowded around because of the cold, and Jeremy did not complain about his one bare foot. Though unplanned, his self-disrobing, prompted by the children, became a nod for the others, who all shed their costumes with similar enthusiasm. In a frenzy, they seized back from the accumulating pile, bits and pieces of clowns, broomsticks, feathers, crowns of thorn, ribbons, one only Golgotha cross, gloves, socks, pipes, masks, psychedelic bed sheets, Jeremy's brassiere (where he got it no one knows, as it was that time in the historical record for a natural look), hats, pillows, any object of potential disguise, and soon the community re-emerged, re-dressed in identities that lacked coherence and meaning, but asserted uniqueness in keeping with their growing passion.

As night enveloped, the well-tended bonfire projected scenes onto the trees and the bluffs, even the starry sky where Ursus and her new spirit-brother lurked. Dancing shadows distorted and quivered, forms blended and transmuted into contorted beings, sparks decorated and bedazzled the turbulent images, and the more aggressive embers sought to lodge themselves permanently in the heavens to become extravagant stars. People imitated witches riding brooms, of course the bear too, and goblins and monsters and hunters; the girls spun like diminutive dervishes. Carver twirled in their midst and demonstrated flips and handsprings. Aunt Maddie made a valiant effort to mirror Carver's athletic prowess, but failed miserably on her attempted handspring, landing in the fire. Wade dragged her out. Even old Alice got going with Wade and Jim spinning her in the wheelchair; she waved knobby-clawed hands and hooted horrible noises. MacLeod laughed at the edge of the blazing light and tapped his cane to the beat of the music.

When Jeremy cranked his favourite tape, *Rasputin*, by

Boney M, even the more cabin-fevered bachelors rose from their stupors of alcohol to become inept and unrhythmic advertisements for Stanfield's underwear, Bannockburn wool trousers, and police suspenders. Sebastian soared over the fire, making eagle screeches and talon-grasping images that only he could see. The dogs went mad, formed a pack for the second time ever, and circled the fire, around and around, performing their own version of a primitive war dance - howling, yapping, nipping, and jumping. For the briefest of instants, all check-valves to a pagan blowout malfunctioned, and the people turned their heads toward the Rapture. With the ancient rhythm locked into Boney M's numbing trance, life had become much more than waiting. Time would be forever, and the prospect of eternal bliss an easy reach.

Each time the *Rasputin* tape ended with, *"They shot him until he was dead, Oh those Russians,"* Jeremy raced for the rewind button, and during those potentially painful moments of silence, the community feared the frenzied emotion might sputter and die, while the tape raced back to its beginning, *"There was a certain man, in Russia long ago,"* and never regain the heights of the previous moment. However, Carver came to the rescue to the surprise of all, who knew every word in the long-story-song, and kept the passions flowing during the hiatus, leading his followers with, *"Ra Ra Rasputin, Russia's greatest love machine, It was a shame how he carried on."* The children answered, as they had memorized the lyrics much quicker and more thoroughly than the adults, *"Ra Ra Rasputin, There was a cat that really was gone,"* and that enthusiasm forced the adults to join the chorus too, with Carver clapping his hands and stomping his feet, shouting another two lines, *"Most people looked at him, With terror and with fear."* The whole group answered, *"But to the Moscow chicks, He was such a dear,"* until finally the rewind button clicked, Jeremy hit "play," and Boney M began their masterpiece all over again.

At another rewind intermission, before Carver could take charge of the hysteria, Duende quickly challenged his tenacity in the limelight with a long tortuous howl. Soon the other dogs took his lead, and one after another, each community member joined with their human howls, prolonged wails, not doleful, nor anguished, but real attempts to communicate with the night sky, unleashing their collective memory of primordial beginnings.

Once Boney M started up again, the howls ceased, the dancing resumed, and Jeremy, clutching in each fist the remaining pieces of bearbecued flesh - juices and cinders running down his wrists and off his elbows - threw his arms to the night and yelled above the throngs, "Thank you bear, thank you bear." Everyone jumped and twirled, coupled arms, and stomped their feet. Their screeches blended as one joy. They flipped back their heads of sweat-drenched hair, as though dancing round the golden calf. Tribelike, and with glee, they closed tight their unchristian eyes, rotated shoulders, and vibrated sinuous buttocks – children, adults and the aged – all the cloistered spirits from The Refuge in an impassioned moment of synchronous resonance, the centipedel giant moved as a single organism, except for that one person.

James had kept his eye on Nicole even as he bonded with his community. She had lurked off-stage, in the shadows, not engaging, only smiling mechanically if people whirled by, keeping her distance from the mad night - still costumeless. When the fire flared, he saw the flashing in her blue eyes; her hair and throat appeared indistinguishable from the flames. His old desires returned, and when he thought she could no longer resist the mesmerizing music, Jeremy ran up, clutched James in an enormous bear hug, and growled into his ear, "Make it like this forever?" A surge of exaltation swept through James' soul. Whatever misgivings he had about her leaving were gone – the bear was dead, fear had been vanquished, and the aloofness and loneliness gone as well. The last few weeks had been a temporary stretch of insanity, nothing more. Tonight they prepared for the next day. His paranoid thoughts vanished too - that she might be leaving for reasons other than the bear.

But when he looked out from Jeremy's embrace, with the certain expectation that she would now merge with him and the whole community, Nicole had disappeared into the darkness. In a panic, because the ugly feelings returned in a flood, he broke through Jeremy's embrace and looked for her in their log home, the shadows, and even the outhouse. He searched for her in the swirling crowd dancing around the fire, but she was not there. Instinct told him he must sort this out alone and not ask for help from his friends. He had never brought others into his confidence. Still though, he thought of approaching Alice, but now was not the time, as she waved her thermos and shouted over and over, "What a marvellous night."

A thought flashed, not an instant knowledge of what had transpired in that conversation between his wife and Alice, but the trailing flash he had sensed in the sky the night he killed the bear. And more thoughts flashed. They rained from the heavens, as he had wished, when sitting in the chair. Instantly, James knew where she must be.

A perfect plan formulated in his head. He ran in the dark without his flashlight: she would be in the chair in the sky, reliving the bear scene as best she could, experiencing his side of the affair, and stepping into his skin, just as the children had done yesterday afternoon when they performed their re-creation of the shooting at the beehive site. Yes, a ceremony roared around the fire, but also, a ceremony was about to take place in the chair in the sky at that very moment. Their quarrel had been a little one; the bear was dead, and the sacrifice complete. All would return to its former state once she had finished her work. Were not the sweet smells of burnt flesh wafting into the starry sky and intoxicating the gods?

The darkness in the forest approached absolute, yet he did not feel disoriented in the least. As he ran up the path, easily remembering all the twists and turns, every exposed root and rock, his imagination specified that when he got to the base of the tree she would invite him to join her. Together they would enter into new delights, and together, they would witness the Pandemonium below. Without a doubt there would be room for two in the chair. This was an invitation to a new beginning. Their naked bodies could mesh and meld, just like they had during that first summer on Production Point.

Halfway there, with the music and shouting barely audible, stumbling occasionally but still certain of his way, James saw a light inside a salal bush moving towards him. Growls emanated from inside. The bush shook its branches and rattled its leaves. There should not have been salal in the middle of the path, nor should it growl or emit light. It stopped in front of him and bristled.

"Your light's in my eyes," he said.

"Sorry."

Though the word, *sorry*, was beautiful, a voice from within made James think of sadness.

She turned the light off, and the leaves rustled.

"I thought you were up in the chair in the sky."

She laughed in the dark, and the leaves rustled again. "Why would I go up there?"

"Just a thought."

"I'm putting on a costume like everyone else."

"You're going as a salal bush?"

"Have you got a problem with that?"

"Not really, except you're naked underneath."

"And how's that different from a salal bush, James?"

SEA WITHOUT SHORES

Dancing

Now that Alice had reconsidered cremation, she would prefer an open space in the forest. A damp spot. Where the Alders would grow right through. Where she could hear the songbirds and chitterings of squirrels. A breeze whispering to the green leaves.

She wanted to feel the dappled light on her deathbed where she awaited the embrace of the subterranean creatures.

"I will be fertilizer," Alice commented

Tara asked, "What do you mean, Auntie Alice?"

"Thinking out loud, that's all dear."

Marine operator
-617
CH 2029
Monday

~ 3 ~

Your Dancing Started Me Thinking

"Even to sit here together created a current of feeling that flowed back and forth between them."

Beauty and Sadness, **Yasunari Kawabata**

BEFORE THE first birdsong of the morning, Adam woke in the darkness. He lifted the lid from his stove and stirred the embers. Coals from dense fir bark flickered tongues of blue and green, then dimmed to ash grey. Heat bathed his hand, and the hairs on the back of his fingers curled in protest, the pain no more than an itch. He added more fuel and awaited ignition. Mesmerized at the gate to this sedate inferno, the recluse poked for a more stimulating reaction. Orange flames leaped from the grate, and sparks rushed up the flue. Not content to leave things go their course, again he poked, only this time with an aggressive jab. A chaos of ash swirled around his hand and wrist. Unable to abide what he had initiated, Adam withdrew the poker and refit the lid to contain the further discharge of emotion.

During the wait for daylight, he paced between the table and stove, a distance of several yards, occasionally feeding the fire.

Over the years, these wanderings had worn a tread in the floor - straight and smooth - and the creaks in the boards had lessened, as they accepted the passage of his footfalls.

Near the edge of the stove, his teapot steeped, and over the firebox, where the heat was more intense, the kettle rocked steadily. Swollen beads dripped from the spout and shattered into a spray of lesser beads that skipped across the metal surface and vaporized before they reached the edge. He thought of a broken strand of pearls scattering across a hard shiny floor, the dancer in disbelief clutching at her naked throat. He thought of the joy of school children released at last for summer break and their wild anticipation of freedom and fun. Not wanting to boil dry the kettle, Adam moved it close to the teapot – the practice to have scalding water ready at all times.

He looked forward to another scribbling adventure. Duende's cooperation during the bear crisis had come as a surprise. In compensation for the dog's dedication, he had expressed his gratitude with multiple gifts of the two precious staples. During an extended "happy hour," he had congratulated his assistant on the wealth of material provided during the saga.

A: We make a good team little doggy. I hope you realize we filled Scribbler Number One all the way into the margins. No mean feat, my good sir.

D: A humble servant at your beckon.

A: Maybe so...maybe so, but you have woken from a one-hundred-year slumber. The importance of detail to the imagination can never be overestimated.

Duende changed the direction of their conversation back to the staples.

D: Scotch and jerky go well together.

A: I see your plate is empty. Let's see what we can do about that.

Now Adam angled for a full report on Alice. The investigative reporter calculated that the Pavlovian ritual - information then jerky, more information then scotch - would get him the details he really needed. He had convinced himself, in spite of not knowing why, that revelations from the old woman would short circuit his quest for truth. This next assignment he planted between the mutt's little ears following a few more drinks. He cautioned Duende with the following statement:

A: If momentum is lost, we might never get it back.

Adam couldn't remember the source in his library, or the name of the author, nor the context either, and whether or not he had actually read or just dreamed the quotation; regardless, what did it matter, he did remember the exact wording. This guidepost he gave to the dog as a means to structure the upcoming, fact-finding mission.

A: The road to knowledge detours along a trail of tears.

Scribbler Two:

ALICE SIPPED her coffee and studied the world of The Refuge through her bay window. Wet stones glisten on the beach. Scoter ducks paddle in the ocean and hardly know they are wet. Rain softens the steep bluffs, while the mosses grow greener. Trees stand patiently and wait. The tips of pine needles bulge with moisture, tears that never fall.

Her diesel generator vibrated on the porch beside the front door. Ivy covered her home and the leaves trembled. From a distance the house looked like a giant creature shaking itself dry. Her windows rattled, and exhaust fumes hung under the covered entryway. On windy days, the rattling seemed less noticeable, and the perfumed exhaust more acceptable. Crankcase oil leaked from the seal around the engine's base pan, saturated the porch floor boards, dripped between the spaces onto the rocks below, wept down to the shoreline, and spread a rainbow slick onto the clear salt waters of The Refuge. The slick became worse on quiet, rainy days, but more attractive, developing swirls of cerise, neon blue, volatile yellow, and an intense California poppy orange. Alice refused to fix the leak.

The muffler to the generator had holed itself from wear and freed itself from the tailpipe by breaking a coupling. Alice would not fix the muffler, or the coupling, nor the escape of exhaust fumes. The quote for parts was too high. The better approach was to wait until prices came down. James, Jeremy, Calvin, and many of the others, had offered to fix her generator for free, but she must buy the parts. "For the love of Mary Magdalene, how is that for free?" Alice didn't mind the smell; she had lived with diesel motors, the tang of their oil and exhaust for most of her life. Reg always had at least one smelly engine, scattered in pieces on the kitchen table, or obstructing the entry to the house. The noise was no problem either, as her hearing had deteriorated over the years, but the constant agitation of the house, and everything in it, was another story.

The cure to her generator might be to get it off the porch. Build a shed on *terra firma,* and do the job properly with a cement base for starters. Fix the oil leak with a new gasket. Blow the injectors. Use shock absorbing hockey pucks to cushion the sled frame. The shed walls should be insulated with lead sheeting, the exhaust noise baffled in a cinderblock maze, and a long tailpipe installed that led away from the house. Reg would have done it, but he never had time. She appreciated the offers of help from the community, and the suggestions too, some of them even helpful, but it wasn't their pocketbooks that would get ransacked. Besides, "making do" had been the credo in their marriage, and the present seemed a bit late to reject those vows.

She watched her bone china mug - a gift from a wealthy tourist - migrate across the glass covered side table, the black coffee inside gyrating like a mini williwaw. She thought the vibration from the generator worse. Her ashtray, cigarettes, lighter, lamp, radiophone, binoculars, bowl of liquorice allsorts, and three gold framed stand-up sepia photos (Reg as a young man beside a four point buck, Reg and Alice on their 40th, and Stinky, their faithful water spaniel asleep in a rowboat) advanced, millimetre by millimetre, across the glossy glass tundra like a herd of mixed, nomadic species toward the parlour wall and according to the slant of the floor. She had a stopper strip fastened to the side table (Jeremy had the idea and did it for her, a kid's solution but a good one, which cost nothing) and whenever her treasures bunched up at the edge, she moved them back to their original configuration. If time permitted. Touching the treasures reminded her to have another cigarette, or sip her coffee, or listen to the weather channel on the radiophone, or check the name of a boat she didn't recognize with her binoculars, and think of another story to entertain her guests. Touching old things felt like touching the past, bringing back the good ghosts from a long restful sleep, so that the difference between then and now became barely noticeable.

Someone knocked on the door. Alice could see the different shake of the door compared to the shake the generator made. She put in her teeth and hit the "blab-off" switch fastened with electrician's tape to the arm of her chair. Her TV went silent.

"Come in!"

The door continued to shake from the knocking, and the generator rumble seemed louder. "Come in!" she yelled.

She sure wasn't going to get up and answer the door.

"Come in!" she yelled a third time, maddened at the interruption. The doorknob turned. The door opened, and the sound of the generator forced Alice to cup her ears.

Tara stood at the entry.

Alice beckoned the child in - an irate wave - and Tara closed the door behind her. She kicked off her rubber boots.

"You know not to disturb me when my programs are on."

"I thought they were over, Auntie Alice."

"Not yet."

"Should I go?" Tara put her hand on the doorknob.

"Sit down on the couch dear, but get your liquorice first."

Tara hurried over to the side table and studied the bowl of liquorice allsorts. Alice raised her arm as if she might slap the child's hand.

Tara smiled. "I won't take the pimply ones."

"You better not." Alice pursed her lips so that her smile was hardly detectable.

They sat quietly and watched the *Price Is Right* with the volume off.

Soon Tara said, "Can we have the sound?" and Alice flicked the "blab-off" off.

Her recliner chair had been outfitted with custom-made side pockets where she kept her crosswords, TV Guide, a 1926 edition of the Oxford Dictionary, and a book of quotations, witticisms and wise sayings, from which she produced cue cards, and would later recite these gems of wisdom without acknowledging their author, or source, to deserving visitors. Rarely was the dictionary required any longer, because, "nowadays crosswords use silly words," and to make matters worse, "no one is interested in improving their minds."

Her chair was sinking slowly through the floor and had been shored up from underneath many times. People wanted to move it from the depression to a safer spot over a main support beam, but no she wouldn't. "Why do they keep asking when they know the answer?" The view of the docks, The Refuge, and all the goings on was best right there. She could keep track while watching television. Study Wade play basketball in front of the freight shed. The young girls do their twirling dance until they fall down dizzy and giggling. She could see James serve the customers at the fuel dock. The boats coming and going, the seagulls and ducks, the eagles, the mail plane, the freighter, and the sunsets. And whether or not Jeremy had company, and what sex they might be, and if they stayed overnight. She could keep count of the nights. Alice watched everyone: Sebastian, Peter, Heinrik, Brad and Jim, and the women too, though they were not as out and about like the men folk. A lot to keep track of. The new boy, Carver, and his fishing tricks. MacLeod and Son of Moocho coming for their mail. Once in a while he looked her way, and she would have waved if his eyesight were better. How feebly he tapped along the dock with his crooked cane, his carriage no longer confident and bold, as in the past.

"Crosswords exercise your mind," said Alice, and Tara nodded her head.

"It is your duty to improve your mind," and Tara nodded once again.

"Even at my age, you must pursue self-improvement…it's a way to prepare for the after-life." Tara's toes squirmed in her socks.

Alice looked at her engagement and wedding rings. Her fingers were deformed from arthritis, swollen, stiff and knobby, curved like talons and stained dark amber from tobacco smoke. Her fingernails were painted harlot red and tapered to sharp points. Like a fool, she had willed the rings to a distant niece and now wondered how they would get them off when she died. As first choice, she had left instructions in her will to cremate, and, after a suitable period of respectful time, toss her ashes to the sea – "leave no traces" – just like Reg. But if they had to bury her, they should get the economy model coffin, or preferably have someone local build it, "They're all good carpenters here." D-grade plywood would be fine or rough-cut cedar boards, no bevelling, no planing, no embroidery, no puffed-up shiny satin, no fancy handles, and "for heaven's sake " no lacquered hardwoods. Not like James' parents who went out in style unbecoming their station in life.

"And no open casket please!" Reg had looked awful.

"What did you say, Auntie Alice?"

"Nothing dear. I was just thinking that graveyards are insufferable places."

"Oh."

Now that Alice had reconsidered cremation, she would prefer an open space in the forest. A damp spot. Where the alders could grow right through. Where she could hear the songbirds and the chitterings of squirrels. A breeze whispering to the green leaves. She wanted to feel the dappled light on her deathbed, where she awaited the embrace of the subterranean creatures.

"I will be fertilizer," Alice commented.

"What do you mean Auntie Alice?" Tara asked.

"Thinking out loud, that's all, dear."

Alice had explained to Nicole that her rings would go to her distant niece, "Not because of blood, mind you!" but because there were six women to consider in The Refuge and you couldn't take sides. "How would it look? It wouldn't be fair to those not chosen."

Nicole understood; Alice felt certain.

When the TV program ended, she pressed the generator kill-switch mounted on the wall above her chair. The generator rattled to a stop, and the red cone in her portable electric heater slowly turned grey. Her memories on the side table stood silent, but anxious to again feel the vibrations from the past. The TV screen shrunk to a bright silver speck. Alice and Tara watched the silver eye grow smaller. Without the aid of electricity, the television continued to stare at them, as if staring were all it knew, as if the constricted iris would never avert its gaze, and though it readily grew smaller, it would continue to the point of satiation, and only then, stop the surveillance.

"My brother thinks it doesn't go away but just gets smaller and smaller," commented Tara.

"Well, he's wrong."

Tara fidgeted her fingers. She pressed smooth the wrinkles in the paisley dress worn overtop her jeans. Alice shivered and rubbed her shoulders and arms.

"I'm chilly."

Tara jumped off the couch, lit Alice's portable kerosene heater, and then rearranged the items on the side table. Stinky got a prominent place beside the allsorts. She took another liquorice, and Alice studied the child's face.

"Why did you call him, Stinky?" asked Tara.

"He had a bad case of flatulence, even as a puppy. Do you know the meaning of flatulence?"

"No."

"Well, look it up. Everyday you must learn one new thing." Alice gave Tara the dictionary.

Tara found the "fs," and "flat," and soon her finger came to rest on the word. She looked up at Alice and said, "Farting."

"Stinky could clear a room in seconds."

Tara giggled. Alice took a sip from her mug. "Warm it up for me please, dear."

Tara took the cup into the kitchen, dropped in four sugar lumps, and poured a refill from the pot on the oil stove. She came back into the parlour.

"Do ask your mother to come down…my nails need attention. Maybe tomorrow when I'm not so busy." Alice held out her fingers for Tara to see the chipped nail polish.

"I can do your nails."

"You're not old enough."

"I do mine." Tara took off her sock and revealed sapphire-blue toenails.

"Your mother shouldn't let you use that colour."

"Carver likes the colour."

"What does he know? Young men like Carver have no idea about good form."

Tara pulled her sock back on.

"And tell your father I want a refund from the post office. They forgot my TV Guide."

"I already told him," Tara said.

"The least I should get is a free subscription. A letter of apology won't do."

Tara sucked on her hair, a habit she had acquired from her mother. They both turned to the door and the sound of scratching.

"Let Duende in, please," said Alice.

Tara leaped off the couch and opened the door. The dog headed to his rug under the TV stand.

"Should I give Duo a wiener?" Tara asked.

"You'll find the tail end of a baloney in the cooler." Duende followed Tara to the back porch. Tara stripped the casing from the baloney and gave the meat to the dog. They came back into the parlour.

Tara commented, "He doesn't chew."

"Reg was like that." The dog settled on his rug, and Tara went back to the couch.

"Why aren't you in school today?" Alice asked.

"Laura is too busy to give us our lessons, and mom says she

can't do everything."

"I will have to speak to your mother. What could possibly be more important than your lessons?"

Tara shrugged her shoulders and found another crease in her dress to smooth.

"What were we talking about yesterday?"

"You were talking about MacLeod. You said he danced with you all night…and that he loved you."

"I have never been sure about him loving me. I only meant it as a possibility. You should not leap from one conclusion to the next. And I don't want you telling that story to your parents or anyone else in The Refuge."

"I won't." Tara waited for Alice to continue.

"We were at a dance in the old schoolhouse, right?"

"Yes."

"You should say, 'Yes, Auntie Alice,' even if I'm not really your aunt…it's a sign of respect."

"Yes, Auntie Alice."

"Do you know how Cinderella felt before midnight when she danced with the prince? Not after, but right before, before she panicked and remembered she had to get out of there."

"Yes, Auntie Alice."

"I felt like her…on cloud nine is another way to put it, just so you know what an important moment that was for me." Alice put a pimply allsort in her mouth.

"Did the dances have to be over at a certain time?" asked Tara.

"No, no, I'm just trying to stress the importance of the moment. That's all. An importance beyond any other in my life." Alice searched Tara's eyes for a flicker of understanding, and soon the child nodded her head.

"The dances in the old schoolhouse were always on Saturday nights. That was when lots of people used to live here and came from all around. MacLeod came that night. You should know that he was and is the most shy man on earth…and he didn't drink like your Uncle Reg, who you never met, or like the other men in the bay."

Alice changed her legs on the ottoman. Both legs were bloated and varicosed. Her feet were discoloured with haemorrhages – black and blue and yellow hematomas. She could touch herself anywhere, and a bruise would appear. When people had commented on the bruising, she would often say, "I'm an abused woman. I'm an abused woman," and then she waited for the laughter. The ottoman sat on a rag rug of many frightful colours. Otherwise her parlour had been carpeted wall to wall in sensible dark green, a hotel throwaway. Tara got off the couch and moved the ottoman closer to Alice's chair.

"Thank you, dear. Suffice it to say, the men were all an unimaginative lot. They clung to the walls like limpets and talked uninspired nonsense about motors, spar trees, and the price of fish. The unfair scaling system for logs was a passionate subject too. The only time they moved was to get another drink. You wondered why they came at all. Eventually, they all staggered home. Half fell off the boardwalks and the other half climbed out of their boats before they got to where they were going."

Tara giggled, and Alice paused an appropriate amount of time for the child to fully appreciate the humour.

"They were all cut from the same cloth except for MacLeod. He came to the dances only for a half-hour. Why, I don't know. Maybe he thought it was duty. Maybe he felt lonely, and that half-hour gave him a pittance of relief from his quiet life.

"I have thought about this often. He had nothing in common with the other men and was too shy to look at a woman. He always stood by himself in a corner with his eyes riveted on the floor. And he always hid his hands behind his back because he thought they were too big and too ugly...I can't remember who told me that, but it might have been Molly Jenzen, who was somehow related to Bradley and Jim, and their dad, Perry. Anyway, I thought they were strong, beautiful hands.

"Women danced with women. We had no choice. The men just weren't interested in what we thought important. The generator roared so you couldn't hear the records, and no one in the bay could play a musical instrument. It's the same now except for Sebastian and his zither, but he only plays for his dog."

"I've heard him. It always puts De Gaulle to sleep," Tara said.

"Why is it that all the bachelors have dogs, Tara?"

"Heinrik has Pemah and MacLeod has Son of Moocho."

"It's just an interesting observation, that's all."

"And Jeremy has Moocho, and we have Angel. But nobody has Duo."

Duende opened one eye when he heard his nickname. Tara got up off the couch and stood by the side table.

"Please and thank you go a long way."

"May I have another liquorice, please?"

"You know which ones not to take."

Alice studied Tara's face as the child made her decision. She returned to the couch with another liquorice – white layers outside, then orange, and black in the middle.

"Where were we?"

"You were starting to dance?"

"Right. I don't know what came over me. I think I may have been annoyed with Reg. Anyway, that is no matter. For no reason in the world, I ran up and grabbed MacLeod's hand and pulled him out onto the dance floor. No one had ever seen him dance. As soon as our hands touched, sparks flew between us. Just like sparks flew on the night of the bearbecue. He didn't know what to do. I put his hand on my hip...that was an act of bravery, Tara. And then I put my hand on his shoulder."

Alice sipped her coffee and stared out the window. Skin hung loose on her large frame, where archipelagos of black moles and slack wens gathered. Nicole and the other women had encouraged her to have them removed, but no she wouldn't. "God put them there for a reason." She dabbed at her left eyelid, which sagged and teared.

"Maybe it will clear."

"Duo smells like a wet dog," Tara replied.

"He'll dry out soon enough."

Tara waited for Alice to continue.

"We started with a slow waltz. A Benny Goodman…and his hand on my hip felt like flesh on flesh. Like my dress and underneaths weren't even there. His hand burned as hot as a branding iron, and I loved every minute of it. I thought a mark would be left and looked when we got home…once Reg had gone to sleep of course, which took all of an instant. My entire body glowed for days afterwards, but no one noticed.

"Only yesterday I caught myself in the mirror after a shower. And I examined my hip to see if the mark was still there. I couldn't see it, but I could still feel the burn after all these years. He marked me for life, Tara. It'll happen to you some day."

Alice placed her hand on her left hip. "It was this one."

Tara mirrored Alice, touching her own hip. For both of them, sensations of pain and joy mingled until neither could be separated.

"From time to time, I can force the heat to come back, and then the flesh burns beautifully like a delicious fever. I can feel his hand right now…each finger."

Alice and Tara took a few more moments to revive the beautiful pain. Alice massaged her hip from the safety of a burnished past. Tara kneaded her hip. She moved slowly into herself, with exploring fingers, away from the image of Alice's smoldering fever, toward the enflamed flesh of her own disrupted innocence.

"I often think that he sits in his house and remembers the night we danced. I'm convinced both of us share a similar wound. For me it is the hip, and for him it is the shoulder. I can see MacLeod sitting in his cabin, rubbing his shoulder, and thinking the thoughts that I think…as if our minds can lock onto the same passion, while our bodies desperately try to catch up with the many places our thoughts can go."

The child's look seemed as far away as that of an animal in a zoo, a gaze through bars. Alice lit a cigarette and pondered further on the immortality of love.

"Would you believe he was a natural on the dance floor? And we danced the whole night. Like Ginger Rogers and Fred Astaire. Your Uncle Reg didn't notice, or any of the other men, but the women did. Women always notice the intimate things. None of them said a word to me afterwards...or ever. Maybe Reg noticed. But it never came up between us. That's how relationships were in those days. People kept their thoughts to themselves, even couples. Things are different now. These days you know an event before it happens."

Tara dispensed with her hip. She detected more wrinkles in her paisley skirt and smoothed them with the same concentration of a preening cat.

"MacLeod and I hardly spoke. I can't remember a single word we said to each other. When one song ended, we stood there, stared at the floor, and waited for another to begin. Near the end of the evening, we held hands between songs like two kids on their first date. Tara, he never came to another dance after that."

"He came to the bearbecue."

"Yes, but time has changed everything."

They both stared out the window. The sky began to clear. Wade and Bradley shot baskets, and Maddie, on the *Tom Forge,* from the logging camp in Lewis Channel, pulled up to the gas dock. Her nephew, Jim, helped her tie up.

"Did you have a fight?" Tara asked.

"No, no. We just had one of those moments when the door opens for an instant, that's all."

"My parents hardly make any noise when they fight."

After a time Alice replied, "Some couples are like that."

"Me and Wade hear them from upstairs."

"All couples fight, Tara. It's just normal."

"My mom wanted to leave because of the bear."

"Your mother and I have discussed these things. She's adjusting to her new life."

"MacLeod has a new boat," Tara said.

"Yes, I saw him fuelling at the gas dock."

"Dad says MacLeod wants to see all the old places before he dies."

"I didn't know that."

A self-dumping log barge motored in the channel heading for

Teakerne Arm. Sun broke through the clouds and struck Centre Island.

"Unless you count my secret thoughts, that evening so long ago became the most unfaithful I ever was in forty-three years of marriage. When Reg died, MacLeod brought me a bleeding heart he dug up in the forest. He just put it on the porch steps without coming in or saying a word. I planted it near the bottom stair. You can go out and see."

Tara opened the door and stepped outside to see the bleeding heart. Duende followed and headed along the boardwalk to the government docks, presumably on another mission. Tara came back after a few moments. She stood by the liquorice bowl.

"It has white flowers."

"Someday a man will give you flowers."

"I pulled some of the ivy out. It's trying to get it."

"Good. I don't want my bleeding heart to ever die."

Tara took another liquorice.

"Every day I see you dancing on the dock," said Alice.

"Charlotte and me and the other girls dance all the time."

"I know. Your dancing started me thinking...about how love can survive at such great distances...and grow from nothing... and turn into nothing."

"He has lots of grey cats," said Tara.

"So I've heard."

Alice leaned over in her chair and picked a tiny twig from the green carpet, perhaps tramped in by Tara after inspecting the bleeding heart. Alice studied the twig and then dropped it on the rag rug with the busy design and frightful colours.

"You can't see it anymore," said Tara.

"What you can't see won't hurt you."

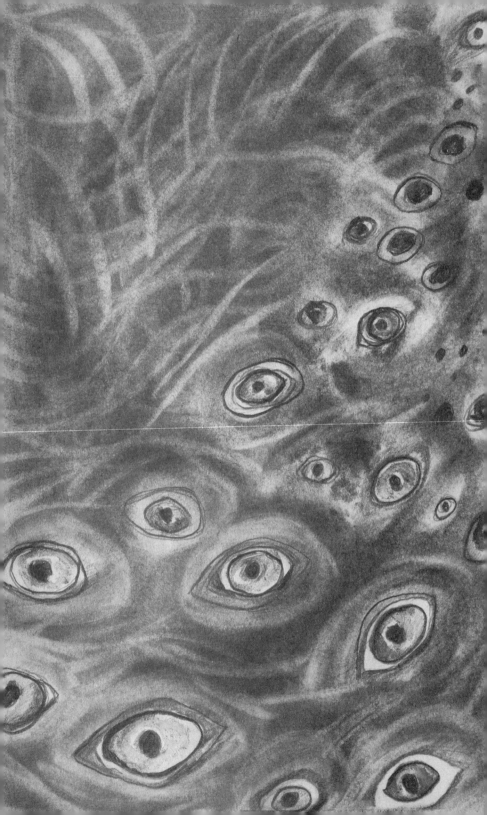

~ 4 ~

Eyes

"But lying at his feet and gazing into the twilit garden without even looking at Pilate, the dog knew at once that its master was troubled. It moved, got up, went round to Pilate's side and laid its forepaws and head on the Procurator's knees, smearing the hem of his cloak with wet sand. Banga's action seemed to mean that he wanted to comfort his master and was prepared to face misfortune with him. This he tried to express in his eyes and in the forward set of his ears. These two, dog and man who loved each other, sat in vigil together on the balcony that night of the feast."

The Master and Margarita, **Mikhail Bulgakov**

DOGFISH (*Squalus suckleyi*) are colour-blind and resolve images poorly. However, the handicap doesn't mean they cannot see. They are grouped in the shark family. The largest grow to five feet in length. Dogfish hunt in packs, like the wolf, and for that reason, some of the older fishermen call them "wolf fish." Those who have been lacerated by the tail barb call them "dagger dogs." They are viviparous like woman. And cartilaginous unlike man or woman. These fish possess an acute sense of smell and can detect minute substances in the ocean from great distances, such as drops of *blood, which they associate with fear.*

D: Fear draws them to the source, not the smell of blood.

Adam didn't realize the dog could read.

A: What makes you so sure?

D: Humans make assumptions about mammals, birds, and fish that stretch believability.

A: I'm too busy to argue. Go snooze in your corner.

Adam was reluctant to challenge the dog for lack of trustworthy data.

D: How come you're not writing in the scribblers?

A: This is my journal. I've kept a journal all my life.

D: I suppose I have, too.

A: You can't write.

D: The handicap of paws doesn't prevent me from making entries on the free spaces in my mind.

Dogfish are particularly sensitive to underwater sounds of low frequency and have fine directional hearing. Organs along their lateral lines and on the abrasive snout enable them to pick up weak electrical stimuli from the muscle contractions of bony fish and other creatures. This combination of refined senses, even without the 20-20 vision that we take for granted, accounts for their evolutionary success, a remarkable achievement.

Fishermen kill a hundred million sharks each year and sharks kill a few humankind as compensation. Human carnivores, especially in the West, are beginning to understand that sharks, including dogfish, taste delicious, but one must bleed and skin them immediately when caught; otherwise, a layer of ammonia between the flesh and skin invades the lovely, tender, white meat. Then the fish tastes of urine.

D: Urine is not the greatest of tastes, but it's not the worst either.

A: Duende, do you want to do my research for me?

D: I'm simply making an observation.

A: I'm not telling you again. Go lay down in the corner.

The dog curled up in front of the stove.

In earlier days, the older fishermen on Cortes Island also called them "piss fish," as did my good friend, Captain Perry Jenzen, now quite deceased, including my younger brother, Darwin, and his crew (my school chums) who unluckily sailed on the last voyage of the Arrogant. Perry once commented, "Don't you think lovemaking would be odd if we leaked piss through our skin like dogfish?" Of course, I had to agree once my imagination startled my biological foundations. With a little practice, and this Perry taught me many years ago, I have found that a pair of pliers, starting at the snout, tears the entire tough skin away, like taking off a tight fitting glove, or, a woman's girdle if one were ever so lucky. Soaking the meat in a mild solution of lemon juice can ameliorate any residue of the ammoniac smell and flavour.

Duende jumped onto his cushion beside Adam. The dog read the last entry in Adam's journal.

D: You're too old for girdle fantasies.

A: How would you know?

D: A hunch.

A: Dogs don't have hunches.

Shark fin soup is an Asian delicacy. Germans call the smoked and curled belly flaps, "Schillerlocken." The English elevate dogfish to "rock salmon." The meat is frequently used in making deep-fried fish and chips, though customers are often unaware of this. The liver is disproportionately large and contains squalamine, a substance that fights cancer by cutting off blood supply to tumours. It also contains large quantities of an ultra-fine oil used to lubricate the cogs and wheels of miniature machines, such as ornate clocks and watches.

D: Ironic that humans need a predator's lubricant to monitor the toll of time.

A: Go to sleep!

D: What's the big deal about dogfish?

A: Go to sleep!

The skin of a dogfish is a useful by-product, leathery and tough, a desert of small sharp pointed scales, similar to tiny teeth, and makes the best fine-grade sandpaper. The Coast Salish, the Nootka, the Lekwiltok, and the Haida further north, still use the skin to smooth their carved masks and canoe hulls. Before contact, they traded the precious commodity with the inland peoples. These artists liken the dogfish to a born leader possessing persistence and strength, unlike modern day Caucasians who daemonize them beyond justification.

D: Dogs are born leaders.

A: I know one or two that aren't.

Wallets made from dogfish skins are easy to insert in the pocket, facilitated by the backward slanting of the scales. Consequently, pickpockets experience difficulty making an extraction. Formerly, when the ocean was teeming - so much so that one could tramp upon the sea - the Portuguese claimed to walk over the backs of codfish during the 16th century on the Grand Banks off Newfoundland; however, not to be out done, the Klahoose narrate stories claiming that they used the million backs of dogfish as bridges from one island to the next. Whenever a dugout canoe wasn't handy, and this is cute, if a family wished to go for a pleasant Sunday afternoon stroll following religious services, wearing their newest cedar garb and giant geoduck shells for shoes....

D: You just made that up.

A: Think what you want.

D: The Sunday stroll and geoduck shoes stretch the bounds of imagination.

A: That's not a sin.

Many fishermen consider dogfish "by-catch," a nuisance fish, a trash fish, a devilfish, and if caught, their bellies are slashed open and thrown back into the sea. Even then you see them swim away, slowly, mind you, to the depths.

FOLLOWING HIS most recent scribblings, another hunch formulated in Adam's head. He now had a new assignment for his assistant and would seek continued cooperation once the mongrel's frame of mind had improved. They sat outside the cabin sequestered on a cold rock by the shore: watching, listening, and smelling. The evening was cold and damp. Moonless. A feeble mist hovered above the ocean, and stars twinkled weakly in a cloudless sky. Insomnia stalked over the patina of gloom.

For warmth, Adam draped a wool blanket over his head and shoulders. One might mistake him for an anchorite from the scriptures, until they noticed that he chain-smoked, lighting consecutive cigarettes with the glow from the last, and the butts accumulating around his slippers, which were soaking wet from the dew-damp grasses. He drank his scotch and allowed each sip to overstay the welcome of his palate, bestowing the illusion that spirits warmed the blood, gave life to a sluggish brain, and generated eternal wisdom. The dog shivered beside him.

Lights in The Refuge homes had been turned off, their inmates gone to bed. Nonetheless, light rose from the sea, not the Eastern sky, as was the custom.

By default, Duende and Adam became silent onlookers to the spectacle of electrified waters. On this night, the bay filled with dogfish, anchovies, and many other sea creatures. They gathered to enact the life-and-death dance – the first dance, the last dance, and the only dance - that had been set in motion long before the Spanish, British, Russians, or even the indigenous peoples appeared on these lonely shores.

Billions of anchovies fled in dazzling streaks of *noctiluca* protected solely by speed and numbers. As the feedfish tried unsuccessfully to darken the sea, the dogfish trailed their flight, like slow propelled burning logs, followed by their long comet tails of endurance.

They're satiated, Adam thought, but take no rest from the dance.

Eyes stared from the ten thousand heads, though the vacant green lights could not easily be connected to their cages of skin and gristle. Pale, white splashes issued from the lethargic slaps of the many tails. In the midst of the commotion, the darkness became more audible, as it swelled with the increasing light. The sea could only be separated from the land by the presence of the dancing bioluminescence. In this ignited murk, eyes looked from the long distances of the late Palaeozoic period, four hundred million years ago, their stares unceasing and selfish, the purpose only to rouse their own seeing. Adam cast a beam from his flashlight against the many thousand eyes, but his light drew no reflexive action.

A: Many years ago, Perry and I sat at this very spot on a sunny afternoon gutting the six blueback salmon we had caught earlier. He cleaned the fish with a wicked knife and seemed content to let me watch his handiwork. My friend had a wonderful technique of opening the fish, severing the head, and pulling in one motion, so that the cavity of guts came loose – the waste, head and all, in one piece. He threw the quivering offal into the water, and very quickly a frenzy of dogfish fought for the remains. As he cleaned each salmon, my old buddy lobbed the offal closer to the shore where he worked. Soon the small sharks thrashed near his boots. We heard the rough rasp of their skin on the rocks, an irritating sound not unlike a fingernail over a blackboard. Their bodies half squirmed out of the sea, reminiscent of pre-biblical times when fish ventured onto the land. Then he took the heart from a salmon - deep maroon, glossy, still pulsing with a methodical beat - and placed the morsel above the tideline on a barnacle-encrusted ledge. A determined dogfish slithered up the rocks, *and upon his belly he did go*, and pecked the heart from the ledge. As he arched his head back, we could see his many rows of teeth - backslanting and multitudinous - the lipless, white, smiling mouth, anal contractions in the depths of the throat, and the luminous vacant stare from his lidless eyes.

D: They make my hackles quiver.

A: Perry cleaned the last salmon and pitched the head and offal high into the sky, where, for the briefest instant, it seemed to glue itself to a patch of blue. Suddenly, the sky darkened. A shadow fell over the ocean, and we heard a giant struggle like clashing armies of wind, the East challenging the West, the tornado against the hurricane. An eagle, as majestic as an archangel, and nearly as big, only a few feet overhead, with splayed wings and feathers – wings so huge it seemed that's all there was – beat back the dense air and talon-grasped the offering stuck to the sky. He flew to a nearby snag to enjoy his portion. I thought the bird could stand on air if need be.

D: Why are you telling me this?

A: It has to do with the eyes. They see things we can't.

D: Or won't.

A: Can't.

D: You've had too much to drink.

A: Not the first time.

Adam had the inspiration to launch the rowboat so they might park in the middle of the bay and become a small, black blob in the midst of the night-lights. Duende, as the saying goes, *came along for the ride.* He sat in the stern seat and made sure his tail was safely aboard. Adam carried a fresh pack of tailor-mades, dry matches, and his finest malt liquor. They drifted and shivered for much of the night, watching and listening to the scrapes against the hull of the boat and the frequent splashes of spray showering both man and dog. They saw that beneath the layer of anchovies and dogfish, there were larger fish, rapid burning torpedoes smashing through glowing schools of feed-fish, concussing some, so that the injured ones sprinkled like an electric shower of fallen angels, to be gobbled by gangs of ever larger flaming missiles. They noticed too, that beneath that layer, another layer existed of even greater and swifter sea creatures that had joined in the fantastical dance. For the man and dog, the thought occurred simultaneously, that the vast illuminated ballroom was limitless in its depth, and they realized also, the absurdity, that light increased in intensity the further one descended into darkness.

D: Was Perry a good friend?

A: We grew up together. We even had the same lovers.

D: Who were they?

A: Marlene, his wife, and her sister, Maddie…and others.

D: I know Maddie quite well.

A: I keep track of her comings and goings.

D: How?

Adam swigged on his malt.

A: Entries on my calendar…entries in my journal.

D: Did the sharing of lovers become a problem in your relationship with Perry?

A: Not for the reasons you might think. When he picked his final crew, he wanted me as first mate, but I made excuses and volunteered my younger brother, Darwin.

D: Why did you make excuses?

A: For certain, it was a wonderful opportunity to go out on the newest tuna vessel in the fleet, but I had concerns about the ship's seaworthiness. It could have been nothing more than that I preferred to stay home and take control of the romances.

D: It didn't work out so well for your brother, Darwin.

A: Did anyone ever say you are the doggiest of doggies?

D: No.

Adam did not wish to continue the discussion with all eyes staring. Perhaps to avoid Duo's inquisitiveness, he entered a boozy trance, a phenomenon that had happened many times before and often had biblical overtones. Upon emptying his bottle of malt, he made a final address to the eyes of the night.

A: When the burning eyes danced all about, the Lord should have said through the voices of the blind, Were a slave owner to strike the eye of a female slave, destroying it, should not the owner let the slave go, a free person, to compensate for the eye? And further, He should have said, Guard as the apple of thine eye and there will be I hid in the shadow of thine wing. And He should have said, If thine right eye causes thee to sin, tear it out, and were it so for the left eye, then be blind. And He should have said more than infrequently, Let us favour an eye for an eye, rather than the cheek for a cheek. And He should have repeated over and over, When thou seest a speck in thy neighbour's eye, look to thine own where a log doth lodge. And He should have exclaimed in wild enthusiasm, What ease with which the camel doth go through the eye of the needle. And He should have lamented, In the twinkling of an eye for all time innocence was lost. And He should have rejoiced through the eyes of the most blind of all and the ears of the most deaf of all, for He knew how to do such things, Look! He cometh. The trumpets blare. Why canst not every eye see and ear hear when we have eyes to see and ears to hear? And He should have noticed that the mind's eye dilated in the face of Him. And with many more voices He could have warned, The eye of the Lord keepth not watch, Of flesh desires the eye unceasingly, His eye resembles most the flame of the fire, therefore beware! And lastly, Who will wipe the tears from the eye when I have business elsewhere?

D: I cannot speak with the biblical flare, as do you, but as a contribution to this amazing night, I once heard a Chinese proverb, "It is better to light a candle, than curse the darkness."

A recent phenomenon, which had annoyed everyone, were the off-season visitors, otherwise known as long haits, who passed through the haven by raft, dugout canoe, de-licensed fish boat, pirate ship, any craft in ruin, preferably full of dry rot, and as a prerequisite must leak! They're attitude of disrespect for the sea - ignoring weather, ignoring tides, and ignoring safety regulations - did not go well with the locals.

A month earlier, two innocents had been rescued at the mouth of the bay: she, Starbright, in a flimsey canoe with a flimsier paddle, fighting a raging Nor'Wester, and he, her 5-month old son, by the curious name, Cacophony, sloshing in the bilge of the

~ 5 ~

Carver

"The pages of the book are clouded like the windows of an old train, the cloud of smoke rests on the sentences."

If on a Winter's Night a Traveler, **Italo Calvino**

HE COULD tell the dog's mind was elsewhere: gratuitous scratching, jerky rejection, elastic strings of drool, occasional whimpers, and an abundance of leg lifting on the beach logs strewn along the shore. When Adam asked, "Marking your territory?" or "Got an itch?" or "Aren't we the quiet one today?" Duende pretended not to hear.

They sat at the water's edge. Another nimbostratus day – damp, dark, numbing, typical, brooding, arthritic, coastal weather fit for muskrats and beaver, a morning to sympathize with Desolation-bound Captain George Vancouver from two hundred years ago, who would have sold his soul for a measly breakfast of sunbeams.

Adam sat on a fir log that had washed ashore on an extreme high tide, full of logdogs, staples, rusted bundle wire, and embedded sand and pea gravel - a nightmare for anyone who wished to mill it into planks or turn it into firewood. The man of solitude feebly threw pebbles into the water, watching the monotonous rings form and grow, to eventually disappear. Duende chased the seagulls, panting clouds of steam as he ran, his tail flaccid, not the usual ramrod pose. Shale squirted out behind his paws but without the gripping passion of his former self. The birds ignored the string of his faux attacks realizing they were no serious threat.

Seemingly on the verge of verbalization, time and again Duende ran up to Adam. The dog gyrated his moist nostrils, licked the humid air, and bent an alert ear, as if he searched for a sign of consent, some indication from Nature that would give him permission to speak his mind. If their relationship had been stronger, if they had been the best of friends since early child-hood days, and if Adam were confident that the canine could withstand the buffets and gales of his caustic humour, then the elderly scribe of scribblers might have teased further with, "Cat got your tongue?"

Unsure of the depth of the dog's unease, Adam let him work through the malaise.

Duende plunked down on the sand beside Adam's gumboot. He scratched behind one ear and then the other. Perhaps he had fleas, ticks, or ear-mites. Adam threw a jerky at his paws, since, in the past, this trick had always brought forth the magic of speech - doggie words, but words nonetheless. The mute dog refused to take the bait. He ran down the beach again and made another pseudo lunge at a gull. Adam picked up the jerky and ripped off a bite. Over the course of the morning neither man nor beast engaged in conversation. Instead they measured the depth and breadth of their mortified silence, the decibels in all likelihood ringing more loudly in the non-human ears. The reverberations of the repetitive plunks of pebbles into the long-suffering sea melted into the oblivion of time, but neither of them cared.

Adam drank. He found himself stuck in the blank pages of Scribbler Number Three. The suspicion grew that his inform-er either wrestled with angels above or devils below. Perhaps a contest manifested beyond the dog's endurance. It occurred to him that Duende may have witnessed a crucial event and failed to report his finding. That possibility seemed likely, given that his demeanour reeked of guilt and obfuscation, as if the Judas mongrel might be complicit. Another possibility emerged that the anal retentive critter might be withholding tidbit delights, simply to annoy the writer. For all one knew, Duo may have been protecting Adam, thinking, incorrectly of course, that the obsessed man didn't have fortitude enough to deal with a dose of truth.

Their relationship - shall one call it a contractual arrangement (though hardly legally binding), whereby Adam accepted in confidentiality the strict particulars of all that the dog saw, heard, rolled in, and smelled, and in return, received jerky and spirits as compensation - had never experienced an off-beat moment until now, not once had their interactions been anything but earnest and whole hearted, and not ever had discord surfaced, or so Adam incorrectly remembered. All the fact finding missions and all the debriefings had been totally above board, Duende reporting the blow-by-blow events, and Adam cherishing his position, scrawling copious notes in his journal, anchoring the community's legend in certainty so that these archives might take a rightful place among eternal things – his scribblers; in fact, become a guidepost to the quintessential quest for order. And, this point needs to be emphasized, had he not painstakingly quoted the canine's exact words and phrases, attempted to capture his inflection, undertones, overtones, mid-tones and minute vibrations? And, to Adam's credit, only once in a wee while did he request that the mutt not bark so quickly, since Parker was no longer as dexterous as other pens Adam had known. Never once did he doubt the pooch's keen senses of observation, which, he gathered, and this revelation had come as a monumental surprise, relied on smell more than any combination of taste, touch, sight, hearing, and intuition. Thus, their *modus vivendi* took on exciting complications. So, as the two moved further into uncharted territories, where they could almost see the future floating in front of their mind's eye, Adam felt obliged to accept Duende's unorthodox way of investigative reporting; for instance, the complete and entire telling of the bearbecue phantasmagoria, and only a few days later, the systematic reportage of the enchanting encounter between Alice and Tara, so that when the double-agent dog mentioned, "The air smelled of sadness in Alice's house," Adam had simply accepted his statement like any good interrogator would, and faithfully made practical use of that haunting emotion, as he scrawled with Parker across the pages in Scribbler Number Two, to convey the mysterious mood of melancholy, though, and this small detail is only mentioned for clarification purposes, Adam did comment at the time, that he was not so convinced of the pervasive phenomenon of *woe*. Yes, he had called the emotion, *woe*; for, being a human by happenstance, and consequently condemned to rely on a myriad of less than stellar senses, rather than that one super sense the dog used to exclusion of all others, our scribbling recluse was therefore prone to scepticism regarding the animal's proficiency when it came to the smell of feelings.

This minute criticism didn't seem to bother the lovable mutt in the least. In a way, this ability to accept faultfinding became the reason why the man and dog made such a good team, each shoring up the failings of the other. Though Adam had conveyed certain doubts about his olfactory prowess, and here a certain question needs to be asked: Did his mute-ish behaviour, on this morning on the beach, arise as a consequence of that unintentional and slightly negative comment on Adam's part? Or? Given that he had promised to take Duende's interpretation of the afternoon meeting between the old woman and young girl into consideration, and then reassured him further by saying that the investigative assistant's extraordinary finding of *moroseness, joylessness, and desolation* (these three nouns Duende had later repeated many times as he progressively succumbed to the attraction of exaggeration and rhythm) would be included in the Key-Tab scribblers, more or less, nose and all, so to speak, as though the emotions were not only Adam's and Duende's, but also, Alice's and Tara's, which, on the surface, satisfied the animal, he hoped, prayed and assumed.

Duende finally broke the silence.

D: I'm heading back to the docks.

A: Wait. You're leaving me without a bone to gnaw on.

D: I've got things to do.

A: If you've got things to do, make one of them Carver. I've been pleading for days now to get the lowdown on the newcomer.

D: Relax.

A: We lack so much in the Carver category. Our file on him is the grand total of one blank page.

Adam had used the plural pronouns to make the cur think and feel and smell as though the project had become their cooperative endeavour.

D: It's not so easy is it?

A: Not so easy, but essential.

D: I agree, essential, but not easy.

Then Adam confronted the doggie.

A: What's your problem little pooch?

D: Carver and I have never bonded.

A: Now's your chance. Bird-dog the guy. Don't you realize that we must always be alert to a stranger in our midst?

Duende ran off leaving Adam without a lead for Scribbler Number Three, which he now had open on page one with Parker vibrating under a full tank of Indiga's high octane. Adam said to himself rather than an indifferent world, Gosh darn dog drives me to drink. In every single instance lately, he engineers a conspiracy to deny me progress. The dog, as I now suspect, could unravel the mystery of this investigation, and my imagination too; he could tear the cloak of secrecy from the shoulders of darkness, to the point of folly, and beyond if need be, and he could scrutinize the many trails he follows, to the point of obsession, no stone left unturned, a scorched earth policy, until the unknown becomes the known, until the thing that the community knows deep inside its growling gut finally thrusts through to the light of day.

Adam guzzled another scotch (What else was their to do?) because his community plant had masqueraded as a nonpareil sleuth, yet failed to honour his commitment.

Scribbler Three:

A RECENT phenomenon, which had annoyed everyone, were the off-season visitors, otherwise known as "long hairs," who passed through the haven by raft, dugout canoe, de-licensed fish boat, pirate ship, any craft in ruin, preferably full of dry rot, and as a prerequisite, must leak. Their attitude of disrespect for the sea – ignoring the weather, ignoring the tides, and ignoring safety regulations – did not go well with the locals.

A month earlier, two innocents had been rescued at the mouth of the bay: she, Starbright, in a flimsy canoe with a flimsier paddle, fighting a raging nor'wester, and he, her five month old son, by the curious name, Cacophony, sloshing in the bilge of the boat, both of them doomed if it weren't for Jeremy and his *Storm Chaser* making a heroic rescue. As to be expected, the obliging man befriended the mother and child for the next several days aboard his houseboat until The Rutabaga Family came and took her back into their fold and garden of tasteless root vegetables. These youngsters never stayed long.

Carver seemed to be the exception – an Adonis - who had arrived during a squall, and now was determined to become a permanent resident, which if it happened, would swell The Refuge population by three point seven percent.

He hitched on a tugboat. And didn't have long hair. His hair was curly and blonde, but short. His eyes glowed green although they stared from a tilted head like the immortal god of beauty with a fairly advanced case of narcissism. The fellow was athletic, handy, strong. He fixed up a small shed behind his uncle's dilapidated machine shop and marine ways, which soon subbed as his home. Some wondered if MacLeod even knew he had a nephew.

Rather briskly Carver had become a favourite in the bay. The keynote to his celebrity was the possession of a rabbit's foot, either that, or he had learned a trick or two from Jesus Christ Himself fishing the Sea of Galilee. As an absurdity, Carver had no acquaintanceship with the marine environment - much like

Jesus – a city boy come to show up the locals. People clamoured for his company and fought amongst themselves for his presence on their boat. The Adonis clone easily cadged invites to dinner because he supplied the main course. And he ingratiated himself further by jumping up from the dinner table and washing the dishes. No longer did people ask, "Did you get any?" They asked instead, "How many did you get?" In a hubristic show of excessiveness, the newcomer would ask, "Would you like a red spring, white spring, or maybe the marbled variety? The pantry is full."

CARVER WALKED into the general store. Duende slept on the welcome mat so the newest resident to The Refuge was obliged to step over the dog. James tallied invoices on his adding machine and failed to notice the young man waiting for service.

"If you don't mind, James," Carver asked, "I need some change?" He flashed a ten-dollar bill.

"Nickels and dimes?"

"Make it quarters. The girls demand a raise."

James laughed. "I wish I could get paid for stacking wood. You're spoiling them." He walked to the cash box, took out a roll of quarters, and placed the ten-dollar bill under the change tray.

"I have to do MacLeod's wood, the Blacks, and the Smiths. You'd think they'd do it themselves," said Carver.

"They think they're too busy."

"Even fussy old Adam wants his shed filled, but it has to be first growth fir bark."

James laughed again, "The old-timers think we'll always have fuel like that."

Carver opened the roll of quarters and sluiced them into his jacket pocket. He gave the wrapper back to James. "Better put up another roll."

He left the store, stepping over Duende sleeping in the doorway, but soundly clipped the poor mutt's snout with his boot heel. The newcomer turned to the dog and commented, with some glee, "Doo-Doo, ha ha, got you."

During dinner, Peter told
Laura and Charlotte about the
results of the plankton tows and
related something he had ~~seen~~
never seen before. Instead of
swimming erratically, as was
usual, the scallop larvae swam
in their few drops of seawater
on the slide of the microscope, and
they spun, each larva equidistant
from the other, each spinning
clockwise, propelled by their feathery
cilia, but the group as a whole
turned counter-clockwise!

    Mother and Daughter had studied
bivalve larvae through the
    microscope only once before.
The animals on that occasion
were sluggish, but Charlotte had
been fascinated by the fact that she
could see through ~~th~~ their clear shells
and watch the internal
organs pulse & wiggle. She had said
to her mother, "They've got no ~~s~~ clothes
on, Mother!"

~ 6 ~

No Space for God's Breath

*"No doubt I am now, in some sense, mad: but, as
you may know, these things are merely a question of
perspective."*

The Emigrants, **W. G. Sebald**

BEFORE ADAM went to bed the barometer had shot upward.
Soon drafts infiltrated the cracks in his cabin. The Bute wind
funnelled out of the central province over the Homathko gla-
cier and down the reaches of Bute Inlet. The wind tumbled from
its steep pressure slopes and stirred the waters into dementia,
spreading through the warren of channels engulfing the northern islands of the *Sea without Shores*. While lying there, unable
to sleep, he smelled the wind's interior origins – dry and clean
with hints of sweet sage and tumbleweed, a change from the
coastal pong of kelp and sea lettuce.

An eerie, lunar brilliance sailed with The Bute and set his
room aglow. The light penetrated the corners of his cabin and
painted the ceiling in a silver radiance, as if washed with the
sea's bioluminescence. Adam, too, was awash in the same light,
and his skin came off as a dull pewter pallor.

Not only did the moon sail with the wind that night, but also
an image manifested from previous thoughts and observations.

A look-a-like to the child, Charlotte, entered his home. Her likeness whirled at the foot of the bed. She wore a flared dress spun to sheen, a white satin material. Her sleeves billowed with the voracity of her spinning, and, as an incongruity, red flames issued from around her feet and coiled up her legs as though she pirouetted on a delicate sun. Her exaggerated fingers gave the impression of terminals of a soaring bird's wing, one splayed toward the ceiling, the other to the floor, suggesting that the apparition might be a conduit to the Above and the Below. Aluminum hair flung out like folds of a tinselled dress, and her head tilted backwards, more than humanly possible, so that her unblinking eyes saw the twirling room and Adam upside down. She twirled so fast that he saw her eyes straight on. This fixed gaze was unlike her real, flesh-and-blood, moocow look. The doppelganger's eyes welled, and soon tears riddled him with a searing, briny liquid. She begged to be free of her dance, and her pleading went thus: "I want to stop the dance, I want to stop the dance."

Near daybreak, well after the image had spun into another dimension, Adam watched the moon – squat, pumpkin orange, a rotating ellipsis – set overtop of Cortes Island. In the channel, the outrageous Bute had mellowed, but still harboured vigour. Off and on, veils of spindrift curtained both entrances to The Refuge. The wind said, "I can come inside if I want," and manufactured small contingents of dervish waterspouts to unambiguously make her point. They hovered on the face of the waters, augured holes in the sea, and stirred the ocean into foam.

"See what I can do," she boasted.

Adam wrote "windy" on his calendar.

He should have written, "All hell broke loose."

His head spun. Following such a disrupted sleep, he had difficulty putting words together, mainly because the words spun. They generated an internal energy. And wobbled. Collided. Exploded. The pages in Scribbler Number Four fluttered. He worried that the windstorm from last night would return and rip the pages from their binding. Adam thought, If I can stop the words, even for an instant, then I'd trap them, and choose which to keep and which to throw away.

When he looked though, they scurried over the pages like frightened mice. He wanted to swat them like flies, give the kiss of life only to those that persevered in the golden quest for truth.

Though temporarily destabilized, he mustered an observation that verged on an innovative theory: Everything spins. Duende chases his tail and will never catch it. The girls spin on the dock, and the centrifugal force will catapult them beyond their centre into a world of outer rings. Wade's basketball spins even when left unattended. And The Refuge spins.

He concluded: Things that don't spin now, will spin later. Spinning is contagious. There is no known antidote. A pandemic approaches.

Scribbler Four:

ONCE THE wind had subsided, Peter spent the morning collecting plankton samples, and in the late afternoon, he analyzed bivalve larvae. His small crew had managed the grading and packaging operation without supervision so he could enjoy a day of marine biology instead of terrestrial business.

His eyes had wearied from staring into his microscope. He decided to take the clinker rowboat home, the only boat he owned that didn't smell of shellfish offal and didn't have a cranky motor. Lately, running the shellfish operation had been more about fixing machinery, rather than probing the mysteries of the sea.

He watched Laura and Charlotte on their little dock, waiting for him to row home from the seafarm. Laura sat on a geoduck crate, whereas Charlotte spun on her tiptoes. She gave pretence of vertigo and stumbled into her mother's lap. The child was dressed in standard garb: rubber boots, sweat shirt, warm jacket, jeans, and a knee length skirt over the jeans. The child contained her hair in a red kerchief.

As Peter placed the oars into their collars, the sea exploded into a marvellous array of shimmering sun-spangles. A thousand million suns shattered, as playful gusts rippled the water's surface and reeled in all directions. In the late light, the trunks of trees along the shore burned fiery red, and so did the faces of Charlotte and Laura. Peter imagined that the trees and his family thirsted for the same sun for the same reason.

He weaved his way through the longlines and styrofoam floats. Bonaparte gulls circled above. A flock of diving ducks, a mix of surf scoters and buffleheads, stripped bare the wild mussel set on his mainlines. Perched on top of the floats, black cormorants balanced with their wet wings partially extended, drying - ready to take flight if necessary. None spooked as he paddled by.

In the channel, he heard the wind, and saw the splashing of waves on the rocky, outer point. Peter looked up at the eagles soaring in the sky and then shipped his oars. He raised his binoculars and counted nine adults and four immatures. The piebald young looked bigger than their parents, fluffed with an under layer of down. The birds loved the nor'westers from the inlets. Years before, his caretaker, Sebastian, had once told him, "Eagles define their territory in ever widening spirals from the still point of the nest to the beyond." Peter picked the point of origin from the nest on Centre Island and traced the invisible cone structure, as he presumed the birds did also.

His rowboat turned slowly, captured in a small coiling breeze that managed to gain entry to The Refuge. Peter relaxed and put his binoculars down. First he saw his own wharf, home, and family, Sylvia's cabin near the gap to the lagoon, Production Point, MacLeod's clutter of buildings, and then bluffs and trees. He saw Alice's house, James' log home on the hill behind the general store, the government dock in the form of a U, Laura's little schoolhouse, the fuel station and a small tug taking on diesel and water. He saw Wade playing basketball at the freight shed, Jeremy's houseboat, Brad and Jim's houseboat, Centre Island, the seafarm with his floats and longlines, and Sebastian's floathouse. He saw the grouch, Adam, sitting on the porch of his rundown shack, drinking his scotch, hardly aware that the world watched him watch the world. The slow turn of Peter's rowboat brought him back to his family again.

He aligned the boat and paddled home. When he arrived, Laura tied the bowline and Peter fastened the stern. Charlotte began to dance again. She tilted her head back, flung her arms out, and spun rapidly. She seemed unaware of her father and said, "The eagles are almost gone, Mama."

Peter grabbed her, as he thought she might fall.

"You'll get dizzy, honey."

The birds weren't *almost gone*, but specks in the sky. The family shared the binoculars. The eagles orbited deeper into space, carving spirals into the blue. Her father helped Charlotte hold the heavy glasses.

"They're still getting too far away, Dad," she said.

"This is the wind they love."

During dinner, Peter told Laura and Charlotte about the results of the plankton tows and related something he had never seen before. Instead of swimming erratically, as was usual, the scallop larvae swam in their few drops of seawater on the slide of the microscope, and they spun, each larva equidistant from the other, each spinning clockwise, propelled by their feathery cilia, but the group as a whole turned counter clockwise. Mother and daughter had studied bivalve larvae through the microscope only once before. The animals on that occasion were sluggish, but Charlotte had been fascinated by the fact that she could see through their clear shells and watch the internal organs pulse and wiggle. She had said to her mother, "They've got no clothes on, Mama."

Peter questioned the orderly behaviour of the scallops, the individual rotations, and then the group counter-rotation, "How it is possible?" He had not seen this phenomenon with other bivalve species either, such as clams, mussels, and oysters. "Possibly they set up eddies and that makes the group spin the wrong way, but how do they get organized...and for what reason?"

Charlotte said, "They're just like us girls, but way smaller."

Laura shrugged her shoulders, "Yes, but you girls spin the same way."

Thinking more, Peter said, "They looked like soldiers in formation," but corrected himself, "No, more like a troupe of ballet dancers...the swans in Swan Lake."

Peter had only seen one ballet in his lifetime and recalled the way each swan pirouetted in one direction, yet the dancers as a troupe spun across the stage in the opposite direction. At the time, he thought it only an illusion.

Charlotte carefully considered her father's story and came up with a solution to the puzzle, "Maybe they were being tricky, Dad."

The night wore on. Laura read Charlotte a bedtime story (Alice in Wonderland). Charlotte brushed her teeth, got tucked into bed, and fell asleep quickly. Laura and Peter made a pot of tea and talked over their day. Laura said her students were doing well except for Wade who had a devil of a time learning to read, and Sarah wasn't the bully like before, which was a relief. The twins, Mary and Elizabeth, remained inseparable and indistinguishable, while Tara seemed preoccupied.

"The twins both misspelled *column*, they left out the *n* in the last test," said Laura.

Peter laughed, "I think I made the same mistake when I was their age."

Laura told Peter that Charlotte benefitted from being around the older girls, and since it was the season, Sylvia had agreed to give the children a crash course in fungal identification. She had promised to take them to a special place where mushrooms grew in fairy rings.

Laura reminded Peter of his promise to give marine biology lessons.

"I'll do it soon."

Remembering the dinner table discussion, she said, "Spinning larvae doesn't seem all that strange to me, but the equidistant bit sounds odd...and the counter rotation is really weird."

"Maybe they're just being tricky like Charlotte said," commented Peter.

SO FAR, things hadn't gone as Laura's imagination had constructed the day.

Before setting off on the field trip, the teacher had hoped her students would receive an orientation session. She knew Sylvia possessed a mushroom library and felt the children needed a frame of reference before romping off into the forest. Laura expected an introductory talk on the general aspects of mycoflora, perhaps a handout with illustrations, and, only then, the forest walk to the fabled fairy rings. Once back in the classroom along with Sylvia, her students would take spore prints and learn the principles of identification and classification. Hopefully, they would find enough edible mushrooms to have a good feed. Her imagined day seemed like the proper way to proceed given the educational purpose of their outing. Instead, their guide had waited at the front door of the little schoolhouse as everyone arrived, and announced, "In the sylvan solitude sorrows are stilled...let's go."

Sylvia's boots were two over-sizes and mismatched, one from each pair belonging to her late husband. Her mortal beloved had died in a boating accident during a sou'easter storm on the *Sea without Shores*. She wore his boots every day, the least she could do to honour his memory, even on dry, sizzling, summer afternoons when the rest of the cloistered community gambolled in flip-flops. The soles lacked tread entirely so it was hardly surprising that she lost footing on the slippery rocks and muddy trails.

The boots leaked. They were as thin and holed as her socks, which had belonged to him too. The soles of her feet had calloused in compensation. She made frequent use of a rubber repair kit, and over the years, each boot had been patched with red, round pocks, and looked as if they nurtured a contagious disease.

Three days prior to the accident, Sylvia had arrived at The Refuge on the *Quillchine Princess* with all their possessions to begin as newly-weds. Not an experienced sailor, the Lord, as the saying goes, *chose to take him away*. An odd thing had happened though: not only did her husband drown on that stormy night, but a pretty young woman. Far more pretty than Sylvia. Their naked bodies were strapped together with life vests and ropes - much too closely. Sylvia was twenty years old when those events took place, ready to embark on a life of romance and adventure. At this moment in time, her clock strikes forty and sounds like the tolling from a cracked bell.

A WESTERLY blew above the forest, sounding as many voices. The stalwart trees spoke in whispers. They noted the remoteness of today's high wind, and how it had become such an effort to articulate under these conditions. Nevertheless, they discussed their own rootedness and compared their progress in reaching out for the illusive moisture in the soil. An old and garrulous fir tree commented on the cloudless day, how it never ceased to amaze him that his green needles really did compliment the blue in the sky. He held a branch above the canopy, where a small updraft swirled and shook his foliage, for the others to admire. A cedar, with an exaggerated taper, who had lost her top during a nasty gale many years ago, interrupted this perfect moment of contemplation to alert the others to the approach of visitors.

"Don't be alarmed, it's only Sylvia with the school children," she said.

A hemlock beside her commented, "I smell a dog."

Below, shafts of light danced on roped carpets of emerald moss, an intertwining structure of endless complication. Eight humans flickered on and off as they passed through the prisms of light. After an hour of hiking, when no one dared to speak a word, they arrived at the base of a giant fir tree. Sylvia addressed her group.

"Link your hands around the Standing One."

The children linked hands as they were told; yet, fingertip-to-fingertip, they could not encircle the tree. Laura joined her pupils and still they could not close the circle. Sylvia took a place between the twins, Mary and Elizabeth, and completed the circle.

"Look up," said Sylvia.

They looked up. The top of the ancient fir disappeared from view; tree-sized limbs jutted from the trunk hundreds of feet above, and small patches of blue sky filtered through. Laura felt her anxieties and expectations melt away. Though no instructions had been given, she closed her eyes, as did the others. Laura could not be certain: either the fir rotated on its base, or, hand in hand, they spun around the tree.

An eternity encased each vital second.

Suddenly, Sylvia broke the connection, and they continued on their journey. She said, as if this the only explanation required, "The Standing One unlocks the entrance to the valley."

Little Charlotte asked, "Did we unlock it?"

"Of course." answered Sylvia.

The widow chose a corridor into a deeper wood, but before continuing on, gave instructions, "Off with the shoes and socks." The children and Laura obeyed.

Every tree appeared as majestic as the fir they had just encircled. They floated as ghosts on the soft forest floor, not intimidated by the deepness when they sunk into the cushioned greens. All shapes were curved and gentle. Their feet fell without sound, the imprint only temporary. Beneath their feet and between their toes, insects traversed on subterranean missions. Every step became a galaxy, and they became a part of this new universe.

Decay blanketed everything. They saw fallen branches sprouting scaly, leafy lichen, and they saw feathered, moss leggings creeping up decomposing stumps. Not a sharp edge projected into the world. The mushroom hunters barely breathed.

At a rotting hemlock log, Sylvia raised her hand and commanded them, "Stop." There they counted drops of water that oozed from colonies of white fungal pillows. Collectively they watched the parasitic assemblage grow larger, while the host log imploded inward, the slow metamorphosis bewilderingly beautiful and measured, with nothing ever lost. These moments were seen by the colonial organism with linked perceptions – sixteen tentacles reached out from eight separate entities.

As the group came upon an opening in the forest, fairies appeared and danced within their fungal rings. They leaped from twisted pipes to burgundy brushes; the gnomes stooped to smell their homes of white-warted fists and purple-pruned wrists. Elves meditated alongside false brains - dark, red, and wood bug chewed. Some fairies sat on stools for green toads and others stepped over slippery, slimy, slug trails connecting nibbled chanterelles to hedge-hogged and coral-clustered outposts from sea-ancient lineages. All around oyster-hued angels hugged deadfalls - stemless, wings of fire, frilled and gilled. Porous honeycombs with latticed veils hid ribbed and meaty knees. Yellow umbrellas rained magenta spores, while champagne glasses awaited the uncorking. Jelly-beaned bubbles pushed relentlessly through the dampened earth.

The children formed a circle around a fungal ring, and the fairies twirled inside. Laura, not wanting to disturb the scene, yet unable to resist a fascination, touched a speckled puffball. Clouds of white powder swirled, as if they might be the reagent for this particular day. Pungent with earthly smells, the clouds seduced her. She left her companions and the dancing fairies, and followed a winding trail that opened upon a stream where the thirsting for eternal youth could be quenched, but that place did not interest her. She passed a kind of eating establishment where strangers talked like old friends, but she did not stop to listen. Laura walked further and stepped inside a hollowed stump, the entrance to a vast cave. The walls were covered in sparkling alabaster, and soft music emanated into the chamber. On a bed of down, silken sheets covered a radiant body. She realized this was her destination and sensed that the radiant body had awaited her arrival.

A century passed.

Sylvia touched her on the shoulder. "Time to go."

On the way back to The Refuge, still swayed by her euphoria, Laura realized she had forgotten to take photographs. They had forgotten to eat their lunches. And no one thought to collect specimens. To go back now, or search elsewhere, would have spoiled their outing and spoiled the mood that had settled over everyone. In the alabaster cave, she believed that she had vanished. Laura wondered if the children had similar experiences to hers. Her own experience was so wonderful, and wonderfully absent of shame. She reflected that each of her students might have a similar and private memory to take home, though perhaps not quite as sensual as hers. She wondered if life in the forest was always like this for their guide.

That evening, Charlotte told her father, as he tucked her into bed, "I danced with a fairy, Dad." He smiled, brushed a few locks of hair from her cheek, and kissed her good night. In their own bed, Peter, wishing to discuss problems on the seafarm, found Laura surprisingly extravagant. Between their naked bodies there was no space for God's breath.

Immediately below the image, Brad had installed an alter shelf, and in each of 7 drilled holes stood a lilac coloured medicine bottle. A full box of medicine bottles, containing various amounts of a dry white paste, sat on the floorboards. The 12-volt light in the ceiling gave off a frail, yellow glow. With such poor interior visability, the bottles could have been mistaken for miniature sentries, or simply eye-witnesses.

A wooden barrel head branded with "Arrogant Fish" hung on the wall below their alter. Their gallery table was piled high with files and medical texts. A thick journal lay open, and Maddie noticed that, on the exposed pages, Brad had transcribed the eulogy, R.I.P. Shipmates of the Arrogant, written by Adam Wilks in 1945 for the magazine, Western Fisheries which she had shared years earlier with her nephews. Intermittently, the bilge pump cycled

~ 7 ~

Devotees to a Scripted Life

*"Occasionally someone makes it back from this dark
world though, and it's from these people that we know
what drowning feels like."*

The Perfect Storm, **Sebastian Junger**

OVER THE years, Adam's camp cot had moulded to his shape –
a cadaverous bundle. Beside the cot stood a three-drawer dress-
er (drawer at the top - underwear, socks, gloves, scotch, loose
change, and three malfunctioning wristwatches; drawer in the
middle - shirts and sweaters, scotch, and one necktie; drawer at
the bottom - pants, scotch, belts, and suspenders). Jackets and
rain gear hung on nails beside the front door, while slippers,
shoes, and boots lined up by the back door. The walls in his cell
remained barren, reflecting his minimalist lifestyle.

At the heart of the cabin stood the stove with a cavernous
warming oven and burnt-out water jacket, outlined in nickel
plate, no longer airtight if it ever had been, and suited to someone who baked (not Adam). Beside the stove sat a large wooden
box, more often than not, filled with first growth fir bark, a fuel
almost as efficient as coal. The porcelain sink supplied gravity
fed water (cold only), and the matching drain board and back-

splash (cracked and stained) had been purloined from a logging camp, where Adam had worked as a watchman many years before. His makeshift kitchen countertop of D-grade plywood remained unpainted, knot proliferated, grease congealed, and unhygienic. Underneath, for the counter-top support, he used wooden pop crates, which doubled as cupboards for pots, pans, dishes, and non-perishables.

Perhaps his bookshelves (not the stove) served as the heart of the cabin, maintaining their own fire. The long, four-shelf bookcase had been cobbled from salvaged boardwalk planking. The library overflowed with a lifetime of reading, pages dog-eared without shame, any old thing used for a bookmark (feathers, strips of arbutus bark, and dried leaves with only the skeletons remaining), and the whole collection organized into four divisions: top shelf – reference material; second shelf – science; third shelf – coastal history and myth; and fourth shelf – philosophy, art, and fiction. Within each category, his books were organized by author from A to Z, the Xes and Zeds to his embarrassment not once represented. That's a white lie. He owned one novel by Zola, *Germinal*. Adam had underlined many passages in these fine books and used two headed arrows to connect unusual words or phrases – a nuisance for future readers. A generous supply of chicken scratches and asterisks tracked beside the margins expressing his pleasure or displeasure with the author. Three books missing from the top shelf were the Bible (Annotated Oxford 1973, and newly purchased), the Oxford Dictionary (Fifth Edition, 1964) and the annual BC Tide Charts (Queens Printer, 1974), which he kept on the kitchen table for quick reference. Duende and Adam had come to argue over trifles, and these three resources gave him an advantage in most informal confabs, debates, polite conversations, raging brawls, and internal dialogues.

Between the bookcase and bed lived his stuffed easy chair, again moulded to the shape of the present occupant. Unfortunately, by force of habit, he picked the cotton stuffing from the padded arms when he read, so that the wooden frame had become quite exposed. Something worse, he had taken to excavating splinters from the soft wood with his fingernails, which the appreciative carpenter ants packed off to their nests inside the cabin walls. Only when Adam put down a book did he realize the destruction done.

For illumination, the self-taught man used two wall-mounted naphtha lamps, one above the armchair and the other in the kitchen nook where he wrote in his journal and filled his Key-Tabs. He prided himself on making the fragile mantles last two years, a feat few in The Refuge could equal. The lights cast a brooding yellow glow - a *Potato Eater* scene - at times so feeble they actually seemed to increase the dark. And the likelihood of a severed ear. Nevertheless, the lamps performed much better than kerosene lanterns, not as smelly and not as messy.

Adam used a straight-back, wooden chair on the front porch of his hermitage for the days that were too warm or too frightening to be inside. There he watched *every winged bird of every kind*; the soaring eagles, wise old owls, trickster ravens, myriad small songbirds, blurs of hummers, flocks of diving sea ducks, lonely loons, and the ubiquitous gulls. He listened to their calls and songs, at times answering with poor renditions.

ADAM AND Duende sat at the table, drinking. The stove burned vigorously. As they studied the arbutus tree outside the window, man and dog seemed lost in thought, until Adam stirred from his reverie.

A: The Salish name for the arbutus is kʷum kʷumay.

D: Didn't know that.

A: Arbutus only occur within a mile of the ocean.

D: Didn't know that.

A: The Latin name is *Arbutus menziesii*, the species name given in honour to Archibald Menzies, Captain Vancouver's ship's surgeon and naturalist.

D: Dogs call them the sunburned tree.

A: The arbutus is sacred for the Salish.

D: As far as I'm concerned, all trees are sacred.

A raven with scruffy white feathers and penetrating blue eyes alighted on the kʷum kʷumay. The restless bird moved from foot to foot. He stropped his beak in the crotch of a branch, as though sharpening a broadsword. The creature had visited Adam before, always choosing the same limb. Adam took the calendar off the wall and wrote an entry in the November 7 square: *damn bird won't leave.*

D: You don't see many white ones.

A: This is the only white raven in the world.

D: There's probably more than one.

Knocking his research assistant off the cushion, the researcher rushed to his bookcase and extracted his bird and myth reference material. He hurried back to the table with a pile of books. Duende jumped back onto his cushion, and Adam read to him.

A: "Raven was once white. He was hungry and snuck into a smokehouse. The people banged on the walls and the soot covered his feathers."

D: What about the blue eyes?

A: The legends don't tell us anything about blue eyes.

Adam continued reading.

A: "Raven is sometimes called, Black Bird. He was given the responsibility of opening the clamshell and allowing humankind to crawl forth."

D: That was a mistake.

Adam thumbed through a few more pages.

A: "White ravens are harbingers of good luck. They travel as guides with Chinese shamans to assist lost souls in their journeys between realms."

D: Around here they would be local shamans, not Chinese.

A: Sylvia is our only shaman candidate.

D: She wouldn't get along with a white raven.

Adam opened another reference book.

A: "The raven is much more intelligent than a crow."

D: I doubt that.

A: His call imitates other birds. Raven makes noises from the recesses of his throat, which sound like drops of water falling into a deep well, or, if his mood is one of abandonment, a child crying in the wilderness, and, if he wishes to manifest repentance, the mutterings of an old man from a purgatorial wasteland.

D: You made that up.

A: My imagination just fired on one cylinder.

Adam threw a jerky onto Duende's plate.

A: Once I heard a breeze rustling the leaves in the trees, and another time, a wave rolling the fine gravel onto a beach, but it was Raven creating the complexity of sound.

D: They're tricky that way.

The bird flew off.

A: Look, there he goes.

D: In search of another clam to open.

A: He wants to see if what crawls out is any better than his original sin.

D: Maybe you just fired on two cylinders.

Scribbler Five:

DUENDE JUMPED aboard, as *Tom Forge* pulled away from the fuel dock.

James yelled out, "You've got Duo."

Maddie called back through the open wheelhouse door, "I'm just going over to Brad and Jim's."

Sheets of thin ice floated on the surface of the bay, and Maddie maneuvered around them. A grey pallor hung in the sky. The wind chill had dropped the temperature another five degrees. Shivering, Duende came into the wheelhouse and parked at Maddie's feet. She looked down at the dog and said, "I'm going to visit my nephews. They're just as crazy as ever."

The dog sniffed her rubber boots and then looked up with a quizzical expression. "I don't know why I still feel responsible for those guys," she said.

The dog sniffed her boots again.

Maddie berthed alongside the log raft. Brad came out of their little houseboat and helped her secure the *Forge*. He wore slippers, a rag of a T-shirt, and cut-off jeans.

"James says Jim's sick."

"He's okay. The recovery time is longer now that his threshold has increased."

"Meaning?"

"It probably has something to do with the colder water this winter."

Maddie crossed both arms and rubbed her cold shoulders. "Brad, explain in ten words or less."

He hesitated and then said, "People, especially children, are able to stay under longer in colder water."

Brad added, "In a sense, Jim has always been a child."

"I still haven't got a clue what you're talking about."

"It's advisable to understand the difference between voluntary and involuntary apnoea, the concepts of laryngospasm, ventricular fibrillation, mammalian diving reflex, asphyxiation, and lung tidal air capacity in order to comprehend the phenomenon of drowning."

She closed her eyes and shook her head. " I doubt I'll take your advice."

Maddie took off her gloves and threw them into *Forge's* pilothouse. She sucked on her cigarette through cupped hands and exhaled a cloud of smoke. "I thought you guys gave up your drowning experiments. Don't you have anything better to do?"

"We started up because of Jim's dream."

"Great idea!"

"It's freezing," said Brad. "Let's go inside."

Duende ran ahead and pushed the door to the houseboat. Maddie followed. Brad picked up an armload of wood for the galley stove.

Jim slept in his small bunk. Duende jumped up and licked his face, but Jim gave no response. The dog curled in close to Jim and continued to lick his face. Maddie noticed their father's logbook in Jim's left hand. He appeared to grip it so that made her feel more hopeful. She pulled gently on the *tori book*, as Jim had always called it, and the resistance reinforced her feelings of hope. Perry's ship's log seemed thinner than before. She presumed that Jim had lost some of his pages.

Though Maddie was quite familiar with the interior of their houseboat, she now, for the first time, noticed a small shelf above Jim's bed holding two matching crystal bowls, one filled with brittle yellow paper fragments and the other only a third full. She made a mental calculation about whether or not Jim would need a third bowl to accommodate all the pieces the passage of time would chip from his father's logbook. She touched Jim's hand, which immediately warmed her fingers.

Three pans on the stove boiled vigourously, filling the single room of their houseboat with a dense vapour. The interior consisted of two bunks, a small galley, and two chairs at the galley table. Their clothes hung on wall hooks along with their cooking utensils. Wood screws secured to the wall a black-framed photograph of their father's ship, *Arrogant*. Maddie could see the elbow of the operator at the starboard window of the ship's wheelhouse. Another crewmember stood at an open galley doorway with one hand on a railing and the other in his pocket. The picture had been taken in Vancouver Harbour, perhaps on the eve of the *Arrogant's* maiden voyage. The vessel looked ultra clean and shipshape. Brad had once insisted to Maddie that the elbow belonged to his father.

Immediately below the image, Brad had installed an alter shelf, and in each of seven drilled holes stood a lilac coloured medicine bottle. A full box of medicine bottles containing various amounts of a dry white paste sat on the floorboards. The 12-volt light in the ceiling gave off a frail yellow glow. With such poor interior visibility, the bottles could have been mistaken for miniature sentries, or simply, eyewitnesses. A wooden barrel head branded with *Arrogant Fish* hung on the wall below their alter. Their galley table was piled high with files and medical texts. A thick journal lay open, and Maddie noticed that, on the exposed pages, Brad had transcribed the eulogy, *R.I.P. Shipmates of the Arrogant*, written by Adam Wilkes in 1945 for the magazine *Western Fisheries*, which she had shared years earlier with her nephews. Intermittently, the bilge pump cycled on and off, and the whirr of the motor progressively laboured under the continuous load of incoming seawater.

"Your battery needs a recharge," Maddie observed.

"We'll have to go up on MacLeod's marine ways. The bottom needs a repaint."

"You'll need more than a repaint," commented Maddie as she took off her wool jacket. "The temperature in here is a bit above Hell."

"Jim has to warm from the inside out. It takes a lot of steam to get his core temperature back to normal."

Bradley picked up the journal from the gallery table and thumbed to the section, RECORDS. "This column on the left is the time submerged, and on the right, is the time from haul out to wakefulness. As you go down the columns you'll notice that the duration increases, but I think we are bumping up against his limits."

Brad turned a page. "Here are some graphs."

"I don't understand graphs and I don't care to. Have you given him tea?" Maddie asked.

"He doesn't have a swallowing response yet. We always start the recovery with steam."

"How long has he been unconscious?"

Brad looked at his journal. "He's not unconscious; he's just sleeping. I fished him out yesterday at 11:34 a.m."

"You're going to kill your brother. You know that don't you."

"I can't stop him."

"Yes you can."

"If I stopped him, he'd sneak off and do it alone; then there would be no one to bring him back."

"The *Forge* can make Powell River hospital in four hours."

"We just need to make steam. They'd do the same at the River."

"Make me some tea."

Brad opened a box of Nabob Orange Pekoe and put a bag in each of two mugs. He poured boiling water from the smallest pot on the stove.

"Black," said Maddie.

"I know."

They waited for the tea to steep. During their silence, Maddie revisited the past: Perry, the crew, Adam, her sister Marlene, the tragedy, the bad press, a clutter of unwelcome memories.

She looked at Brad. "Give me your shortest version of his dream."

Brad moved his chair closer to Jim's bunk. While he related the drowning dream, Brad petted Duende, as though he needed the dog's permission to tell the story.

"In his dream, Jim was the only person in The Refuge. He stripped naked and dove off the dock. The day was warm and windless. An eagle glided overhead and disappeared beyond the entrance to our bay. The sun shone brightly, and the surface of the sea appeared mirror-like. He probably meant *glass-like* because he said, 'Da sea were a mirror.'"

Maddie interrupted, "The preamble isn't necessary."

"Jim gave me these background details as if they were somehow important, so that's why I include them. He said he dove into the water because the bottom looked 'white and sandy and sparky.' He meant *sparkly*."

Maddie interrupted again, "You don't need to translate. I know Jim-talk."

"When he arrived at the bottom he tried to resurface, but a swift current - he called it a 'liddle wind' - knocked him over. Each time he tried to get to his feet, another gust hit him. Soon he rolled like a ball along the sparkly bottom."

"You're not giving me a condensed version."

"I'm trying. Jim and I have gone over the dream many times, especially during these long winter nights when people seldom visit. In the evenings, we sit around the stove and talk about the dream. Lately, there's been little else to discuss.

"The dream is the subject that interests him most. Each time we go over it, a new detail emerges, and that's what makes it intriguing. For instance, he spent a great deal of energy trying to explain why the dancing girls were not on the dock, and the same goes for Wade and his basketball. It could be important information, but I haven't been able to sort that out yet. He brings their absence up, because it bothers him, and he worries over things like when he said, 'Why was da girls not dancin?' or, 'Why was Wade not in da dream, dat a big mystery?' You can be sure there's much more that I have left out."

"Let's stick with what happens," said Maddie.

"Each time he planted his feet in the white sand, another underwater current hit him. His ears ached and his chest felt like it might explode. Part of him wanted to panic, as Jim put it, 'no bref lef,' whereas another part of him wanted to investigate the beautiful sparkly sand. The river gust bounced him along the bottom, and he rolled over the sand like a ball. Soon he could no longer hold his breath. His mouth opened involuntarily; millions of air bubbles rushed to the surface, and his throat, lungs, and stomach flooded with a roar of sea and sand.

"Following the pain, he said he experienced peace. Actually he said, 'Happy now.' He sat on the ocean floor and sifted his hands through the beautiful sand, which had taken on all the colours of the rainbow. The 'liddle fishes' swam all around him. Columns of sunlight pierced through the ocean, struck his body, and warmed his fingers and toes. To my way of thinking, along about his fifteenth retelling of the dream, Jim made a rather sophisticated remark. He said, 'body dead, brain not.'"

Brad picked up one of his medical texts from the table, moved his chair closer to Maddie, and passed the book over to her. "If you read Chapter 13, you'll realize that is precisely what happens when someone drowns. The last organ to shutdown is the brain. I find it amazing that Jim has figured that out."

She accepted the book, though she didn't open it. "I'm not much of a reader, Brad."

Brad went back to patting Duende as he spoke.

"It's important to understand that life can go on for quite some time, that a condition of consciousness extends much further than most of us realize, and the nature of the consciousness overwhelmingly includes euphoria until all electrical activity terminates…and since the state is euphoric, the drowning person experiences a timeless moment. From the point of view of a drowning victim, their bliss is eternal, as is their life."

"A comforting thought," said Maddie, "but what's the end to the dream?"

"Jim claims, at least, this is my interpretation, that during the euphoric phase of his drowning death dream, while he warmed his hands in the sunlight, and other times let the 'fishes' filter through his fingers, he noticed another creature float toward him, but it was neither finned, gilled, nor scaled; in fact, the being was dressed in slickers, with a lifejacket held under each arm. He still had his boots on, an odd state of affairs as everyone knows that the first thing a fisherman does when he goes overboard is kick off his boots."

At this point in Brad's description of Jim's drowning dream, tears collected in his eyes and soon overflowed onto his hot cheeks and into his beard. Some of those tears intersected his lips and Brad licked the saltwater back inside. He leaned his head against Maddie's head. Their contact persisted until she eventually said, "It's cooling down in here."

Maddie recharged the fire and refilled the pots, which had nearly evaporated all their water. She lit another cigarette. Duende slept alongside Jim. Brad thumbed through his journal. Noticing a point of interest, he said, "The pearl divers in Japan can stay under for five minutes. Jim stayed down for four minutes and eighteen seconds this time. He's hoping to encounter the being again, but now realizes that a more extensive visitation is conditional on a longer immersion…his entire life's focus is in preparation for a grand reunion."

"Is that the case for you, too?" asked Maddie.

"I don't have faith like Jim has faith. If the dream had been mine, then I might feel differently. The dream is his, and I have accepted that fact. If the presence ever reappears, then it will be through Jim and for Jim. Aunt Maddie, I'm content to live my life helping my brother make contact."

Though his muscles ached,
he gathered his rake and net bags, and
carried both lanterns this time.
In the darkened ~~cap~~ canyons between
the tall boulders, he began the clam
harvest. He spit on his first clam, an
offering of thanks, a habit he had
acquired from his Sliammon brothers
in Malaspina Inlet, who had taught him
the proper ways. One his knees, he
dug Manilas, and left behind the Natives,
knowing ~~what~~ Peter's customers wanted.
The ~~absolute~~ long tines of his rake
turned the ground easily. He raked
toward himself and backed up as he
worked carefully not to injure the
younger stock, vulnerable on the
overturned ground. The clam smell

~ 8 ~

Transformation

"Perhaps you will think it passing strange, this regret for a savage who was of no more account than a grain of sand in a black Sahara."

Heart of Darkness, **Joseph Conrad**

ADAM MADE an entry in his journal: *Colour alone determines the shape of the sun as it sets over Cortes Island.* By way of irony, he read a historical footnote to Duende from another of his resource books.

A: "Cortes Island was named after the Spanish conquistador, Cortés, Hernán Ferdinand 1485–1547, champion of New Spain and the New World, thought by the Aztecs to be Quetzalcoatl, the sun god, bringer of light. One late afternoon Hernán Cortés arrived from the east, astride a white stallion horse, and both shone brightly in their polished coats of armour - white horse, white beard, white skin. The confused sun worshippers, squinting into the dazzling, reflected light, thought they saw one being - man and beast fused - a deity. Prophesied. Two arms and four legs. They had never seen a horse before."

D: Then they should have called Cortes Island, Quetzalcoatl Island.

A: Quetzalcoatl Island's a mouthful.

D: For your tongue, not mine.

A: You didn't let me finish reading. "The sun god slaughtered the Aztecs. Cortés built cathedrals on top of their sacred places and gifted them holocaustic diseases." He was not a nice man.

D: Apparently not.

A: What do you mean, *apparently*? I give you a fact and you place conditions around my fact, so much so that now I feel obliged to supply documentation.

Ignoring his glass, Adam took a large swig from his bottle of scotch.

D: You're over-reacting.

A: You're under-reacting.

D: You're floundering.

A: I'm doing quite well, thank you…despite your lack of support.

D: I see you doodle in the scribblers.

A: So what?

D: Just making an observation.

They both sipped their scotch. Correction: Duende lapped, Adam gulped. In the face of ill feelings developing between dog and man, Adam had in mind a review of his work. At this point, he was not so concerned about the precision of the details, as they would make their edited way to the surface eventually, but now he wished to get Duende's take on tone, to see if he thought the timbre were appropriate in each of the scribblers, or did he have reservations about any scribbler in particular?

A: Forget Cortes, forget Quetzalcoatl, he just sauntered into my brain because of the sunset.

D: It is rather nice.

Duende scratched an ear.

A: I was wondering if you would like me to read a selection from the scribblers, so that you might witness your own input?

D: From time to time, I have wondered if the words you use, or should I say our words, represent the world as we both know it.

A: Oh.

D: Yes, definitely, I would like to spend a few moments in a quiet corner reading the scribblers.

A: No, I would read to you. Your paws are not meant for turning pages.

D: Humans have extraordinary digital dexterity, but dogs have their own methods.

Duende looked at his paws, and then at Adam's hands. Adam read envy in the dog's countenance, and then thought, Dance on my words with dirty paws – never!

If truth be told, he had grown weary of the investigative model, as it revealed so little, so slowly. Was that not always the complaint of the Washington Post to Woodward and Bernstein? Adam now leaned in the direction of feral imagination, a model, which had potential to uncover more, much more quickly.

A: I see your saucer's empty.

D: A refill might prevent me from giving a responsible and thorough read.

A: Throw caution to the wind. Let your hair down. It's the weekend.

He poured the beast a stiff one. Adam now realized it had been a mistake to invite the dog into the collaboration. Best to keep him in the submissive role as long as possible. Before long, as the sipping and lapping continued into the night, they discussed how truth had locked itself inside beauty, new directions in creativity, the proliferation of alleged solar deities, ancient drawings of helicopters, primitive tools, eagles, clams, oysters, giant rocks, and what the hell was Sebastian doing on the beach? All sorts of useless stuff.

ADAM PUT the glasses on the caretaker of the seafarm. Sebastian sat on the shore staring intently at a giant boulder. He remained in that meditative pose for three full hours before the incoming tide forced him to quit.

The monolithic rock - located mid-intertidal - rested close to Seb's floathouse. Adam had noticed in the past that when the tide flooded and the house floated, it thudded against the boulder. And on an ebb tide, his home often grounded on the boulder and leaned at a precarious angle. The granite annoyance stood the height of a man and occupied the volume of a Cheops building block, though the dimensions less perfect.

Adam tried to understand Sebastian's fascination with the rock. Did he search for a vulnerability? Were his eyes, X-ray eyes? Could he see through to the inside of hard surfaces? Adam's guess, after he had become quite bored with his own voyeuring, was that the man only wished to tell the rock his troubles, as there was no one left in the world capable of hearing his worries.

On the following morning, our feral scribe watched Sebastian employ a skill from a previous century. Seb used a small claw hammer and pail of nails – a mix of many sizes. He tacked pins at the narrowest gauge of a seam in the rock, no doubt the seam discovered during his long meditation the day before. As he tap-tap-tapped along, following the circumference of the rock, progressively using bigger nails, a fault slowly emerged. The fault grew in width, until it became the diameter of his largest nail. No longer bored with his voyeuring, now Adam sensed contentment in Sebastian's industry and imagined that the man could tinker for an eternity. Adam wrote in his journal: *Sebastian takes no rest from his deconstruction project.*

Seb put down his nail pail and picked up a coal chisel. He inserted the chisel into the seam and gave a single swift swing with a small hand-sledge. The monolith halved as easily as slicing a watermelon. He retrieved his nails, as many as he could find scattered on the beach, and began opening a new seam on one of the halves. He tapped on and on, opening new faults from the newer pieces. Adam wrote: *His ultimate goal is to find an indivisible piece.*

Adam's scotch-and-jerky-craving assistant scratched on the door. He let the mutt in. Duende jumped up on the cushion.

A: It looks like Seb got tired of living on an angle.

D: He found a solution.

A: Let's put it this way; he's finding a solution.

D: Agreed, it will take time.

Though still early in the day, Adam poured some malt into the dog's dish.

A: Often I imagine the treasures in his home falling everywhere.

D: One day I gained entry to his floathouse…I hardly remember the pretext…and I saw that the interior was so cluttered that navigation amounted to squeezing through narrow winding trails.

A: Even for dogs?

D: For me it was easy, but for you it would have been impossible.

A: I can confirm that the man is a collector. He's never emptyhanded entering his home.

D: I noticed overhead bracing between the canyons of stuff. Things probably never shift very far.

A: Something of the junk shop quality about his home?

Duende lapped at his dish.

D: More like museum.

With unexpected candour, the dog embellished further.

D: Seb's home is like a storage room of artefacts, but the objects are of no conceivable value except to him. I saw an instinct to collect, arrange and display, but no logical thread to follow. It reminded me of just too much stuff.

A: You said you saw a museum quality to his home?

Then Duende became ostentatious, seemingly a new feature to his personality. For the sake of brevity, a truncated version is provided.

D: …the power of Sebastian's collection lies in its ambiguous layered meaning and the metaphoric implications, nay, I clarify, meteoric implications, which, if one employs…then a pattern of…emerges, and we are left with a thirst for his planned flight into fantasy, which must inevitably lead to a forfeiture of certainty, an Armageddon of despair and desolation, and….

Adam decided to ease up on the alcohol, and pour the coals to the jerky.

Scribbler Six:

SEBASTIAN SNORED when he slept on his right side, but didn't snore on his left. He slept with his deaf dog, De Gaulle, so how did it matter? When the alarm chimed at 1:30 a.m. in late December, neither dog nor man heard the ringing, but the dog felt the vibrations and crawled up to his master's head – only the front legs worked.

The sleepy animal licked Sebastian's face until he woke.

Christmas had slipped by without notice. After months of inactivity, the man and his dog planned to pick oysters and dig clams for Peter on the night tide. Sebastian and De Gaulle should have been out during the build-up to the holiday season, a busy time in the seafood industry, but both were sick: Sebastian with violent stomach cramps and a headache that never went away, and De Gaulle with arthritis, diarrhoea, persistent dry cough, spasms, loss of bladder control, and bleeding gums. What an exhausting job keeping the dog, who was nineteen (but looked older), alive.

Peter had visited often during this time of seclusion and had encouraged them to get out of the floathouse.

"Seb, what are you doing in there? You and De Gaulle need fresh air."

Sebastian never once let him inside, never once told him what he was doing in there, and only nodded at the doorway, as if he agreed with whatever Peter said. Then he slammed the door. When the visits became too frequent, when Sebastian was maddened by the interruptions, he had used eagline postures and screeching assaults to send Peter away.

It didn't take long to get ready for their expedition. Seb had prepared the gear earlier - slickers, gloves, rakes, lanterns, shuck knife, and the ubiquitous red onion sacks used by the shellfish industry. He had fuelled the *Oystercatcher* and pumped the bilges. Food? They would find food on the beach. He dressed in multi-layers of wool, survival suit, rubber boots with safety toes, black balaclava over his head and face, and a sou'wester tied under the chin. He wore wool liners inside his rubber gloves. Wool liners weren't available in the general store, so he had sewn his own from sock remnants.

Sebastian wrapped De Gaulle in two blankets, tucked in a hot water bottle, and placed the dog in the doggie bunk at the *Oystercatcher's* covered bow.

The aluminum skiff looked anatomical. Hoarfrost traced the weld-seams and rub-rails. He fired up the outboard engines and navigated through the maze of white floats and longlines on the seafarm. He motored slowly from the bay into the open channel. A nor'wester breeze issued from the inlets. Above, the stars shivered. A large moon crested the mainland peaks and cleared a buttery trail over the *Sea without Shores* that led to Corby's Point opposite the mouth of Teakerne Arm. Beyond, a boundless depth opened onto the night. He throttled both engines, and the boat sliced through the small chop. He steered down the middle of the brilliant band of light, as if driving the yellow centre line of a desolate highway.

The scamper of his boat over the electric highway invigorated the shell fisher. During the trip, he shouted above the roar of the outboards to the invasions of his mind. These oratorical moments occurred frequently, were practice for a far off time when his inadequate human speech would transform into a new language and then saturate the sky. His monologue engaged a host of phantoms, which, if they cooperated, could be shaped to any fancy. On this early morning, the phantoms became a subservient audience filled with reverence for the speaker.

He gave an impassioned address, interrupted with slashing hand gestures to manifestations of the supreme judges at the World Court in The Hague: the theme - interlocking conspiracies planning the destruction of all living things. He had brought along his long-suffering fuchsia plants by way of demonstration for his assembled audience. How ill they looked. Before the noble gathering, seeing himself dressed in bowler hat, tuxedo, and eagle tail feathers tied to his long braids, he made a convincing presentation. Sebastian, buoyed by a standing ovation, permitted an airy thought, If I were standing on a precipice, watching the eagles soar, wings, of their own accord, would sprout.

At Corby's, he stopped both engines and drifted towards shore. He listened for motors from other nighttime harvesters, but heard only a tinkling slop against the metal hull of the big skiff.

A tug pulled a boom far inside Teakerne Arm. He saw the tow and mast lights, but couldn't hear the engine rumble - the breeze had carried the sound elsewhere. When the bow of his boat gently grounded on a patch of fine gravel, a shoal of loligo squid splashed and flipped in the moonlight streaming over the mainland mountains.

He tilted his engines, unloaded the boat, and carried his dog and gear to the top of the beach. To keep from grounding, while the tide ebbed, he pushed the boat far out and moored it with a trip anchor. Sebastian had five hours to work before the flood tide would force him to quit.

The dog shivered in his blankets, the warmth from the hot water bottle mostly extracted. Sebastian lit a fire with bark chunks from a fir blowdown straddling the forest and shore. He built a windbreak of beach drift to protect De Gaulle from the nor'wester chill. Sebastian took off his survival suit and put on slickers. When satisfied that De Gaulle rested peacefully, he walked out onto the beach.

The rising golden moon paled the stars.

Boulders and tidal pools covered the beach. This bivalve Holy Land bisected the worlds of water and air. Oyster shellstock lay loosely scattered between the three-and-five-foot intertidal level, not windrowed in long arcs, or bunched in piles against rocks, as might be expected on an exposed beach. Still aware of the finer points, he opened two oysters with his shuck knife and ate them. The adductor muscles were strong; the soft white bodies tasted creamy, plump, and sweet. In the freezing air, nectar crystallized in the shells.

He chanted, "Soft bodies in hard shells, soft bodies in hard shells," and hopped, birdlike, from foot to foot.

Then he chided himself – a quick blow to the side of the head – for using human words and singing human songs, embarrassed that his tongue remained welded to their terrestrial beginnings. His headache – talons clawing deeply inside the scalp – had returned, a reminder of his true mission. His stomachache had disappeared.

As the oysters looked so white, and the night so lunar, he decided not to use the lanterns. Sebastian picked the cocktail grade into his sacks, the size Peter preferred. He sung, but this time another song, *Freight Train Freight Train Going So Fast* – that ditty mastered years ago, when self-learning the zither. Again, realizing the regression into the old tongue, he slapped his mouth. The grit on his glove embedded in his beard.

He worked diligently, and an hour passed, the tide still a long way out. When he had harvested forty dozen perfect oysters - round, deep-cupped, sized, fluted colourfully with sharp, shell growth, unfouled by common barnacles or tuberous worms - he placed the sacks in a shallow tidal pool so they would not freeze.

Seb walked back to the fading fire carrying a half dozen oysters. De Gaulle wagged his tail. The blankets had fallen off. Seb collected more bark chunks and recharged the fire. The flames flashed in the dog's eyes, and Sebastian saw a brightness that hadn't been there in years. He balanced the oysters on rocks nestled in the hot coals. When the bivalves hissed open, he poured the steaming juices into the dog's dish – a large, empty geoduck shell - and then waited for the liquid to cool. He chewed a cooked oyster into mush and regurgitated the mess into the dish. The dog ate like a bird. While De Gaulle worked over his plate, Sebastian ate the remaining oysters from their hot shells.

The golden night transformed into a silver bloom – the high moon now corralled in an expanding corona. Down channel, a trifling patch of fog tumbled out of Malaspina Inlet and seemed to lift Haystack Island from the sea. The fire spit cartwheeling embers; the Lilliputian meteor shower delighted both man and dog.

Though his muscles ached, he gathered his rake and net bags, and carried both lanterns this time. In the darkened canyons between the tall boulders, he began the clam harvest. He spit on his first clam, an offering of thanks, a habit he had acquired from his Sliammon brothers in Malaspina Inlet, who had taught him the proper ways. On his knees, he dug *Manilas* and left behind the *Natives* knowing what Peter's customers wanted. The substrate looked loose and perfect, the littlenecks large, so he knew that other diggers hadn't molested the sacred place.

The long tines of his rake turned the ground easily. He raked toward himself and backed up as he worked, careful not to injure the younger stock vulnerable on the overturned ground. The clam smell, coaxed into the night by his rhythmic scratching, intoxicated his other senses. He inhaled deeply and frequently, smelling and tasting the tang in the beach air. His own breath dissolved with the night, and the night enjoyed his contribution to this stunning moment. The lanterns hissed beside him, their light frail compared to the moon.

While turning the ground, he practiced a vocalization in the back of his throat, like the grating and grinding of gravel in the bottom of a bucket, a replication of the secret mutterings of eagle mates content in their lofty nest - words of endearment. After hours of digging and vocalization, the incoming tide forced him to stop. He sluiced his catch into a large mesh basket and sacked the clams. He placed them in the tidal pool beside the oysters. On the way back to the fire – very pleased with his progress – Seb hopped, birdlike.

Sebastian banked the fire and put on a pot of clams to steam. De Gaulle slept and shivered. The nor'wester breeze abated. He decided to wait for sunrise before heading back to The Refuge. A single bright star lay low in the heavens, and the window of dawn kindled behind the coastal mountains. A wolf howled across the channel near Poverty Bluffs. Hyperactive, winged spirits danced in his fire, and he sang to them.

"The big beach… you come to me on the big beach…you guide me on the big beach." He chanted with his new avian tongue.

The shellfish harvester took off his slickers and put on the survival suit. He wrapped himself in a blanket and fell asleep beside his dog, a cocoon around the pupa. The moon's light fell. The sun rose, but they slept on.

Suddenly, he woke to a loud thwacking sound. Sparks flew in his face, spray drenched the fire, empty red sacks scattered, and his hat blew away in a snarled wind. A Labrador helicopter - official distress yellow and orange - hovered offshore. The down-draft dug a hole in the sea. The chopper moved down the beach and landed, the rear door opened, and helmeted and uniformed men ran toward him. Sebastian gathered De Gaulle in his arms and scrambled into the forest.

They called after him.

"Wait."

They called again, louder, and the helicopter blades whirred. One of the men waved a burlap sack over his head.

"We saw your skiff and sacks. We want to buy clams for New Years."

~ 9 ~

Winter

"He set off from the deepest of hatreds and arrived, from deep below, and from far away, from so far below and so far away – that then, at the beginning of the beginning, he had not the slightest idea where he was heading,..."

Seibo There Below, **Laszlo Krasznahorkai**

ADAM READ Duende a quote from another historian of note.

A: "In 1792, when Captain George Vancouver and Commander Juan Francisco de la Bodega y Quadra met at Friendly Cove and drank the best Madera wine from Quadra's private cellar, they carved up their section of the New World whilst the indigenous folks looked on in astonishment. As the Captain restrained himself on that pleasant evening, and politely encouraged Quadra to devour a second and then a third bottle, Vancouver thought he gained the better part of the negotiation. As a result, in a gesture of intended and perpetual friendship, not to mention that his generosity was meant also as a metaphor for eternal relations of peace and harmony between England and Spain, he lit on the notion of calling the three-hundred-mile, long island they dined upon, *Vancouver y Quadra Island*. But alas, when the admiralty in London got hold of his survey maps a few years later, they had no hesitation in striking the addendum, *y Quadra* from the chart. The British did make a concession however, as the Captain and an irate contingent of Spanish diplomats would not cease with protests and appeals; so, happily for some, but not for others, they called the puny island between Vancouver and Cortes Islands, Quadra Island."

This quotation prompted a repartee between the erudite man and the belligerent dog.

A: Three islands – Vancouver, Quadra and Cortes - think of them as coffins for three great men, rafted one beside the other, and slowly sinking into the *Sea without Shores*.

D: That's an interesting point of view. Did you know the Salish call them floating islands?

Surprised that Duende knew such lore, his master was not about to let the mutt get the better of him.

A: Once I read that our islands drift from the mainland at a rate of one-quarter inch per year, on a collision course with the volcanic Hawaii archipelago.

D: Not imminent.

A: But destined.

The beast grew haughty, almost a totemic figure.

D: Then I ask you to recant your sinking coffin illusion and opt for three ships sailing with hapless captains, and a skeleton crew, in search of *terra incognita*, without stars for navigation, sextant, charts, the secret *rutter* journals of the Chinese, knowing latitude and ignoring longitude, yet, their course is steady as she goes.

These discussions stimulated Adam.

A: Bring me a ruler, atlas, papyrus, and quill.

D: Get them yourself.

Raising the flag of victory, the drunken bastard ran off with his tail ramrodding the sky.

BAD WINTER. Depression. Gum disease. Desolation. Loose teeth. Pneumonia. Green spittle...swallowing razor blades.

Rain. Coughing. More rain. Sleet. Snow. Heavy dose of evil.

Tea, chicken broth, outrageous depression, soda crackers.

Mini ice age cometh.

Long wait to get better. Death creeps. Closer. No taste for scotch. The over-abundant universe drying, shrinking. Endless storms…free-wheeling. Firestorms. Brainstorms. Of depression. Dances…of delirium.

No time. For a loveless life.

Then comes the crisis phase.

Fever…a thought that all is gone. Sweat. Rivers of sweat. Saline drops puddled onto bed-sheet shores. Dried up Aral Sea, where ships cruise on sand, refuel with sand, and sink in sand. Preserved. For eternity. They await…an alien archaeologist. To report on the vicious sand storms.

Cry for the land. Cry for the sea. Cry for the air. Cry. With tearless eyes.

Forge beached on a sandy *sea without shores*.

HOWEVER! When least expected, spirits lift. Adam moved Wade's October drawing of the *Forge* and pasted it onto January - a frozen Niagara Falls. He asked Duende to drag over the scotch that had been sitting unopened for too long. For once, the dog did what he was told. But, the beast continued as if he were the mentor. Adam adjusted his position at the table to denote an attitude of rapt attention while Duende lapped at his scotch.

D: You have kept the good wine until the last.

A: It's not wine.

D: I refer to the New Testament.

A: The Feast of Canaan, I presume.

D: They probably didn't have jerky.

A: I suspect not.

A team perception. They could see white. Looking through the window. White land. White sea. White and grey sky. Adam wrote *dirty snow* on his calendar.

D: I notice that you are writing again.

A: It feels good.

D: Two words, but a start, no?

A: Yes, the rapture of words.

D: The fireworks of words.

A: The dance of words.

D: They'll melt the snow.

A: They'll uncover the mystery.

D: This is a community story. Everyone should take part in the telling.

A: You think I don't know that?

The dog jumped down from his perch at the table and curled up by the stove. He covered his ears with his paws, so there would be no more talking to him.

Adam taped around the gaps in the window frame in an effort to keep out the damp and cold. The window had recently taken to clouding over. Physical exercise boiled down to leaping up every five minutes to rub away the condensation on the glass. At last, he was active. Looking at his face. In the window. And beyond the window. The dirty snow. And the dirty snow covered the face of The Refuge. And The Refuge stretched out before them.

People sat idle, unable to work outside. Adam continued to sprint between the table, the wood box, and the stove.

Things went well!

But Adam coughed through the night.

He commissioned Carver to replenish the wood supply. The young fellow cut and stacked fir bark in the woodshed. He didn't say much. Just worked, collected his pay, and left. Sort of a miserable guy. Nevertheless. Slowly, but certainly, Adam took control of his life. Steps on the stairs. One then another. Soon he would deface pages in the Key-Tabs at an alarming rate. Parker, and his favourite ink, Indiga One, longed for Adam's return. And so did the old man in the bottle. Again and again and again.

The white withering winter weather went wonky. One dark night a freezing torrent bounced from the sea, bounced from the roofs, and bounced from his brain. The wind ransacked the nooks and crannies in the houses. In the morning, the temperature suddenly dropped, and the entire bay froze over. A vast sheet of salted ice. Jagged and treacherous. He sat at the table and listened to the ice crack and groan. Yowls. Whimpers. Sobs. Carping and bellyaching.

Not yet able to begin another scribbler, though certain his old form would return, he wrote in his journal: *My empathies go to the birds.* The ocean had solidified quickly, very quickly; their feet and wings had stuck in the ice. He watched them perform their death dance – haughty carriage, wings as shawls and fans, and rhythmic beaking at the indestructible ice. They flapped and tapped, lurched and twisted, and slowly entered the purgatory of freezing fire. He counted eleven seagulls and six diving ducks scattered on the ice over the bay, dead. Adam watched Sebastian salvage an eagle carcass. It took him three full days to break a trail through to the bird. The recovering scribe wrote: *What happened to the eagle? What will he do with a dead eagle?*

With the *Storm Chaser,* Jeremy spent days breaking the ice but finally admitted defeat. The trails he carved grew over. The seafarm closed, no boats coming or going. Each Monday, Wednesday, and Friday, the Refugees watched the mail plane fly over the bay, unable to land.

People rarely visited. When they did, they travelled over land. Duende, the miracle dog, made his rounds, so that Adam kept appraised of his observations, but only if the tired and sick man supplied refreshments.

Laura cancelled school. Believe it or not, Wade still played basketball on the dock. He played in the gloom of each waning afternoon, the gathering dusk, the arctic dark, and the illuminated dims of hell. Though ice sheeted the dock decking, the boy had the foresight to scatter the small section below the basket hoop in rock salt and sand. He bundled in layers of wool clothes and wore wool socks over his boots. The boy managed to cut the net off the rim as it had frozen in an odd shape and would not let the ball fall through. The ball sounded dead as it hit the backboard. But there was a pattern. No dancing girls in this weather. No sign of the *Forge.* Where was the white raven?

Smoke billowed from MacLeod's chimney. Jim and Brad holed up in their houseboat and never came out. Carver tried to walk across the ice in the U of the government dock, but fell through. James saved him with a pike pole and took him home to warm up. Nicole spent the day pouring in hot liquids.

Everyone worried about Alice in her rickety house, trying to stay warm with a sooted oil stove. James forever tinkered with the carburetor. Alice lived on tins of cold beans and raw potatoes. Nicole sent Tara down with hot meals. Alice fumed because her generator wouldn't start. No television.

Adam watched the last embers of each day die.

SEA WITHOUT SHORES

wade,
malt
paper
erkulcks!
wicks!

pvo
va
l day
Nicole

"Dear Tara"

I go for a walk on the beach every morning with my dog, Buster. Yesterday he dug your bottle out of the sand. A storm must have buried it. I got out the charts to guess the route from Refuge Cove. I have never been to your community, but it sounds like a lovely place. My name is Bruce Harris and I'm an old man. If you would like, I would enjoy being your pen pal. Please write to me by real mail at the address on the envelope. It might take too long if you send the reply by bottle again (ha. ha.). The weather is nice here too. I guess you were just being funny when you asked for "HELP" and gave the longitude and latitude.

Yours Sincerely,
Bruce Harris (Mr. Nobody ha ha)"

~ 10 ~

Message In A Bottle

*"... when her future was a closed book and the curiosity
of opening it had not yet been born."*

Blindness, Jose Saramago

Scribbler Seven:

THE ONE room school building stood immediately beside the
general store - to the right of the ramp leading from the dock
- a small structure, shingle sided, shake roofed, uninsulated,
perched defiantly on squarely hewn timbers, and porched on
the waterside with railings and posts of split cedar, the hallowed
tree of the First People in this great land of theirs. A Canadian
flag – frayed, sun-struck, and lifeless on the still morning - hung
at half-mast on a pole attached to the northwest corner of the
building. Smoke coiled from the chimney. Close by, a full woodshed stood, connected to the school with an overhead roof and
planked walkway.

The school, a former bunkhouse, from an abandoned logging
camp near the mouth of the Brem River in Toba Inlet, had been
moved on a log float to the present location by James and volunteers four years earlier. Historically, buildings such as these,
many still scattered about the coast, were precursors to present-

day mobile homes made from the inorganic materials invented by modern man. James and crew had dragged the bunkhouse off the float and joggled it up the shoreline with the aid of blocks, wire cables, and a winch. They levelled the structure with Gilchrest jacks, underpinned the building to creosoted cedar pilings, and cross-braced the supports. These "skid houses" were rarely erected *in situ* due to the transient nature of coastal loggers; rather, they were constructed elsewhere with skids under them and reinforced (floor boards installed on 45 degree diagonals as were wall battens and sheathing) in order that they might be moved safely, and without injury, or distortion, from one location to the next. Handloggers became so adept in moving these dwellings that bread baking in the oven, as the building was dragged over rocky shores and up steep bluffs, never fell. The good wives and mothers, busy with their household chores inside, hardly noticed the change of scenery, the incline of declension, nor their toddler teetering in his or her highchair.

Though a clear February morning, the sun had not yet peeped over the hills behind The Refuge to share its warmth with the southern shore of the bay. Only local vessels were moored at the dock. Six children played basketball in front of the freight shed, one boy and five girls. Laura and James leaned against the porch railing of the general store overlooking the game. They wore gloves to protect their hands from the cold, drank hot coffee, and chatted amiably. As a precaution against falling off the dock into the chilly waters, all students wore bulky lifejackets. The straps, clips, and padding detracted from shooting the basketball accurately, a liability acknowledged by the parents and reluctantly accepted by the students.

The children referred to the dock area and vicinity as "Downtown." No one had painted black and white lines on their basketball court, since the edges of the dock and tie-up rails served that purpose most admirably. To all appearances, the ball went out of bounds too often, plopped into the ocean with a mighty splash, and drifted away depending on wind and current conditions. The children retrieved the ball with a long stick and sometimes an old dip net. Wade tied his canoe alongside the dock adjacent to the freight shed in the event that the ball drifted farther away than the length of the stick.

Laura, noticing a disruption in the game, yelled, "Quit hogging the ball, Sarah."

The teacher's intervention had little effect on the course of the game until Charlotte swatted the ball and sent it sailing into the middle of the U. Wade untied the canoe and fetched the basketball, but with some difficulty, as a tiny gust of wind, perhaps only to tease him, skittered the ball away every time he approached. Each plunge of his paddle through the surface of the *Sea without Shores* exposed the ambiguous third dimension, a concept not yet entirely internalized by the children. While Wade was so engaged, the five girls - a gay, gaudy and rambunctious sisterhood of femininity - began their twirling dance, presumably in order to stay warm while they waited for the return of the ball.

Laura commented to James, "The students will have letters for the mail plane today. We're studying letter composition and salutations, all that stuff."

He nodded and then said, "They sure dance a lot."

"They're trying to stay warm," she replied.

"But they do it when it's warm."

"James, they just like dancing."

Wade returned with the ball, and the game began anew. Laura ran down the ramp to the dock, snatched the basketball, and ran back to the schoolhouse with the children trailing behind.

Rubber boots cluttered the covered porch, and the basketball sat in the wood box. Jackets hung on outdoor pegs. Angel whined at the door until Tara let her in. Soon, no man's dog whined, and Tara let Duende in. Inside the schoolhouse, the barrel heater roared in the corner. Laura assigned Wade to stoke it. Both dogs quickly fell asleep on a scatter rug by the heater.

Laura had covered the walls of the cheery room with arithmetic and spelling exercises as well as paintings and drawings – the theme revolving around the notion of Valentine's Day, with red the prevailing colour. One large table served as communal desk for the children. They sat around the table wearing fur-lined slippers; the floor had never been insulated.

Laura asked, "Does everyone have the date for your letters in the top right hand corner?"

The children answered, "Yes, Laura."

Sarah erased her date from the left side of her page and put it where it belonged.

"I want each of you to read out your salutations. Mary, you go first."

"1345 Cook St. Victoria, B.C."

"Mary, that's the address."

"Elizabeth, can you read your salutation?"

"Dear Aunt Louise?"

"Very good...now Tara, it's your turn."

"Dear Anybody."

The class learned that it wasn't Tara's intention to post her letter on the mail plane. Instead, she would place her letter in a corked bottle and send it out to sea. The child explained that *Christopher,* in her bedtime story the previous night, had done a similar thing, and she saw no reason why the idea wouldn't work for her, even though his bid for help occurred two hundred years earlier. Apparently, the brief message Christopher had sent, stated longitude, latitude, and the single word, "HELP."

"Did he get help?" asked Charlotte.

"I'll find out tonight," answered Tara.

Tara further explained that, since she didn't know who would receive her letter, she couldn't address the salutation to anyone in particular. In other words, "Anybody" would do. Though some of her classmates ridiculed Tara's unorthodox plan, Laura supported her student for thinking creatively. She rested her hands on the child's shoulders. "There's always room for thinking creatively in this classroom."

Following recess, the teacher and her students walked to the store. The dogs followed. Each student had a letter to mail in the conventional way, except Tara, who carried a corked wine bottle with her letter rolled and stuffed inside. At the post office window, James cancelled parcels and envelopes with his date-stamp hammer. Five residents in the bay huddled around the space heater, drank coffee, and discussed the weather, while waiting for the mail plane. The children lined up to have their letters cancelled and dropped in the mailbag. Laura explained why the letters had to be date-stamped and the importance of return addresses. Tara stood to the side with her bottle. James pretended to smash his thumb each time he swung the date hammer.

He asked his daughter, "Where's yours, sweetie?"

"I'm sending mine in a bottle." The store rang with laughter.

The mail plane arrived, and everyone ran down the ramp to greet it. James straddled between the edge of the dock and the pontoon of the single engine Beaver. He gave the pilot, Blackie, the outgoing, and took the incoming in return, three bags full. The plane taxied into the middle of the bay, and the children cheered when the pontoons lifted off the water near Hope Point. The Beaver made a circle around Lewis Channel and flew back over The Refuge onto the next stop in Pendrell Sound on East Redonda Island.

Laura approached Tara. "Now it's your turn."

The child walked to the edge of the dock and heaved her bottle. It splashed, and for a moment, looked like it might not resurface. It did. The students watched the bottle bob, but quickly their interest evaporated, so Laura let them play basketball. Tara refused to join in the game. Instead, she sat on a tie-up rail and watched her glass envelope. Duende and Angel joined her. The bottle drifted back to the edge of the dock. She picked the bottle out of the water, threw it again, and Angel barked at the splash. The two dogs and Tara sat down and watched it drift slowly back to the dock.

MacLeod arrived in his rowboat, Ark. His dog, Son of Moocho, accompanied him. The old man walked up to Tara.

"Why aren't you playing with the others, dear?"

"I'm waiting for my bottle to float away. It's got an important message inside."

The three dogs engaged in sniffing rituals. Tara and MacLeod watched the bottle. Twice he leaned forward and tapped with his cane, encouraging the encapsulated message to vacate the bay.

In the late afternoon the bottle bobbed in a corner of the U of the dock. Tara sat on a tie-up rail, crying. She drooped her small body over her dog, Angel. Duende rested his head on her boot.

James called from the store porch. "Let's go home Tara. We can watch your bottle with the binoculars."

MacLeod offered to keep watch until something happened. He related a truism in an effort to stay her despair, which even Tara, at such a tender age, had heard numerous times before.

"The tide will turn."

He gave the bottle a few more taps of encouragement with his cane.

TARA SAT at the bay window of her log home holding the binoculars. Her bottle bobbed in the corner of the U. Angel and Duende stood beside her, on their hind legs with their front paws resting on the windowsill.

"It's trapped," she said.

Wade consulted the tide table. "The outflow started at 16:35 according to Point Atkinson."

"You have to add on twenty minutes for the difference up here," said James.

"I already did," replied his son.

James walked over and checked the tide book. He looked at the eight-day clock on the wall and said, "Right."

Suddenly, Tara rejoiced. The bottle had started its journey, slowly drifting parallel to the long finger running out to the plane dock. MacLeod kept pace until he could go no further. Son of Moocho barked the bottle out to sea.

During the next hour the family members took turns with the binoculars and watched the bottle catch the outflow. Tara looked as if she lived inside a warm glow. Angel and Duende went back to their rug behind the wood heater.

James gave his daughter further encouragement as the container approached Hope Point. "There's a nor'west forecast for tonight. Your letter will head for civilization once it gets beyond the point."

MacLeod and Son paddled home in the *Ark*, presumably also satisfied that Tara's letter was on its way. At dusk, the nor'west wind picked up. A murder of crows blackened the sky, heading for their rookery.

DURING THE remaining weeks of March, Tara seemed perpetually grief-stricken, especially when the other children received replies to their letters and had the honour of reading them in class. Each mail day she checked with her father to learn that there was no reply to her bottled message. Whenever any resident of The Refuge saw her, they asked if she had received an answer. However the question so upset the child, they soon stopped asking.

Often, the regulars waiting for mail around the space heater speculated on the likelihood that the bottle had survived the storms. They reached the consensus that a glass envelope would have smashed somewhere on the intertidal rocks. In deference to her feelings, these conversations were not related within Tara's hearing.

On a Monday morning, MacLeod showed up at the general store to wait for the mail. He produced a chart of the local area, showing three possible routes for the drifting bottle.

"Look at this, James," he said, "I've checked the winds and tides every day since Tara threw her bottle. There are three possibilities, but the most likely is the north end of Savary Island."

"That's a nice thought," replied James.

"It's all sand."

"I know."

Jeremy came over to check on the calculations. "Not a chance, MacLeod. I'm out there every day. It smashed on Kinghorn rocks, and if it got by Kinghorn, then the Raggeds took it out."

Heinrik, Carver and Sylvia came over to look at MacLeod's chart. After some deliberation, Heinrik said, "I agree with Jeremy."

Carver chimed in, "No frickin' way did that bottle survive."

"Give him some credit," said Sylvia, "you guys did bugger all, and MacLeod researched the shit out of it."

Through the tail end of winter, the fate of the letter had dominated conversation in The Refuge. Concerned over Tara's broken heart, Calvin wanted to send a counterfeit reply to her message in the bottle. Nicole counselled him out of this action. Heinrik remarked that disappointments like this would prepare her for the harsh realities of an adult life. Sylvia, upon hearing him, stomped out of the store. The only time Sebastian appeared for his mail, he commented with eagle screeches and the precise geometry of eagline gestures. Alice kept abreast of the news with visits from Nicole and the other children. She had pledged to pray for Tara. Jeremy promised, though no one believed him, and perhaps only out of sympathy for Tara, to keep a lookout for the bottle on his forays for beach logs. The Blacks came and went and said nothing. Jack and Vivian Smith gave Tara candy as a way of appeasing her disappointment, as this was how they handled the twins whenever they had despaired. Jack, who laughed loudest and longest at his own jokes, said, "Does she expect the reply via bottle return?" No one enjoyed the man's pathetic sense of humour. MacLeod could often be seen standing on the dock looking out to sea, as if his eyesight stretched for miles beyond these shores. Peter, trying to be helpful, encouraged her to write another letter. Brad gave her an exceedingly convoluted explanation of "corks," and their natural ability to thwart deterioration. Laura had tried every trick in the book, even tactics taught her at university, to pull Tara out of the deep hole into which she had fallen. When the teacher assigned a story writing exercise, none of the children could get beyond one feeble sentence, and Tara's effort was by far the worst attempt, though she was considered the best writer in class. As for her school pals, their adult behaviour should be commended, as they treated their friend with the respect due someone who suffered.

LAURA HAD finally been successful enlisting the adults as volunteers in her educational program. Jeremy completed a course in knot tying, one of the oldest skills known to humankind: slip knots, clove hitches, half hitches, sheepshanks, cat's paws, bowlines, overheads, squares, figure-eights and grannies. Once a week, the students visited Alice to hear local historical lessons, though she tended to repeat herself, and these ramblings often ended in platitudes like, "make do for that is all you'll ever have," or, "refrain from gossip at all costs," or, "your reward will be elsewhere." James broadened their educational horizons beyond the post office to the cash register area, where he taught the children how to make change, and then onto the stockroom to go over the principles of inventory control and pricing policy. Peter took them to the shellfish farm, following much nagging from Laura, where they learned the mysteries of marine biology and phycology. The students looked through the microscope, discovered the confusing terms for measurement, such as micron and millilitre, and soon could separate monoflagellates from dinoflagellates - in their sleep even - and free-floating from motile algae. They studied the wonders of photosynthesis, upwelling and downwelling, benthic organisms, how the wind and the sea interact, and the value of agar and carrageen. They memorized the Latin names for the local shellfish, *Crassostrea gigas, Mytilus edulis,* and *Tapes philipinarum,* remarkably none of these indigenous to the B.C. coastline, and they learned also the cycles of the poisonous tide, frequently red, but also brown or green, of the genera *Peridinium* and *Gymnodinium.* As an aside, Peter told them that two hundred years ago, two of Captain George Vancouver's crew died of paralytic shellfish poisoning while eating mussels near the present town of Prince Rupert. Brad and Jim gave the students a glimpse into the subtleties of haiku poetry from their father's logbook. Neither Laura nor the children bought into the notion that lists of fish lures should be classified as haiku. Heinrik gave a hurried lecture on bee culture, otherwise known as apiculture, the terms delivered almost entirely in a rare Germanic dialect. Nicole presented an art program, her own aptitude in the spheres of collage and found objects, of which there were plenty in The Refuge. The paintings and sculptures that emerged were entirely abstract, as if the world of illustration must never be breached. MacLeod, from his Books of Knowledge, taught them the first six letters in the Hebrew, Arabic, Greek, Russian and Sanskrit alphabets and often the children could be heard reciting, *aleph, beth, gimel, daleth, he, waw;* or *alif, ba, ta, tha, jim, ha;* or *alpha, beta, gamma, delta, epsilon, zeta;* and so on. Calvin, in a disorganized way, taught them the principles of the combustion engine. Only Wade took interest. Sylvia, following their outing to a secret valley the previous fall, agreed to bring her resource books to the school along with sample mushrooms. The children took spore prints and learned to recognize the more common fungi. Laura became upset with Sylvia however, when she introduced two specimens, not in her mushroom books, and took the liberty of naming them herself: the red one, *Hiroshima penultima,* and the yellow one, *Nagasaki ultima.* The fungal discussion veered into consideration of nuclear fission and fusion, radiation, numbers of dead, mortality and morality, and the unusual nature of infinity. Laura had anticipated none of these topics.

On an unseasonably warm day in March, Carver conducted a physical education class near the freight shed, where he taught the rudiments of gymnastics and tumbling. The students rolled out two old mattresses on the dock. Carver rigged a sawhorse as a gymnasium horse with two, large C-clamps securely attached as pommels. He fabricated a makeshift springboard from a twelve-inch fir plank. The students learned somersaults, front and back flips, how to fall like a row of dominoes, and various statuesque and pyramidal group formations. They practiced for a public performance planned later in the spring. Tara and her classmates became so engaged in their gymnastics practice with Carver that they failed to notice, or hear, the arrival and departure of the mail plane.

Soon James appeared on the porch of the store, along with a small crowd of well-wishers.

He called down to the dock, "Tara." He waved a letter.

She ran up the ramp, followed by Carver, Laura and the children. After taking a quick glance at the return address, Tara commented, "Mr. Bruce Harris on Savary Island sent it."

"Probably lives at the north end," said MacLeod.

The child trembled as she read her letter to the community.

"Dear Tara,

I go for a walk on the beach every morning with my dog, Buster. Yesterday he dug your bottle out of the sand. A storm must have buried it. I got out the charts to guess the route from Refuge Cove. I have never been to your community, but it sounds like a lovely place. My name is Bruce Harris and I'm an old man. If you would like, I would enjoy becoming your pen pal. Please write to me by real mail at the address on the envelope. It might take too long if you send the reply by bottle again (ha, ha). The weather is nice here too. I guess you were just being funny when you asked for 'HELP' and gave the longitude and latitude.

Yours sincerely,

Bruce Harris (Mr. Anybody, ha ha)"

Imagine the old fellow strolling the beach of his remaining days: rain or shine, sleet or snow, breeze or gale. Buster his only companion. Mr. Harris walks there daily, kicking the odd clam shell as he trudges the long sandy shore, yet he is willing to be Mr. Anybody to a chance encounter, which on this particular occasion was unearthed by his dog, a shaggy and faithful terrier willing to play fetch into eternity, or dig holes to China. The sea had engineered a coincidence of introduction, coincidentally engineered by a bedtime story, about a frightened, though resourceful, child shipwrecked on a deserted island.

Now Bruce waits for his answer with the same misery, as Tara had waited for hers, only this time trusted to the vagaries of the postal service. Hopefully, answers would multiply and reciprocate, grow to a shoebox full on the Savary side and a lunch bucket full on the West Redonda side, answers that presumed and pondered questions, and evolved toward less evasive missives as each writer felt his or her way through the sea of humanity that had narrowed to two human beings in search of trust and understanding. Tara took the first step. Bruce took the next. These complete strangers, one old, one new, male and female, naïve and experienced, opposites in so many ways, both with pasts and futures, though differing in length and intensity, and presently protected by distance and anonymity, they would soon explore the secrets that lived inside their prisons. Had it not also been written? "Sooner or later, everyone tells their story."

A GENTLE breeze blew in the channel. The dock bustled with activity. One noticed an assembly line aspect to the festivities, as well as more hands than needed. The adults piled crates of empty wine bottles in one area, all compliments of Jeremy. A small table had been set with corks and corking plunger, again, compliments of Jeremy. The children had carried down the large table and chairs from the school to the dock. They wrote letters furiously, with Laura supervising spelling, punctuation, and sentence construction. Jeremy rolled the completed missives into tight cylinders, inserted them into the bottles, and plunged the corks.

MacLeod encouraged everyone. "Hurry, the tide's perfect."

He carried the tide book and consulted with others for reference. This time he speculated on new destinations: "Twin, maybe Hernando, the south shore of Cortes, let's hope its not Kinghorn because its too rocky…what if their bottles get into the open Strait of Georgia…it's too hard to tell until we see what the weather really does, we don't want them to go up Lewis Channel, because they'll get lost. No one lives there except Maddie and Jake…I'll have to do more calculations when I get home. It's good the children are sending lots of bottles. I hope Jeremy does a good corking job…we should have better containers than glass. My recommendation would be not to bunch them up."

Sarah urged, "Remember longitude and latitude."

"What is it again?" Charlotte asked.

Tara answered, "It's exactly **Longitude** 124.847 and **Latitude** 50.1275."

"Who told you?" Elizabeth asked.

"My brother."

Wade said, "I checked it on the charts."

The dogs raced; almost as excited as the humans, barking at ducks, seagulls and grebes, nipping at each other's tails, charging from the plane dock all the way around the U to the gas dock and back again.

"I've done six bottles, so far," Mary said.

And her twin sister, Elizabeth, said, "Me too."

Jeremy served the wine. "Our primary responsibility is to free up envelopes."

In a moment of uncharacteristic exuberance, Sylvia said, "Drink! Drink! Drink!"

When it had become so important to use the correct word, a question loomed. What would a collection of glass envelopes – linked by common purpose, housing fantasy and fact, clanking against each other for reassurance, bobbing on an abyssal surface, hopelessly optimistic, yet totally beleaguered by inexperience, their destinations unknown, their recipients unknown, heading on an outgoing tide for Hope Point and other hopeful points along the way, containing letters of introduction and pleasantries on the weather, though knowing full well conditions could change without warning, and specifying origin by longitude and latitude – be called? Congregation, shrewdness, cete, colony, sleuth, unkindness, litter, intrigue, herd, drove, packet, cowardice, pack, gang, richness, pride, cackle, troop, team, passel, prickle, warren, crash, pod, flock, dray, scurry, streak, brace, wake, clutch, gulp, horde, convocation, charm, stand, gaggle, wisp, murmuration, company, fall, descent, agglomeration, army, shiver, hover, grist, murder, bed, intrusion, plague, swarm, or bevy?

And then the other perplexing mystery that loomed: following the lead of their notable companion, Tara, why did the other children also write urgent requests for HELP in each and every letter? Why did each child capitalize the single word, in some cases give the word multiple exclamation marks, encase it with quotations, and underline the four letters, not just once, but many times?

The day turned into a party. All bottles had been cast into

the troubled waters. MacLeod worried them out to sea. Carver cast from the dock and reeled in rock cod, lingcod, salmon, and perch, to later become a fine kettle of fish. The adults ate and drank: bread, sardines, wine, dill pickles, and potato chips. Dogs begged for leftovers. The people put aside other plans for the rest of the afternoon. Even James forgot his mental "to do" list. Alice watched with her binoculars through her parlour window. Laura cancelled school. Once in awhile the adults looked up and checked the progress of the glass envelopes, still an assemblage, but later when the forces of Nature would rise to the occasion, each would have to find its singular destiny. Wade went back to his basketball. In the distance on Centre Island, Sebastian kept watch from high in a fir snag. Above him, eagles cruised on warm thermals intersecting their widening gyres. The girls ran off to the gas dock and performed their twirling dance, five spinning tops in a Sufi mesmerization. Rushing to God. Rushing away from a god.

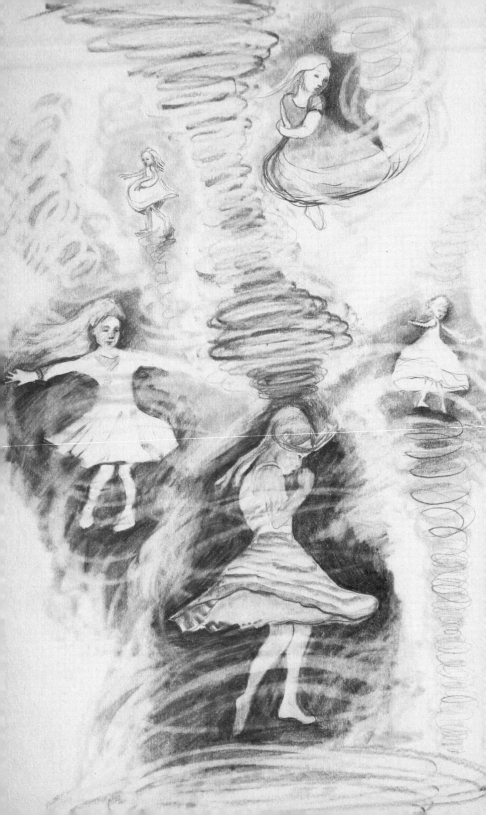

~ 11 ~

Cru Fik Shun

"He tried to talk to God but the best thing was to talk to his father and he did talk to him and he didn't forget."

The Road, Cormac McCarthy

UP TO his knees at the water's edge, a blue heron measured the ups and downs of the tide. Adam watched the long-legged bird study his reflected self in the shallows. So far the bird had struck three times - the beak, head, and neck so much quicker than Adam's eye. For the effort, Mr. Lightning swallowed three sculpins. Adam wrote in his journal: *He sees himself, his reflected self, but that self is not himself.* He put down Parker and drained another scotch. He took up Parker again and wrote: *He moves when movement can't be seen.*

The scribe sat in his nook. He watched Bradley and Jim climb into their rowboat tied near the gas dock. Duende leaped aboard and took his place at the bow. Adam suspected that James was sending them over with mail, newspapers, and supplies. He hoped Duende would have an update.

The Jenzen brothers used any excuse to visit Adam, as he had been a close friend of their father, Perry. His grown children often pressed for memories of the past, however, the accounts had to be positive, monumental, inspiring, beautiful, and heroic.

For his part, Adam had many questions left to be answered in his investigation. More accurately, one could say that his ratio of questions to answers tallied at 100 to 0. The brothers, he thought, might provide leads. Almost in a manipulative sense, Adam decided to negotiate a barter. He would tell Jim and Brad about an adventure he had with their father, and in return, he would expect them to explain the bizarre game Jim and Wade had been playing every day on the dock. Recently, he had witnessed Jim staggering under the weight of a timber and Wade urging him on with the snap of a bull kelp. That theme had been played out between Jim and Brad during the night of the *bearbecue,* but now the game had blossomed into a Jim-Wade obsession reminiscent of the girls' dancing addiction. Somewhere within that obsession, he hoped to force a grain of truth to surface.

DUENDE SCRABBLED his paw at the door. The door opened easily, and the dog took his cushion beside Adam. Jim and Brad squeezed into the nook opposite them.

"We brung da mail," Jim said. "You gots da nib."

"James thought you'd need your new nib for Parker," Brad added. He passed the package over to Adam, who also noticed a brown bag containing his preferred nectar and a backlog of weekend newspapers.

"I'm having a wee dram, does that interest either of you?"

Jim shook his head, and Brad said, "No thanks. Our father wasn't much of a drinker and we follow in his footsteps."

"There were occasions when he took the drink."

Jim said, "Tea an milk an cream soda."

"Jim is correct," Brad said, "those are the only liquids mentioned in our father's logbook. It was our mother who took the drink."

"It look lak wader," clarified Jim.

"Yes, I remember that Marlene had a preference for vodka," commented Adam.

"Not smell, not ever a bit," elaborated Jim.

"I'm sure you're both correct, but there was that one special celebration we had during the war years...did I ever mention the story about the floating Japanese bomb?"

Jim jumped up from the bench and pushed Duende off his cushion. He sat down on the cushion beside Adam and said, "Tell tori." Duende trotted over to the stove and lay down, his tail signalling a pissed-off viewpoint.

Jim tugged on Adam's sleeve and repeated, "Tell tori."

"Well, here goes then. It was early 1945, and your father fished *Pride II*. The *Arrogant* was still under construction at that point. He asked me to crew, because his most recent deckhand, Conners, who had a major drinking problem, messed up during their last trip. Do you remember Conners?"

"He and Aunt Maddie were fond of each other," Brad answered.

"Just a temporary liaison," said Adam.

"Him dead now."

"Yeah Jim, he drowned," said Adam.

"Tell pa's tori."

"We fished off Langara that summer. One morning on the way to the grounds, we noticed a porcupine-like object floating close to shore. When we approached, we realized that it was a mine, which had most likely floated over from Japan. You may not know, but the Japanese used floating bombs to protect their shores from U.S. invasions, and sometimes the mines broke loose from their moorings and drifted on the Japanese Current to the shores of Vancouver Island and the Queen Charlottes. For years after the war, many were discovered stranded on the beaches from Oregon up to Alaska.

"Rather than report the sighting to the naval authorities, your father thought it best to dispose of the danger immediately. 'This is our chance,' your father said, 'to contribute to the war effort.' When I asked what he had in mind, Perry said, 'Go get the .303 and bring an extra box of shells.'"

"What 3 0 3?" Jim asked.

Bradley answered, "A rifle, Jim. 3 0 3 is written in a margin of our father's logbook."

"We positioned ourselves about a half mile from the mine, turned the engine off, and let the ship drift. The sea was calm, but the slow ups and downs of the ground swell meant that the changing horizon often left us without a target. We took turns firing three shells each and soon realized that hitting the bomb would be close to impossible. Your father said, 'Let's get closer.' We slowly motored within 400 yards of the mine. Even if one of us hit the target, we had no idea if the bullet would trigger the device, and had no idea how significant the impact would be.

"We emptied one box of shells and then half of the other. On three occasions, your father hit the mine, and we heard the smack and saw sparks fly. Perry was a much better shot than me. 'We have to hit a spike,' he said."

"Tori scary." Jim moved off the cushion beside Adam and cuddled along side Duende in front of the stove.

"The mine had drifted onto the shore and bounced on the rocks each time a swell moved it. Your dad fired up the engine again and moved to within 200 yards. He took up the rifle and with the first shot hit a spike. The blast flattened the forested shoreline, and boulders and beach drift erupted into the sky. The concussion blew out two wheelhouse windows, and a rock snapped off the forward guy-pole. As if that were no big deal, Perry said, 'Now we can fish.' On the way to Langara, we tipped back a quick shot of rye whiskey... a toast, nothing more than that."

Jim moved back to the cushion and said, "Good tori."

"How about a drink boys?"

"Maybe when we have something to celebrate," Brad said.

Upon seeing his opportunity, Adam asked, "Now it's your turn to tell a story, Jim. What about that game you play with Wade on the gas dock?"

Jim seemed quite pleased to be asked for a story, but he needed a few moments to gather his thoughts. He soon replied, "Cru fik shun da game."

Bradley intervened, "It's a game we played as children, before the logbook came into our lives, when any diversion from his unhappiness was welcome. At the time, it didn't seem like an outrage to turn the crucifixion of Jesus into fun."

Jim reached into the back pocket of his jeans and pulled out the logbook for Adam to see. Then he put it back. "We tend stuff lak gettin whipped an nailed to da cross an da hammer noise ringaloud."

"Very interesting, Jim, but why have you started up the game so many years later?"

Again, Brad intervened on behalf of his brother, "Jim started up the game with Wade some weeks ago. Why I don't know, and why he chose Wade as his playmate is not clear either. Perhaps it is because they have become basketball buddies, or that they have intimacies I do not share. In any event, the day I became aware of Jim's invention, I noticed him from the window of my sanctuary bedroom some twenty-five years ago, when we lived in Vancouver. He struggled with an old timber that he'd dragged from our father's lumber pile, and when he got it into a grass clearing, he went back for another beam, which was shorter, nicely squared, and of similar dimension. He dragged that piece out and laid the shorter one atop the longer one. For a moment, though I had no hint, or reason to reach such a conclusion, or any experience in such matters, it seemed to me that the two pieces were made for each other, and had, in fact, only been waiting for a craftsman to come along and jig them together. Then Jim proceeded to lay himself upon the timbers and began a long sequence of teetering, tottering, wincing, and writhing. I remember thinking that despite his diminutive stature, Jim had inordinate strength wrestling with those timbers, but I could not make head or tail of the agony he portrayed so brilliantly in our backyard. More than a little fascinated, I abandoned my bedroom sanctuary and went to the scene he had prepared.

"I asked, 'what doin?' and he replied, 'it a game.' The props consisted of nothing more than the two beams, a long, sharp-pointed stick, and a length of blackberry cane with vicious thorns. He then proceeded to give me instructions on how I was to enact my part. He gave me the stick and said, 'it a peer.' I held the spear, and because my mind was able to rush ahead or behind with the fewest of cues, I had little difficulty traveling back two thousand years to become the centurion on Golgotha, making ready for the final blood letting. Jim lay on the cross face up, but since the top beam teetered on the bottom one, he balanced unsteadily. Once in position though, with both arms outstretched, and legs straddling the main beam, he told me to proceed and 'fro peer.'

"I threw the stick, and on purpose, it landed a few feet from his rib cage. 'Fro bedder.' We went on like this for sometime, throwing and retrieving, Jim insisting that on each throw the spear must land closer and closer. 'More close Brad,' he repeated. On my final throw, the spear grazed his chest raising a slight welt, I only discovered later, but Jim smiled and congratulated me, 'Good at game Brad.'"

Jim interrupted at this point and commented, 'on da rib," and then rubbed his rib cage, as though he could still feel his earliest days of hurt.

Adam asked, "Does your rib still hurt?"

"It a big big pain."

Bradley continued, "I should mention, since you have already introduced the subject, that our mother was busy cinching up her courage to face another day, which consisted of multiple cups of black coffee, cigarettes, one after the other, and then the noon switch over to the clear liquid. Only a few years had gone-by since the disappearance of the *Arrogant* and the loss of our father.

"She never witnessed the embryonic beginnings of our inventive obsession; an adventure, by the way, that she needed to assume responsibility for, as mother was the one who threw me into a carnivorous Catholic boarding school as well as exposed Jim to the nuns, the liturgy of the Holy Mass, the darkness of the confessional, the plethora of church ritual, relentless indoctrination, and the abuse of bodies and souls, which we have never been able to shake free from, or forget.... I should mention too, later that day, we played 'cru fik shun' one more time, and we developed procedures for the use of the thorn laden blackberry cane, which produced minor scratches on Jim's head."

Jim placed both hands on his head, and presumably, rubbed in the places where the thorns had penetrated. Then he smiled. During this enlightening parley, Duende had begun to snore. Adam had assumed that Brad, as proxy for Jim's story, was just warming to the topic. However, the brothers stood up to leave. Duende apparently hadn't been asleep, because he jumped up, gave a stretch, as all dogs do, and then pawed the door open. The three of them made their way down to the rowboat.

Cradling his single malt, Adam followed. The sun had set behind Cortes Island and the incoming tide had floated their boat. Jim and Duende climbed into the stern.

The investigative reporter asked, "Jim, why did you start playing the game again after all these years?"

Jim hesitated. Adam thought that perhaps the question was incomprehensible for the miniature man. In due course, Jim answered, 'a sac fyc.'

Brad must have realized that Adam did not understand his reply and entered into another soliloquy from the bow of the boat, pinning it to the gravel beach.

"Why he resurrected the game at this point in our lives, I have no idea. But I do know that things like this happen for a reason, and in the fullness of time we will have an answer. After years of the pastime, after exploring the entire fiction of all fourteen stations of the cross by way of intense study of the four gospels, and many other reference materials, including our missals, catechism books, cradling our rosaries in hypnotic states, kneeling on sharp rocks, fasting for days and nights - to mention only a few influences - Jim came to understand, at least this is what I have concluded after much thought and circumspection, that Jesus sacrificed himself for all of mankind. Most of us understand this, but it took a considerable number of years for the fact to gain prominence in Jim's own unique belief system. The repetition, the embellishments, fabrications, deviations, reversals, and exceptions that we introduced into his invention eventually fanned his imagination, so much so, that he may have developed a more clear understanding of the Golgotha saga than even I had acquired.

"To clarify though, Jim did not study in the true sense, since he was handicapped in too many ways, but, to give credit where due, he did participate every step of the way, watching intently, pretending to read the books we had accumulated, holding tools, fetching tools, admiring tools, mumbling pretend prayers, commenting with a 'good' or 'dat bedder' or 'too bad,' if, for example, I made some blatant bungle in squaring the two beams of the cross. In particular, Jim and I focused on the second station initially, where Jesus receives the cross, the fourth, where Simon of Cyrene is forced to carry it for him, the three falls – the third, seventh and ninth stations, and then the twelfth, which is the 'ringaloud' nailing, as he always calls it.

"The humiliation, the burial, the removal of the rock by the angel, and the resurrection, all came with time. The stations became a super script for the development of new rules, and in each future session, we devoted our energies to one station solely. At least that was the case in the beginning. I suppose I travelled beyond reason, which has become a pattern in my life, as many things bothered me about the crucifixion, and of these concerns – let us say the shortcomings – I was able to convince Jim of the need for complexity.

"There were practical considerations, which we dealt with first. The beams required a fitted saddle notch, and as I was the de facto man of the house, it fell to me to take on the carpentry jobs, flourishing chisels, saws, and mallets acquired from our father's stockpile in the basement. We studied the brass Jesus on a wooden cross in our hallway entrance, studied the grand crucifix at our church above the main alter, and we patrolled the fourteen stations, seven hanging on each of the church's long walls – the Via Dolorosa – sneaking into church whenever there were no services. I studied all the crucifixes at boarding school, and it seemed like there were thousands, Jesus looking down on me whenever I looked up, and the two of us locking into a stare, which I could never hold beyond a few minutes.

"Usually on weekends, or those many weekdays when I had

played truant from school, well after I had cobbled the two beams together in a fairly secure fashion, for instance, we'd do Station Two, where I would heft the cross onto his little shoulders, and then he'd drag it around the yard, in and out of flower beds, which hardly mattered as they were so grown over. Jim was content to simply drag it from here to there and back again, until he was completely played out. My brother was never bored. Soon the yard consisted of dry or muddy trails, depending on weather, with the small islands of green shrinking, shaved into smaller and smaller units as Jim persisted with his expanding passion. Whenever I looked down from my bedroom window, I saw an intricate maze under construction, the kind that invited a wandering in the wilderness for forty days, then forty years, and now we continue to wander with the Satan tempting us every step of the way, just like he did with Jesus.

"Jim learned the numbers of the stations and would call out '3,' while we were in the middle of '7,' so then he would stagger, stumble, and drop the cross, and I would feel obliged to become a bystander along the Way of Sorrows, allow myself to get pressed into service, and put the cross back on his shoulders. 'Tanks Brad,' he'd say."

Jim jumped out of the rowboat and ran down the beach and fetched up a beach-worn log, perhaps ten feet long and six inches in diameter. He placed one end on his shoulder and then trudged toward Adam, Brad, and Duende, saying, 'dis is 7,' all the way back to the rowboat. He dropped the log, ran to its other end, hiked it up onto his other shoulder, and then plodded on down the beach, saying all the way, 'dis is 3.' He continued with his demonstration, while Bradley finished the story.

"Only sparingly, did he call out '4,' which was the cue for Simon of Cyrene. I assumed this role and would traipse around under the most immense of burdens to feel what it must be like for Jim, but also, what it must have been like for Jesus to bear the millstone of humanity's sins, a burden which grows in numbers and density as the centuries click on by, the weight forever growing. One could say that in this experience, we approached ultimate empathy.

"With '12,' we developed new variations. At first, I nailed Jim with smaller nails, but made certain that I pounded well clear of his hands and feet. As he gained confidence, and as I acquired accuracy, we agreed to use our father's biggest spikes. Jim would say, 'let do da big one Brad,' and away we'd go. Now I used the sledge, instead of the paltry claw hammer, and found that with both hands I could be quite precise. I no longer pounded the spikes clear of Jim's hands and feet, but drove them between his fingers and toes. Jim would lie there, staring into a blistering sun, often with a smile on his face."

Meanwhile, Jim lay down on the beach with the log in his embrace and squinted into a brilliant sunset, occasionally looking towards the rowboat, perhaps to make sure that everyone was watching his performance.

"I assumed Jim was wondering why his father had forsaken him. Or, maybe he was wishing that life could be repeated to bring a different result. Or, simply, he forgot that he should be writhing in pain."

When Bradley said, "writhing in pain," Jim looked away from the sunset, and repeated his earlier statement to Adam, "It a big big pain." Then he smiled.

"As I nailed him to the cross, my hand gripped the sledge our father once held, a joy for me. The closeness of being joined through a tool gave us a peace, not absolute, but comforting nonetheless. To the best of our knowledge, mother ignored our industry.

"At school, I took an interest in catechism, bombarding Brother Cavanaugh with questions such as, Does Golgotha really mean skull? How heavy was the cross? Why did they put the sponge on the stalk of hyssop and what is hyssop anyway? Did the nails go in the hands or the wrists? Why did they break the legs of Dismus and Barabbas but forget to do Jesus? and, Do you think Simon of Cyrene carried the cross just as a favour or was he forced? The 'Cav', our nickname for Father Cavanaugh, once we knew what he was all about, answered some of these questions quickly, but for others, he needed to do his own research. He didn't know what hyssop was and wasn't clear about the leg breaking. I devoured the gospels, Mark, Luke, Matthew, and John. Luke's gospel was the longest, 148,000 words, whereas Mark came in at a little over 50,000. It seems that John was in an ecstasy when he wrote his account. Eventually, I started calling my brother, Jesus, and he liked that – this we only did amongst ourselves, never in public, or in front of mother, a habit we eventually dropped once the logbook took over our lives.

"I'd say in a voice, which I thought could have sounded like Pontius Pilate's, 'Jesus, admit your guilt,' putting emphasis on *Jesus*. He'd say, 'nope,' and I'd whip him until he'd say, 'o k.' Then I'd wash my hands of the whole affair in an old galvanized washtub of green scummy rainwater, where mosquitoes bred, and pollywogs swam, eventually rejecting their tails as they metamorphosed into sonorous, croaking frogs. Some days, I played Mary Magdalene washing his feet. I used a towel as a stand in for her long trusses of hair, and later the towel conveniently took the role of the Shroud of Turin, which became the centrepiece for a shrine we assembled from our father's junk. Other days, I would become Peter weeping in a dark doorway after denying three times any knowledge of the man called Jesus, the role performed by Jim, or become Judas throwing thirty pieces of silver into the sky – we used our father's silver and chrome lures - and then hanging himself with our father's ganion lines, or become the centurion sneaking off with the robe – one of father's motheaten wool blankets, and one weekend, I worked the two full days on a sign for the cross, King of the Jews, carved into the reverse side of a barrelhead, branded *Arrogant Fish*. If my intensity went beyond Jim's threshold, he would usually say, 'cared Brad' or 'too com pi caed.' Then I would ease up, but always be ready to push the game further, once I had determined that Jim had cinched up his courage or achieved enlightenment."

Duende gave Adam a quizzical look, as he and the brothers rowed off to their houseboat moored to the government dock. Adam overheard Jim say, '3 0 3 gotsa be in da tori book.' And Brad said, "We'll check when we get home."

They stopped at Production Point. The night bite seemed

promising with rings of feed erupting from the deeps, a downpour smacking up from the sea. Carver fished there too, in MacLeod's new boat, and some of the girls fished with him. The brothers cast buzz-booms, and Jim got a strike. Adam saw his rod double over and heard the reel zing and scream into the darkening night.

The lonely scribe went inside for a refill, disappointed that the information had not advanced the project in any measurable way. A half hour later, Duende scratched on the door.

A: You swam.

D: Didn't have a choice.

A: Any dogfish out tonight?

D: If there were, this doggie wouldn't be here.

A: So, we didn't learn much from Brad and Jim.

D: They got the better deal in the barter.

A: How do you mean?

D: Their obsession needed sustenance; the porcupine story became the fuel.

A: Well, I've been of service then.

D: You've reinforced abnormal behaviour.

A: Now I feel like a failure.

D: I could have told you the crucifixion game would lead nowhere.

A: I should have asked.

They cracked a new bottle. Their relationship had improved somewhat, though at times, it seemed that Duende had taken unnecessary charge of the partnership. Before they both passed into oblivion, Adam felt quite sure that the dog had said, "Completion of the scribblers will bring the atonement you crave."

SEA WITHOUT SHORES

As if all these affronts weren't enough, another incident occurred that morning, which for him amounted to the last straw. An innocent woman, who had not read the fine print of the exchange rules, attempted to trade her five, bottomshelf Harlequins for the top shelf "Catcher in The Rye." Obviously, she must have presumed this a fair exchange. Heinrik only discovered the atrocity after she returned to her boot with one burger, two fries, three coffees and one Salinger. Though the line of customers stretched forever, he somehow managed to notice the Harlequins sitting in the place where the Salinger had resided. He abandoned his post, grabbed the lower class excuses for literature, and stormed down the ramp onto the dock, where he found the offending woman on her boat. He boarded, uninvited, and seized back Salinger. He threw the Harlequins overboard and lectured the woman uninterrupted for twelve long minutes on the subject of what constituted good literature, and what did not, how, in some cases, especially this one, equivalency could never be achieved, no matter the number of the Harlequins offered up. His tongue-lashing ended with " why would someone

~ 12 ~

In Defense Of Literature

"When I woke, the earliest dawn light was coming into the room. It was a pale, bluish light, as though just one layer of darkness had been removed."

When We Were Orphans, **Kazuo Ishiguro**

IF ADAM had been thinking more clearly the other night, he would have followed up on Duende's unusual statement. Certainly, the "atonement" comment had been an invitation to engage in a meaningful interaction, lately absent in their chats. Determined to rationally explore the subject, Adam took advantage of a temporary, sober morning.

A: How's the woofy dog today?

D: Not all that woofy.

A: I've noticed.

D: Have you got any jerky?

Adam put two jerky sticks on Duende's plate.

A: What did you say that I craved the other night?

D: Atonement.

A: How so?

D: You carry a burden, and the way to let go of the burden is by performing a creative act.

A: Do you refer to the scribblers?

D: Don't you see that your addictive behaviour has everything to do with unburdening your soul?

A: Hadn't thought of it that way.

D: The bid to uncover The Refuge mystery is your final chance for redemption.

A: You sound emphatic, even a bit Hollywood.

D: I get frustrated. That's why I descend into hyperbole.

A: I wish you'd just stick to facts. Getting information from you is like pulling teeth.

D: For an experiment, why don't you let Parker do the writing?

A: That could mean less jerky for you.

D: I doubt it.

A: And less of the cherished liquid.

D: I doubt it.

A: You'd lose your job as assistant.

D: I double doubt it.

Scribbler Eight:

FOLLOWING DOMINION Day in Canada, the summer invasion of boating tourists came to pass, and the cloistered folks entered their annual busy phase as shrewd entrepreneurs: Heinrik opened his Burger Palace and book exchange; the children sold lemonade on the dock; Nicole, ahead of her time, made sushi and Nanaimo bars; Wade bagged ice for his dad from the new ice machines for a dime a bag; Jeremy ran an afterhours bootleg operation and garbage disposal unit for a buck a bag; Peter sold oysters, clams, and scallops from his seafarm; and Calvin monkey-wrenched motors, replaced spark plugs, rewired starters, and charged batteries. James maintained the general store and fuel dock with a contingent of five, including Jim and Brad. Carver hired out as a fishing guide. In the little spare time available, he ran extra freight in the store's de-licensed aluminum herring skiff, often taking the children along as swampers.

Heinrik's Burger Palace had become a popular destination for boaters, an eatery for delicious food and free knowledge. Heinrik's dog, Pemah, rode Downtown each morning and back each evening in her master's packsack instead of running ahead, or behind, as was her normal routine. She took to this privileged position due to the cougar. As an aside only, it should be mentioned that she did not always bear the name, Pemah. When a puppy, the beekeeper had called her Grushenka, but she would never come. He tried many names – Evgenia, Heidi, Hilda, Gretchen, and Varvara – until one day he called out "Pemah" and the dog jumped into his lap.

On arriving for work, Heinrik found cougar scat on the porch of his hamburger stand. His alarm shifted to anger when he discovered that his book exchange had taken on a state of disarray. Later, he learned that these incidents were unconnected.

His lending/swap library comprised six shelves for customers to browse, while they waited for burgers, French fries, and coffee. Harlequin romances sulked on the bottom two shelves. There were so many, too many, and they threatened to overtake the shelf above, which was supposed to be occupied by science fiction, but on this particular morning, the Sci-Fi had landed all over the place. Two shelves of murder mysteries came next in the collection, from which he extracted nine Harlequins and threw them into the waste bin. The misplaced Sci-Fi's he put back where they belonged. The upper shelf housed a smattering of classics with a few meritorious modern novels intermixed, and thankfully, nothing there was amiss.

Heinrik operated a knowledge-for-free service - commendable in this present day and age. He had posted rules in the event that boaters wished to make a swap: fifty harlequins begat a classic, ten harlequins one science fiction, three mysteries yielded two Sci-Fi's, two mysteries one classic, and one for one within genre (or sub-genre) went without saying. Even with the rules posted, the patrons were often confused and asked questions when Heinrik should have been concentrating on cooking. And there were other disturbances too, which annoyed him. Sometimes the boaters wanted to give books to his library that didn't fit any of the categories. A week earlier, a poor woman had tried to donate ten children's books and he had refused outright. Other times, they expected him to give a quick synopsis of some particular novel, as if he had nothing better to do than read every book that came his way, and then offer the latest findings, as in the New York Times Sunday edition. Three days earlier, he had scolded a beautiful woman offering a collection of verse by Emily Dickinson, "Harlequins, sci-fi, murder mysteries, classics and selected modern – that's it!"

"I think Emily's work is classic," she said.

"It's poetry," remarked the disperser of knowledge.

Heinrik also forbade books of religious tone and temperament. Exceptions to the rules of trade were tomes on pure science. Though rare, these books appeared from time to time and he took them home never to regain circulation. Heinrik excelled in mathematics, chemistry and physics, but none of the soft sciences.

In addition to the upset of the cougar scat on the porch, as well as the mixing of genres, he found three women's magazines tucked behind the Agatha Christies. These careless exchanges by non-obedient customers made it difficult to focus on his entrepreneurial skills: peeling potatoes, slicing potatoes, cooking patties, slicing buns, warming buns, buttering buns, melting cheese on patties for those who had ordered cheeseburgers, frying onions until they were barely translucent, slathering his special, tangy relishes, deep frying French fries, and brewing coffee – extra strength only, cream or sugar not included.

As if all these affronts weren't enough, another incident occurred that morning, which for him amounted to the last straw. An innocent woman, who had not read the fine print of the exchange rules, attempted to trade her five Harlequins for the top shelf "Catcher in the Rye." Likely, she must have presumed this a fair exchange. Heinrik only discovered the atrocity after she returned to her boat with one burger, two fries, three black, unsweetened coffees, and one Salinger. Though the line of customers stretched forever, he somehow managed to notice the Harlequins sitting in the space where Salinger had resided. He abandoned his post, grabbed the lower class excuses for literature, and stormed down the ramp onto the dock where he found the offending woman on her boat. He boarded, uninvited, and seized back Salinger. He threw the Harlequins overboard and lectured the woman uninterrupted for twelve long minutes on the subject of what constituted good literature, and what did not, how, in some cases, especially this one, equivalency could never be achieved no matter the number of Harlequins offered up. His tongue-lashing ended with, "Why would someone who reads trash want Salinger?" Later, the embarrassed and frightened woman, as she watched her Harlequins float out to sea, told a group of sympathetic listeners, "Saliva sprayed everywhere."

Of course, the meat patties were charred when he got back to his workstation, and the waiting line had increased by the power of six. His customers remained silent and patient, since no other eatery in this section of the wilderness existed. Pemah, nee Grushenka, like the customers, also remained silent when Heinrik returned from his mission. Only she saw, until Heinrik noticed, and then all the patrons, the cougar standing on the boardwalk ten feet from the doorway of the burger stand, dressed in its tawny magnificence, fur-shiver dancing on a ridge line along the back. The cat slowly lowered into a crouch stance, the tail swished and twitched at its very extremity, and the cat's eyes burned brightly at the dog, who was afraid to bark, even to whine, petrified in her bed outside the door to her master's Burger Palace.

Without thought for his safety, Heinrik raised his hamburger flipper over his head and ran menacingly toward the cat, but tripped on the boardwalk, wrenching his back. The cougar, even though he or she had temporary advantage, became as frightened as the Harlequin offendee. The cat darted into the underbrush. Pemah refrained from the chase. The patrons captured the fleeting moment in their memories – this, the wilderness adventure they had hoped for, these, the stories they would take back to the cities of their lives.

Let it be said: the rich and famous - for the first time ever - learned the meaning of hunger, as he closed early and limped home with Pemah and Salinger in his backpack.

A lagoon stretches behind the Refuge. Most call it a lake, as few ~~can~~ care when words are used properly. The easiest route passes by Silvia's home and garden, but at all costs refrain from picking a bean, pea, or zuchini unless the ~~agony~~ of a witche's wrath tempts you; quickly run past her "Keep Out," "Beware!" "Vicious Dogs" and "Trespassers Eliminated" signs, avoid the snarling cats, then as long as you have not lost conviction entirely, scramble over the old boardwalk ~~built~~ alongside the two hundred ~~yes~~ yard flume that separates the lagoon from the ~~ocean~~ ocean.

~ 13 ~

Hot Tub

*"Lolita, light of my life, fire of my loins. My sin, my soul.
Lo-lee-ta: the tip of the tongue taking a trip of three
steps down the palate to tap, at three, on the teeth.
Lo. Lee. Ta."*

Lolita, **Vladimir Nabokov**

ADAM AND Duende watched the boat traffic entering and leaving the bay. They sat on their favourite beach log in front of Adam's cabin.

A: Have you ever seen the gas dock this busy?

D: Never.

A: I thought the tripling of fuel prices would be the death knell for James' business.

D: Logic never prevails when it comes to commerce.

A: I noticed you were busy on the dock the other day.

D: How do you mean?

A: That poodle was twice your size.

D: She comes in every year. Last summer we ran off to the lagoon.

A: An old flame?

D: You'd call it an open relationship.

A: Does she drink?

D: Nope.

A: Did you know that dog spelled backwards is god?

D: Everybody knows that.

Duende licked Adam's glass.

Scribbler Nine:

A LAGOON stretches behind The Refuge. Most call it a lake, as few care when words are used improperly. The easiest route passes by Sylvia's home and garden, but, at all costs, refrain from picking a bean, pea, or zucchini unless the agony of a witch's wrath tempts you; quickly run past her "Keep Out," "Beware," "Vicious Dogs," and "Trespassers Eliminated," signs, avoid the snarling cats, then, as long as you have not lost conviction entirely, scramble over the old boardwalk built alongside the two hundred yard flume that separates the lagoon from the ocean.

Loggers built the walkway near the turn of the century from hand sawn fir planks, some thirty feet in length, two feet wide and four inches thick. Such exceptional timber no longer exists. Over the years, the constant tread of logger's caulk boots had gradually chewed the boards away. Presently, the structure's footings are rotten, and the planks so thin, they may collapse when walked on.

To prove a point - whether the body of water were lake or lagoon - Carver held his breath and dove down twenty feet to retrieve a water sample from the bottom. He also wanted to demonstrate his athletic prowess. Watching from the shore, his companion for a day only, Sheila - a visiting niece of the Blacks, and in no good mood since she had been frightened by Sylvia, intimidated by her cats, fallen through one of the planks on the way up the flume, and skinned her delicate shin - gagged when she took a sip of this unequivocally brackish water. She retched by sticking her finger down her throat and brushed at her tongue with the back of her hand to remove the foul taste.

"It's pukey and salty!"

He laughed at her, perhaps for too long, until Sheila silenced him with a shrew stare. His muscles danced under his skin, as he swished the water from his wet hair.

Over the course of Carver's short stay at The Refuge, he had learned the history of the lagoon from his so-called uncle, Mac-Leod, and hoped to impress the pretty girl with this local knowledge. Though her mood for listening attentively had expired, even before the demonstration, he explained, "Fresh water floats on salt water."

"Do you think I'm stupid?" replied Sheila.

"On high tides the creek reverses direction and fills the lagoon."

"Lake," insisted the urban girl.

He then elaborated on the construction of the flume. "The loggers widened the creek bed, they cleared out the larger boulders, built a shoot of wooden sidewalls, and a dam at the narrowest spot so that after a few years the lagoon rose to the height of the dam."

"Impossible," she said.

"Finally they were able to raise the dam gate at a high tide and float logs down the flume where they were bagged in the salt chuck."

"The tide can't go that high!" yelled Sheila.

Carver persisted, "Just like cattle going to slaughter," now grooming his golden locks with a rat-tail comb.

He took her back to the Blacks; accompanied also by dark thoughts via a cheater trail that by-passed Sylvia's.

A day later, Sheila screamed over the engine rumble from the deck of the *Quillcene Princess*, "It's a lake and that's an ocean," gesturing warlike at the waters of The Refuge. Carver never forgave her for embarrassing him in front of his friends, in particular, the children. The whole community watched as the freighter pull away.

THE LAKE or lagoon (depending on point of view) is three miles long, bent like a dogleg, shallow (no more than a twenty-five foot depth in the deepest spot), shoreline irregular, dotted with islets, and uninhabited. During the early part of the century, when logging flourished, a floating community of eighty persons lived there. They even ran a school. Today, the bottom of the lake is littered in sunken timber (as logs often lack buoyancy if the salinity is low), and there they are preserved (like pickles), waiting the day when quality timber becomes scarce and expensive. A rusted donkey winch on rotted-out cedar skids and a beached carcass of a box-like steamboat, once used as a tug, remain from that historic time.

Carver met Karen, an anthropology student, off one of the yachts. Karen's father was disposed to let him escort his daughter on the lagoon tour, as the night previous, the competent young man had shown the yachtsman how to catch a salmon. They caught six fish, one a record-breaking, twenty-eight pound coho.

This time Carver took precautions with the young female student, using the path along the shoreline rather than the boardwalk. They passed by Sylvia's, but on the other shore of the flume. The two adventurers stopped at the dam, and Carver explained how his uncle had taken his own initiative and saved the returning salmon run, both coho and chum, by brailing them over the gate each autumn. Now the responsibility had fallen to him, as MacLeod was too old and too frail for the annual chore.

"The coho come up in October and the chum in November and December. Both runs are small, but I still managed to transfer six hundred last year and nine hundred the year before. I've got the dates and figures back at the cabin if you want to see them."

"Do you get paid to do it?" she asked.

"Hell, no. My next project is to clean the gravel beds in all the creeks."

He explained that he had an application into Fisheries to build a fish ladder.

"I'll do the labour *gratis*," he explained. "They just need to supply materials."

"Good for you!" Karen said.

He judged her to be about twenty-five years old, older than he was used to. She wore glasses that hung low on her pretty nose. She carried a notebook, and every once in a while, he ceased from his talk so that she could make an entry. Karen wore hiking boots, knee high socks, and no-nonsense shorts cut a trifle tight.

"I bet you could give me some pointers on writing proposals," he said.

She smiled, "It sounds to me like you don't need help."

They headed for an indigenous archaeological site – the lure that got her to go on the adventure located near the dam. Mac-Leod had told Carver about the bowl carved into rock. After two days of searching, he had found it filled with mud and debris. The bowl, or hot tub as he liked to think of it now, measured four feet in diameter, a perfect circle, and three feet deep. The sides had been smoothed and sloped to the centre. His uncle didn't know what the bowl was for – "either cooking or washing."

When he and Karen arrived, the sizzling sun had heated the bath for the anticipated communal wash.

"Imagine the time to grind that hole into the rock with the tools they used," Carver commented. He had worked for an entire day cleaning the tub and filling it with fresh water.

She seemed to know everything about these bowls.

"They are not that unusual. I know seven locations on the coast where they can be found. The Klahoose people from *Tu7kw*, originally from K̲w'ik̲'tichenam used rock pots for cooking by heating the water with hot stones. My guess is that they used this one to prepare cattail, *Typha latifola*. The roots, or, more correctly, rhizomes," as she clarified, "were an important nutritional source for native peoples when other foods were scarce. The young shoots, though I've never tried one, are reported to be very tasty, the mature tubers starchy like potatoes, and the fibrous stalk and leaves can be processed to make string, mats, and furniture."

She spoke with machine-like rhythm. The attractive archaeologist pointed to a marshy area some fifty yards away and said,

"See, there are some *Typha*."

Pleased with herself, she continued, "Redwings and ducks love to nest in this habitat. They use the fluff for bedding material. Oh, I almost forgot, cattails have medicinal value. Many cultures used the roots to treat intestinal maladies and burns, and the absorbent tops are used during child birth and for menstruation."

Carver wished to know none of this.

The student congratulated Carver (in a manner suggesting he was a good boy) for cleaning the site and treating it with respect. She took a picture, looked at her watch, and said that her mom and dad were leaving soon so they should get back. "Besides it's too hot to be out in the sun."

She gave him her telephone number, if ever he happened to be in Vancouver, and on the way back, by rote, recited the finer points of her master's thesis ("The Message of Functional Art in Coast Salish Culture"), which had something to do with native basket design.

He chucked his bar of soap in the bush.

IN HIS spare time, which had become increasingly rare, what with fish guiding and fetching the store's freight, Carver had managed to build a lean-to over the water straddling two islets near a far shore of the lagoon. He patterned the structure on a large outhouse with the end walls missing, as rustic, remote, and picturesque as his fantasies permitted. The floor of the hideaway perched at a perfect level (as long as the loggers didn't monkey with the height of the dam) for hanging his legs over the side and wriggling his toes in the cool water after a long hot summer night – and if he was lucky, a long hot night of good fun. This was his perfect place to greet the morning sun and drink his first coffee of the day.

"Hot, black and strong," he had instructed Moon Dance, a hippie from Galley Bay, who seemed to care less about whether or not she would ever return to her commune.

He sipped his coffee and heard the loons give their lonesome cry out of the fog. Soon the birds would fly through the gap into the channel, and he would hear the whistle from their wings. He had a speech prepared about how they acquired their necklace. That story always impressed overnight guests, especially if they thought he had constructed the yarn himself. He would forego the tale today though, as the girl beside him knew the story.

The few patches of blue sky above seemed to move rather than the mist below. He decided it was time to leave even if the fog hadn't lifted. If they got lost, it would be her fault. His morning coffee routine had been upset with the addition of powdered milk. Had not his instructions been straightforward?

Seb set up an information booth on Monday morning located near the fresh water outlets close to the fuel docks. He placed 5 fuscia and 5 begonia potted plants on one side of the outlets, and another five and five on the other side. He posted 2 signs:

"XXX water" and "skywater."

The first sign, the XXX one, had what could be taken for lightening bolts slashing all around the edges, and smoke-stacks in each corner belching black ash over a sterile forest with dry creek bed running through. Skulls and cross bones appeared everywhere. So much went on in his presentation that the viewer could hardly see the phrase "XXX water." The latter sign portrayed rain gently sprinkling from clouds drawn above the word, "Skywater!"

Eagles flew everywhere, enjoying the happiness of flight. Again, as in the first sign, the word "skywater" got lost in the activity of the scene. In both plant groupings, whether fuscia or begonia, the eagle-approved group were vibrant, whereas the XXX-rated group looked dreadful — wilted leaves, blossom end rot,

~ 14 ~

Ecological Calamity

*"I have nothing in common with this structure, with
these perspectives, and these perspectives are not even
made so that I can exist in them, so that I don't even
exist, I only howl, and howling is not identical with
existence,... "*

Animalinside, Laszlo Krasznahorkai and Max Neumann

Scribbler Ten:

THE FUCHSIA-BEGONIA project consumed Sebastian in
early August, a debut whereby he paraded a message of concern
to his community and the greater public. He conducted his protest from nine a.m. to two p.m. daily, and continued the vigil for
the remainder of the month.

Seb set up an information booth on a Monday morning, located
near the fresh water outlets close to the fuel dock. He placed five
fuchsia and five begonia potted plants on one side of the outlets,
and another five and five on the other side. He posted two signs:
"XXX wader" and "skywader." The first sign, the XXX one, had
what could be taken for lightning bolts slashing all around the
edges, and smoke stacks in each corner belching black ash over a
sterile forest with a dry creek bed running through. Skulls and cross

bones appeared everywhere. So much went on in his presentation that the viewer could hardly see the phrase, "XXX wader." The latter sign, portrayed rain gently sprinkling from clouds drawn above the word, "skywader." Eagles flew everywhere enjoying the happiness of flight. Again, as in the first sign, the word, "skywader," got lost in the activity of the scene. In both plant groupings, whether fuchsia or begonia, the eagle-approved group were vibrant, whereas the XXX-rated group looked dreadful – wilted leaves, blossom-end rot, blackened stems, and mould. The display implied that the plants watered from the store's water system – the source a pristine creek in the valley above the store - were compromised, whereas those irrigated with rainwater, which Sebastian had collected and stored in barrels, flourished.

Nicole, the first to see the mini-protest, studied the situation before grasping a possible meaning. She immediately became concerned that Sebastian had not accurately conveyed his true intention.

She thought the signs looked produced by an unruly, all-boys, grade-one class. The lack of professionalism - hunks of delaminating cardboard, grease pencil used for a marker, misspellings, the multiplicity of images, and the meaning entombed therein - encouraged her to take the initiative.

"Seb, no one will understand what you mean. Would you mind if I make a few suggestions?"

He, by this time, had arranged himself into a simple elegance on the dock - a lotus position holding a feather in his left hand, the longest feather from the tail section of an eagle. De Gaulle shivered alongside on his blanket. Remembering that Seb refused to speak, she hoped that at least he could hear. "Your signs try to illustrate too much," she explained. "You should just have words. The plants will tell the story all by themselves."

Seb seemed not to notice her, preoccupied in stilling a restless mind.

She went away for an hour and returned carrying new signs, constructed from pieces of smooth doorskin – one foot by two feet, a white latex background, and perfectly spaced letters painted in black, as if applied with a stencil and ink roller.

While in university, she had read *Silent Spring* by Rachel Carson, and now sensed the same angst in Sebastian as she had in Rachel.

"Do you like these?" Nicole held each sign in front of his face so that he would see them.

"I thought 'Hose Water' instead of 'XXXwader' because I know you are concerned about the aerial spraying by Forestry, and I thought 'Rain Water' instead of 'Skywader.' Is that okay?"

"Maybe I should have just said, 'Run-off'?"

"The paint is still wet so don't let anybody touch them."

"I'm going to take down your signs and put these up. Is that okay?"

"Shake your head or do something if you want me to stop."

Nicole took his signs down and carefully laid them beside De Gaulle who wagged his tail. She put her own signs up.

"Try these just for today. We'll put yours back if you don't like mine."

Nicole rearranged the plants thinking the groups too close together.

"The rains are quite beautiful," she said, "but keep them separate from the run-offs," and then she left.

Heinrik, along with Pemah, in a hurry to open the Burger Palace, stopped at the fuel dock for naphtha for his Coleman stove. Pemah sniffed the plants and sniffed De Gaulle who continued his shivers. Like Nicole, Heinrik needed a few moments to digest the situation.

"Seb, you need proper controls for your experiment," he finally said.

It may be that Sebastian heard the anguished voices of the run-offs and the soft purrings from the rains.

"The experiment means nothing. You need more plants... you need a whole series of replicates. Six is a minimum for any experiment. No scientist would ever use five. And the water has to be controlled...rains and run-offs...and the plants...tested, certified, both."

Sebastian's jaw muscles twitched and his Adam's apple

spasmed. His eyes fixed on a point in space that only he could see. He was barefoot, and his toenail weaponry captured unconditional attention: layers of accretions, especially on the big toenails, brittle from age, upraked and downraked from overcrowding, like misshapen oyster shells that had lived too long, too high intertidal, and had finally expired from the pounding surf and lack of nutrients, not to mention extended exposure from the sun. One hardly noticed his necklace of eagle beaks, the two tail feathers in his hair, and the hand-sewn, loose-fitting shirt and pants – a burlap material sprouting eagle down.

"Don't you think that if there was something wrong," Heinrik continued, "the forest would be all limp and bedraggled like your run-offs? I talked with Forestry in March and there's been no spraying anywhere near here for years."

Sebastian looked to another point in space - something had happened. He carved the air with his eagle feather.

"C'mon Pemah." Heinrik and his dog walked away, but Heinrik could not resist the urge to call back, "Even if they did spray, it wouldn't hurt the water supply or the plants."

As Heinrik was unable to let any matter rest, he yelled across the U when he reached the foot of the ramp, "You need an hypothesis to test. Do science right!"

A yacht pulled alongside the fresh water outlets. A tanned boater stepped out and tied up his vessel. He read the signs, looked at the potted plants, Sebastian and De Gaulle, and began filling his water tank.

Another yacht pulled alongside. The skipper told his wife to top off the water while he went to the store for buzz bombs and ice. He gave her the bung wrench and left. She read the signs too – a man in lotus position, dressed oddly, holding an eagle feather, two sets of five fuchsias and five begonias, sick dog, water hoses with signs on each side – and then asked Sebastian, "Excuse me, is there something wrong with the water?"

She tried another question. "Did the hose water hurt your dog?"

The tanned boater, who had finished filling his own tank, said, "The water's fine."

At that moment, the woman's husband stepped out onto the store porch, carrying four blocks of ice. She shouted across the U, "Harold, the water's poisoned. The ice is contaminated!"

Within hours, boaters were announcing over their radio-phones, "Boil your water if you got it at Refuge." Always known for its pure and tasty water, the safe haven had now become a suspect destination to the boating public.

When James learned that his wife had made the signs for Sebastian, they fought in the nook of the post office for the entire world to hear. He found it inconceivable that she could be an active participant in the destruction of their own business.

"Whose side are you on?" he asked.

Nicole knew what his question referred to, and she replied, "It isn't about taking sides. I felt sorry for him...that's why I helped."

Unable to restrain himself, James said, "You city people always see poison in the wilderness when you should be seeing it in your own streets and sewers."

When Nicole slammed the front door of the store, a row of cigarettes fell off the shelf behind the cash register. James picked them up. Accusations swarmed in his head just as the bees had swarmed over the queen excluder in the time of the bear.

As Nicole left, she addressed a woman listening near the doorway, "You have to live here six generations before outsider status is forfeited." She went home for the day, leaving her husband understaffed.

James didn't come home for dinner; instead he spent five hours on an American luxury yacht drinking excellent Bourbon. The skipper made him feel like a business equal. He complimented James on the well-run marina operation and told him not to worry about the water situation – nobody took the "kook" seriously. They discussed the world at large, the war in Vietnam, the reasons for the tripling of beef and fuel prices, and he found James' economic theories for inflation sound, even enlightening. And when he learned that James owned most of the land in Refuge Cove, he said, "Come and see me if you ever want to sell."

James climbed up the hill to his log home with a gold embossed

– 14 karats – business card tucked into his shirt pocket. He stumbled into the house at 10:30 p.m. and said, "Where's my dinner?"

Nicole stood at the kitchen window watching the last light of day when he came in. She turned and walked toward him.

"I didn't make *you* any."

There was that *you* again.

He approached Nicole but slipped when almost beside her. As he corrected his balance, his arm came up over his head, and then his clenched fist grazed her head and shoulder. He almost fell over. He quickly explained to himself that what had just happened was an accident. He had hardly touched her. If she had not been advancing, and if he had not been advancing.

An aura glowed to the side of her head: orange, pulsing, about the size of her head. Stretching and inflating like a balloon. And twisting and untwisting. Angel got up from her bed and stood looking up at Nicole. James took the time to wonder if the intent eyes of the dog saw what he saw.

James put a narrative together. "I wasn't running at you. I wanted to get into the kitchen to make my dinner, but you were in the way, and that's why I slipped. I was only trying to get around you. I slipped and my arm grazed you. That's all."

She screamed, "Don't *you* ever hit me."

He climbed the stairs to the loft where they all slept. He shook Wade, but couldn't wake him. Then he shook Tara. She wouldn't wake either. He sat on her bed and watched her breathe. She had fallen asleep reading. He turned off her little flashlight and put the book on her night table. He saw a pile of quarters in a dish on the night table. He stacked the quarters, almost a full roll's worth. All James wanted was to talk to his children. To ask them if their day had gone well.

Next day he tried to reason with Sebastian, but got nowhere, as the man refused to talk. He couldn't even get Sebastian to wave his eagle feather as a response or acknowledgement. He put up a much larger door skin – a simple statement, WATER OKAY. Sebastian in no way tried to escalate their confrontation with more or bigger signs. He had done what he had to do, and now others were welcome to take whatever initiative they saw fit.

During the rest of the month, the children mostly ignored Sebastian, except for Charlotte, who often sat beside him and patted De Gaulle. Some days she chattered to him like an exuberant songbird, not caring that he didn't answer. Other days, she cried tiny tears. When needed, she fielded the many questions from the boaters, as if she were lending the protester her voice.

"The dog's not feeling better."

"The man's got a headache all the time."

"The water still tastes good."

"When he holds the feather he can't lie."

"They're pretty when not dead."

'We want him to talk."

The boaters were grateful to receive any information.

The girls performed their spinning routine beside Sebastian and De Gaulle, since the usual location near the freight shed had been taken up with Jeremy's garbage collection depot. The proximity of the dancing girls to the silent protester resulted in the boaters noticing him even more than they would have. Most observers found the two performances absurd and walked away baffled. The thoughtful ones in the audience assumed that somehow both events were related, in fact, shared common values and mechanisms. They perceived that the signs, the dancing girls, the meditative man, the potted plants, the eagle paraphernalia, the shivering dog, and the contaminated water, as a singular and coordinated happening. In this living collage, a story was unfolding, and, as in all great works of art, the viewer needed to be alert, intelligent, and intuitive.

One day, a woman boater, who obviously had a background in the creative world (an art critic by trade), analyzed the live theatre for the benefit of a group of perfect strangers: "One would not expect to find a melding of the protest movement and street theatre in an outpost so removed from their urban origins. This *impromptu* gives us all pause to wonder; namely, do our city egos dominate to the extent that we cannot admit to the evolution of new and important artistic structures elsewhere than under our metropolitan noses?"

She then pointed in turn to the following features: "Please note, if you will, the myriad of dichotomous analogues: youth and age, stillness and motion, sadness and gaiety, nature and man, nature and woman, and then the dog!"

Here she clutched her hands together as if to pray.

"The shivering dog shouts out an incongruity!" she exclaimed, and looked around at her stunned audience, who began to drift away.

In order to stay their departure, she continued, "The new cultural politics of difference is determined to trash the monolith and homogenous in the name of diversity, multiplicity, and heterogeneity; to reject the abstract...."

As the last listeners drifted off, either to the store, or the serenity of their own vessel, she shouted, "You could understand if you would think of vision and reality as two competitors in a race...." As it turned out, she hailed from Chicago and traveled aboard a yacht so large it carried enough fresh water to circumnavigate the globe twice without a top-up.

Divisions in the small community surfaced and people took sides. For some, their support or opposition to the protest was genuine; for others, the fuchsia-begonia debate became a surrogate excuse for re-enacting old feuds. Though they had always been friends, Heinrik and Peter fought about the proper ways to conduct scientific experiments. On two occasions, this jousting took place within Sebastian's hearing, though he seemed not to notice. And during the course of these arguments, Heinrik often reminded Peter that he had been the one who brought the protester to The Refuge in the first place.

Eight years before, when Sebastian still spoke, on a day when he sold clams and oysters to the shellfish plant, he mentioned to Peter that things were weird in Malaspina Inlet, so he needed to move. He added, "The shellfish are dying, the eagles are dying, my dog's sick, I'm sick, and the garden's wilting." Sebastian blamed the forestry spraying program for weed suppression in the forest replant areas and said that all run-off was contaminated. He knew for a fact that toxins had leached into everything.

Why else would he have a headache and stomachache that never went away? Four days later, to his surprise, Peter noticed Seb's floathouse tied to the seafarm. Peter made him the caretaker, not because he needed one, but simply because he felt sorry for the man and his dog.

Visitors informed Alice regularly about the curious activity on the dock. In the past, when Seb did socialize, Alice had spent many evenings listening to his *tale of woe* and learned more than she ever wanted to hear about the different toxins in different sprays, and what they could do to your brain and liver.

Her opinions, she kept to herself.

"It's too early in the day to form an opinion," she said.

"Some things are best left unsaid," she said.

As everyone knew, Alice believed "gossip" would quickly destroy harmony in a small community.

"You have to admire him," Sylvia commented to MacLeod and Son on a mail day. MacLeod had tried to get a fix on the events and asked her to spell out everything, unable to see how, or why, some plants suffered and others didn't, and what made the *rains* different from the *run-offs*. "Science is too complicated for me," he said.

"It's not science. It's sensitivity. He knows something, and feels something, that we are only beginning to grasp."

Carver showed a side no one had seen before. He wanted to throw the plants in the ocean and escort Sebastian back to the seafarm if necessary, and if necessary, chain up his boat so he could not come back to the government dock. Jeremy counseled him away from these rash thoughts and defended Seb's right to protest even though his own ventures with bootleg alcohol and garbage disposal teetered on bankruptcy.

James answered the same question a thousand times that summer: "Is the water really okay?" He tried unsuccessfully to get the federal Harbour and Wharf Commission to remove Sebastian. Apparently the silent man's civil right to free speech would be denied if they interfered. "It's a government dock," the bureaucrat had said. "If it were a private dock that would be different." The diligent clerk also reminded James not to remove the signs. James called Forestry and they confirmed, as Heinrik had discovered, that spraying had not taken place on West Redonda Island for years.

Reluctantly, James dug mud and fresh leaf build-up from the dam - just to be sure - though he'd already done that in early June, and there hadn't been much rain since. He even wandered up the creek bed for a mile in search of a problem he knew he wouldn't find. He arranged to have the water sampled, tested, and the results posted. "Low coliforms, and faecals neligible."

Peter pointed out that he tested for the wrong things; the results hadn't included analysis of chemical or industrial toxins, which could be harmful even in parts per billion. That comment strained their relationship. The seafarmer reminded the storekeeper that few boats had holding tanks, therefore direct discharges into the ocean threatened his seafood operation. James did not see a connection between the two issues and encouraged his friend to stay focused.

By the end of August, the store business had suffered moderately as did the ancillary businesses. To all appearances, neither the fuchsias and begonias, nor their demonstrator, effected a meaningful change in the public's attitude; nor did the protest advance enlightenment in the minds of the local people. Sebastian and De Gaulle abandoned their summer routine and returned to his floating hermitage to prepare for the next stage in their metamorphosis.

The summer came to a close in a heat wave. The ocean seemed the only place to be.

SEA WITHOUT SHORES

~ 15 ~

A Night on the Tom Forge

"And it seemed as though in a little while the solution would be found, and then a new and glorious life would begin; and it was clear to both of them that the end was still far off, and that what was to be most complicated and difficult for them was only just beginning."

The Lady with the Pet Dog, **Anton Chekhov**

ADAM APPROACHED oblivion. He and Duende concluded their argument on a sour note. The dog wanted to investigate a hunch, whereas Adam insisted the hunch could wait. The recluse felt that the "Maddie" *thing* needed to be dealt with first, so that the *thing* between them could finally be put to rest. Then, together, they – Adam and Duende – could concentrate on their mission, the other *thing*. Adam, housed in a fermented fog, insisted that one could not enter the present without first exiting the past.

A: The past is saprife with energy.

D: The present is far more interesting. *Now* shoots up from the belly of the earth and singes my paws. Then I dance.

A: Dancing dogs belong in the circus. They lack profundity.

The fool smells like he's rolled in rotten starfish, hardly worth a curse, thought Adam.

Duende ran off in a huff. Ruff, ruff, huff, huff.

ADAM SAT on his thinking log. Thinking. The tide lapped at his gumboots. He had concluded that the hound suffered from a deficit in mental agility. The pooch thought in linear perspective only – a four-legged freeloader unable to enter the chambers of limitless possibilities. The hybridized beast could not endure the complexity in the universe. The mongrel did not see how things interconnect...sure the crossbreed heard the sounds rumbling deep inside the earth and smelled the emotions that Nature released, and he understood better than most, that Nature was in charge, but he couldn't fuse the myriad interconnections into the beautiful symphony.

Whelmed with guilt, and mustering an unconvincing argument for their bipolar reconciliation, Adam, alone, delivered a speech to the night, not unlike Sebastian had done on his shellfish expedition: "Duende, I have wondered, but don't know how you feel about this; what if...suppose...you had the same official sanction as myself...you heard me correctly, *official*, perhaps we would not be equals initially, but later, when you learned the ropes, took your first tentative steps, so to speak, and we had separated out duties and responsibilities, each doing what he is best suited for, *to the best of one's abilities,* as they say? You could sit on my shoulder, in a manner of speaking, to whisper, shout, or bark if necessary, in my attentive ear, then following on this initial apprenticeship, and a successful completion thereof, might we sit down – how shall I say – to discuss the evaluation of your position...you could operate on a pro bono basis, or a retainer fee, as you wish. Think of Heinrik's venison jerky, think unlimited portions, think of jerky beyond forever...does that not sound like a profitable and profound arrangement? And nectar too...let us not forget the scotch, bottles and bottles of scotch. Okay, do not panic, I anticipate your concern, let us be informal for starters, and forget the wherefores and herewithalls and therebys, and since you have never been shackled by the writing part of the thing, we could consider that your duties continue much as they have been, yet with certain provisos made for the opportunity to review, edit, and comment, the kind of minor changes and critiques that are required in undertakings of this sort, between colleagues...and even actual new suggestions for words and/or phrases, but later, my God, much later, it might evolve, if we are fortunate, that you could suggest for consideration, not just suggest sentences, but, on your own, take the immense burden, yes, write or dictate, however you want to do it...whole long tortuous sentences, and compounded ones for diversity if you wish, declarative sentences, or interrogative, if you so please...consider for instance...fragment phrases used sparingly. And what of the imperative...you see the field is wide open. Together we might dance and sing...do you follow my reasoning?"

Now the tide lapped over Adam's gumboots.

NEXT EVENING, the *Tom Forge* approached his shore in a weaving, non-conventional manner.

"Holy Christ," Adam mentioned to himself.

Maddie yelled, "How about a boat ride?"

"Where?" he shouted.

"Into the channel. We can watch the sunset." She held up a bottle of malt.

"Have you got Duende aboard?" Adam asked.

"Why would I? He's at Jim and Brad's."

"Good."

He rowed out to the *Forge* and tied to the stern. Maddie put the boat in gear and steered for the treacherous opening to Lewis Channel. She was careful to miss the shoals that were not there on Chart 3594. They motored out to mid-channel maintaining a northerly bias. He sat on the back deck railing, wondering.

He had not spoken to her in years. He had not seen Maddie, except to watch her go by in the *Forge*. Once a week. Twice if lucky. Often he put the binoculars on the workboat to see her face framed in the dark wheelhouse window. He could never be sure if she looked his way. He had noted in his journal each time and date she visited her nephews. And how often she fuelled at the gas dock. He watched her walk to the store and walk back to the *Forge*. He loved to watch her walk. He collected the data to pass the time.

He had advanced Wade's drawing of the *Forge* to each upcoming month, so that new drawings of new vessels became redundant, though he never told the boy.

Waiting for the *Forge's* passage oriented his clock. Though he hadn't realized, he used Maddie to wait out time. He thought of her only some of the time, but those were the best of times. For him, she had power over time. And though he didn't know how, she could summon time from a distant universe. To obstruct reality, he had once dreamed that she manufactured time, as a spider weaves a web. And if he were caught in that web, he might tolerate the redemption of time. Though time sped on by, he wouldn't change things, even if he could.

Well, maybe not.

Maddie killed the engine and let the boat drift. She appeared from the wheelhouse with glasses and refreshments, looking as undernourished as ever. And much younger than the number sixty-one should allow; impossibly tight jeans, wide-black-shiny-cinched-up belt, oceans of mascara, glossy red lipstick, unchippable red nail polish, low-cut blouse, dangle-bobble earrings, a gaudy, clacking necklace of plastic beads, and rubber boots with tops rolled down, the latest fashion as now the children in The Refuge dressed that way.

She stood on the open deck separating him from the late day sun. The aberrant touch of her shadow made him shiver, nearly knocked him into the drink.

She put two tumblers on a box of freight and gave him the bottle of scotch. She said, "You pour, I pick."

He threw the screw cap overboard, noticed three measuring lines on the plastic glasses, and aimed for the three-ounce level. Maddie kneeled on the deck and sized them carefully. He saw that her hair had greyed along the neckline. Otherwise, she was still *ne plus ultra*. She picked the most full glass, the difference negligible.

They toasted – a plastic clunk.

"Last time we drank," he said, "it wasn't this friendly."

"It was still fun…some of the time."

"Not much of the time."

The sun grew in volume, took on a crimson hue, and slowly lost its circle of perfection maintained through the day. *Forge* turned broadside to West Redonda Island. They watched the hilltops change into golden splashes and they watched the trees and mosses transform into a rich Venetian orange. The sea turned a brassy red. Adam watched Maddie's earrings take their turns at pulsing prismatic surges. The drinks in their hands flashed and sparkled, and the amber malt aged a few more years.

"What are we doing out here?" he asked.

"I thought we could renew our old friendship."

"Friendship? That word makes our past sound inconsequential."

"You still use big words."

They both sipped on their malt. Adam hoped he could control the craziness sloshing through his brain.

"What about Jake?" he asked.

"We're finished."

He took another sip of the scotch. "Nice."

"James told me your brand."

"I drink anything."

"Me too."

She sat on the deck and leaned her shoulder against some cargo. The warmth on their backs retreated with the setting of the sun. They watched the shadow of Cortes Island slowly stretch its arms across Lewis Channel, envelop the *Tom Forge*, and quickly grapple with the shores of West Redonda. They watched the shadow climb the bluffs and suck the colour from the land. To the northeast, the sky turned pink, as the boat drifted up channel past McGuffey's Bay and Point-No-Point. The tide pulled them in close to Poverty Bluffs.

"Not much left of the Anderson place," Maddie said.

"It never was much."

They glided slowly to Joyce Point at the mouth of Teakerne Arm, neither of them able to speak. The northern and southern tide met there, and swirled in vast gyres, catching and corralling debris: tangles of kelp and witches hair, dirty yellow seafoam, logs lined with gulls, cormorants drying their unwaxed wings, whole trees torn loose from the raging Toba and Brem Rivers, plastic bags, rotten planks, styrofoam floats liberated from the seafarm, a buoyant dishwasher with a hardwood counter top, flocks of contented grebes and golden-eyes, and the *Forge,* trapped for a time. Occasionally, a Bonaparte gull peeped to highlight the silence.

"We're trapped in the Saragossa Sea," he said.

"Never heard of it."

"It's a *sea without shores,* seven hundred miles wide, two thousand miles long, bounded by the Gulf Stream, the North Atlantic Current and…"

"We're a *sea without shores.*"

"The colour is deep blue."

"Our colour is shallow red."

"The sea will never have shores…"

"Same for our sea."

"The various currents collect the refuse thrown into the Atlantic."

"Our currents collect the garbage we threw at each other."

"The sea is named after the seaweed, Sargassum."

"Our sea is named after the land weed, Gout."

She kicked his foot, and he chuckled.

"This time you pour and I pick," he said.

She filled their glasses, but didn't go for precision. Maddie could still handle a drink.

She looked up channel to the logging camp, where she had lived for thirty years. "Jake bought me the old schoolteacher's house in Seaford. And he's giving me some money. Then he's sailing off with a Lund woman."

"Not a bad deal for the Lund woman."

"A good deal for me."

The radio squawked in the small wheelhouse. "MV 2658, Tom Forge, Tom Forge, Come in, Tom Forge, over."

"Damn." She got up and went into the wheelhouse.

He heard her voice, "Forge answering, over."

"Where are ya?"

"Jim and Brad's. They need company."

"They're not kids no more."

"I'll be up early in the morning, over."

"I need that gasket."

"You'll get your gasket. Forge, over and out."

She came out on deck with a pack of tailor-mades, lit one, gave it to Adam, and lit another for herself. They sucked on their cigarettes.

"The sea's calm tonight," he said.

"Like piss on a plate."

"So, things have worked out for you?"

"Of course."

"Me too."

"Cortes is different now," she said, "the hippies overran the place."

"That's not such a bad thing."

"Things have worked out better than I thought."

"Yeah, me too."

Maddie dragged on her cigarette like a movie star from the fifties. She held her head atilt like someone should take her picture for a glamour magazine. His old flame teased him by aiming smoke rings in his face. He didn't mind.

"It'll be different," she said, "but memories'll be hiding in trees."

"Memories never know when to quit."

"I'll have electricity and a telephone, and now there's a ferry to Quadra."

"You'll like that."

"It'll be a good change."

"You'll get to go to Campbell River any time you want."

The gyre at the mouth of Teakerne Arm spit them out. The *Forge* drifted from Corby's down the east shore of Cortes. They sipped on their scotch and watched the boulders and beach logs slowly glide by. Was it the land that moved, or was it the *Sea without Shores*?

An eagle watched them from a snag, and a mink ran along the shore with a small fish in its mouth.

"I'm too drunk to know what to do with tonight," he said.

It took her awhile to answer.

"I just wanted to talk. It's like there's no one to talk to. We always had great talks."

Of course, he remembered and dreamed of…their talks.

"You talked about the big world and wanted to take me down the Amazon River. I thought it would be like African Queen, and me burning the slugs off your back with my cigarettes."

"Leeches."

"Who cares?"

"They were his cigarettes, not hers."

"Who cares whose cigarettes they were."

"I'm trying to get the story straight."

"You were Bogart so what does it matter?"

He couldn't remember the end of the movie. They both sipped on their scotch.

"You would've made a good Hepburn."

"Do you think so?"

"She didn't drink though. You wouldn't have liked her."

He poured her another scotch and one for himself.

"Your hair's the wrong colour," he said.

"I could dye it."

"You've got a tongue like Katherine."

"Nobody ever thought of me as a movie star before."

"She was a humdinger."

Maddie took a big swig and said, "We all had fantasies when we were young."

"Sounds like you still got them."

"Don't you?"

"We'll never wake into the world we knew before."

"That's sad."

He could not force himself to say that he had dreamed about her. Not on purpose, or that he had tried not to, but every once in awhile, she crept into his nightlife, like a whiff of smoke, stayed a few seconds and then vanished on a current of stale air, never leaving her aroma behind, never allowing him to remember the feel of her lips.

Some nights those dreams had woken him.

Broken dreams.

The *Forge* glided by Turning Point, and the dock lights of Squirrel Cove came into view. A tug berthed alongside the pilings of the government wharf. One of the crew played an accordion, and the notes wafted towards them.

Adam pointed to shore where the new navigation light had been installed.

"Below that snag is where they found Georgie."

"That murder changed everything for everyone," she said. "We wouldn't be sitting here if that had not happened."

"That's almost for sure."

"We might have done the Amazon. And then gone off to Africa and done the Nile…and hunted elephants. We could have just kept on going."

"We might not have survived the Amazon."

"The murder opened up everything for our parents and for us, and then it all shut down. Maybe we did what we were supposed to do, but the murder kept making us do things we never wanted to do."

"Like what?"

"You disappeared."

"Well you disappeared into Jake's logging camp."

"When you came to The Refuge, I thought we'd see each other."

"I've watched you go by."

"I've watched you watch me go by."

Maddie got up and went into the wheelhouse. She came out with a blanket, sat down on the deck, and wrapped herself. He tugged on a corner so it covered her bare shoulder.

"Have you got another blanket?"

"No."

The *Forge* approached Seaford. The ebb tide surged, and Lewis Channel emptied into the wine dark *Sea without Shores,* the wine dark *Sea without Shores* emptied into the wine dark Pacific Ocean, and the wine dark Pacific Ocean emptied into the wine dark Universe. And the wine dark Universe?

Adam silently lamented that this dream was going too fast.

He watched his rowboat secured on the long tether. Sometimes it sailed ahead of them, sometimes coasted along side, and other times, stayed where it should, trailing well behind the *Forge*. A three-quarter moon crested the coastal mountains, climbed up Mt. Denman and rocketed past the peak. The night would be almost as light as the day.

"That's my new home." She pointed to a small red building on a bluff overlooking the channel. "It's got a garden and fruit trees…and a damned good view."

"I don't have to look to see it."

"Not even the rich have a view like mine. Since Desolation got famous, the fancy yachts crawl all over my view. I've done pretty good for myself."

"There's not much left of my parent's home. I can see it from my cabin." The building Adam looked at was the furthest south in the small community of Seaford. The roof had collapsed so the structure wouldn't last much longer.

"I don't think I ever told you this, but as a boy, I developed a theory that there were East facing people and West facing people. People who got up with the sun, they were the East facers, and people who went down with the sun, they were the West facers. People who watched it rise and people who watched it set. And everybody took it for granted…but I couldn't. I figured it would mess you up if you changed from one to the other. I thought it had something to do with energies that were opposites, like with magnets, ones that pulled, and ones that pushed. Then, when I moved to The Refuge and became a West facing person, and never saw the sun rise again, except for how it turned the sky pink way off into the distance, so that I could only infer that the sun had risen, but never knew for sure, well, that disorientation hurt me in a profound way, like I was turned inside out, like my latitude became my longitude, or like…."

"You're losing me Adam."

"It's not so easy to explain."

"I guess not. But what about people who lived on the prairies? All they had to do was turn their head one-way every morning, and then the other way every evening. Adam, if you got fucked up, it's got damn all to do with the sun."

"Well, what was it then?"

"You betrayed your community when the *Arrogant* went down along with Darwin and Perry and JJ and my dad. Jesus, it had nothing to do with the bloody sun."

"So that's what we're here to talk about?" Adam asked.

"No, it's not. We just slid into a patch of bad."

"Well maybe we can slide right back out."

"Suits me."

Maddie kicked off her boots. "There's a pillow in the wheelhouse. My ass is sore."

When Adam got up, he realized how drunk he was. In the wheelhouse, he saw her gallery of photos pinned to the ceiling, one of him and one of Perry, when they were both young and thought they owned the world. He didn't recognize the others. But there was a bunch of them. He grabbed the pillow and brought it to her. Maddie pulled it under her ass, and he pulled the blanket over her shoulder again.

"I've always held that men can't talk," she said, "and women just chatter. But, some of the time, if conditions are just right, a man and woman can really talk."

"Like somewhere between the third and fifth scotch?"

"We're on our fourth."

"Fifth."

"If we're on our fifth, then we're near the end of a good talk," she said.

"Hope not."

"I was enjoying our conversation until the *Arrogant* loomed up. We were talking almost like times when we were kids and teenagers…like we didn't realize everything was messed up yet."

"It takes a lifetime to see the mess."

Adam looked toward Desolation Sound. The moon ran a golden trail straight into Haystack Island and turned it into a gentle blaze.

"Let's talk about Haystack," he said.

She looked at the island. "What's the big deal about Haystack?"

"It makes me mad."

"It don't make me mad."

"The charts call it Station Island now, and they call Mink, Repulse Island, and they call Martin, Rebuff Island. They've rewritten all the names in Desolation Sound, but they didn't ask anyone, especially me."

"Why would they ask you?"

"They just sent their hydrographic surveyors around to catch up Captain Vancouver on any trifle. The *Discovery* only had a lead line to toss, but the government had all their modern sounding gear, and some pipsqueak bureaucrat in Ottawa used the opportunity to erase our history."

"Whose history?"

"Ours."

She thought for a bit.

"I got a new 3594 a few months ago and they still have the shoals at the north entrance to The Refuge."

"I wrote our Member of Parliament about that, and the name changes too."

"Just passing the time?"

"Look at Haystack, nothing looks more like a haystack...not even Monet did better and he painted tons of them."

"I don't know many artists."

"My faith in democracy will be restored if we get the original names back."

"If you want the originals, then you got to talk to the Klahoose."

After some thought, he said, "Right."

Now they were off the bay where Perry had found the murderer's stash of money, for which the charts were nameless, though Adam had his own name. One day, while he had clammed on the beach, a long-legged wolf galloped toward him and skidded to a stop thirty feet from where he dug. They studied each other, and then the wolf moved on sulkily. Thereafter, he called the bay, *Wolf Bay,* and would always do so, no matter the fictions of Ottawa.

"If we'd had lots of talks like that naming screw up,' she said, "then I could've been easily satisfied. I would've just coasted through life."

"Let me get under that blanket."

"Fill my glass first. I don't want to be nervous."

He filled both their glasses and said, "Another dead soldier." He threw the empty bottle onto the deck.

"I got more mixed in with the freight. Just rye though."

He got under the blanket with her. They held hands.

"You got soft hands now, not slivered and callused logger hands, and not cut-up smelly fishermen hands."

"I haven't done physical stuff for a long time."

"Like I said, I just wanted to talk…holding hands is a bonus."

He wanted to talk too, but only if he could direct the conversation. He convinced himself that the physical stuff would stay in the past. *Memories saprife with energy.* He was too drunk to remember his conversation with Duende.

"Wade says you're writing stories."

"I'm trying to figure something out."

"He said they were stories."

"That's how I'm trying to figure something out."

"I didn't know stories could do that."

"There's something wrong at The Refuge."

"What?"

"I don't know yet. The dogs know. They smell stuff."

"There's nothing more wrong at The Refuge than any where else."

"You should talk to Duende."

"You've had too much scotch."

"I think everybody knows something is wrong, but nobody knows they know."

"So, writing's the way you'll find out?"

"Maybe."

"When we were kids, you were the best writer in class, and that eulogy you wrote about the *Arrogant* crossing the bar pretty well said it all. I reread that piece once in awhile. Jim and Brad think it's a bloody gospel."

"I wrote it for honourable reasons, even though some people thought otherwise."

"A lot of those people are dead now. It's water under the bridge, Adam."

"None of you realized that Perry changed the blueprints. When Marlene got Halliday to calculate *Arrogant's* stability, he used an old blueprint. The surveyor knew the bait tanks had been fitted one ahead of the other, but he didn't realize they were bigger than drawn."

"I never knew that."

"No one did."

"You did."

"I rescinded the statements I had made to the newspapers about the ship not being seaworthy and encouraged those who went with me on the maiden cruise to do the same. We had seen her list, and hold her list, like she would never come to."

"The papers stepped all over themselves to apologize to my sister and the rest of the widows," said Maddie.

"If I had pressed the issue, Marlene wouldn't have gotten the insurance.

"Don't get so worked up."

"If I had pressed the issue, then I'd have destroyed the myth."

"Perry was more than a myth to me."

"He's a myth for his kids."

"You got that right."

She set her empty glass on the deck and laid her head on his shoulder. He gave her a sip of his scotch. She wiped her wet lips with the back of his hand.

"You crossed your own bar when you went to the papers."

"I made the mistake of thinking truth was everything."

"Old people take secrets to the grave. They know what truth can do."

"Where's the rye?" he asked.

She pointed, "In that box."

He found the rye and filled her glass and his glass, though his glass was half full of scotch.

"Tell me a secret before you end up in a grave," he said.

"Perry and I were lovers."

"That was no secret, not even from Marlene."

"Don't tell Brad and Jim about any of this."

"I won't."

Adam shielded his eyes, "Jesus, that moon is bright."

"Well, close your eyes."

They fell asleep. On and off. Shoulder to shoulder. Hip to hip. He could smell her hair – smoky.

Once, when she woke, Maddie said, "Hold me close you beast," so he held her close. He wanted to cry. He should have cried. They should have cried. Together.

They headed for Kinghorn, slipped by the two shoals that the hydrographic crews had found, sliced in close to the steep sides of Haystack, and made for Desolation Sound. Currents diverted the workboat from entering the Sound near Martin Island. *Forge* never once bumped or grazed solid things.

At daybreak, they bobbed off Hope Point, nearly back to their point of origin. They watched the sun clear the tallest peak of East Redonda Island.

"Nice to see the sunrise," Adam said.

"You're an East facer today."

"So are you."

He felt the warmth.

"I don't feel so well this morning," she said.

"Me neither."

"You know how Sylvia is a bit witchy?" Maddie said. "She told me the *Arrogant* went down in an explosion and the crew died instantly, so I guess I don't buy into the rollover idea."

"You believe her?"

"She has visions."

"So do I, but not that one."

"Once Conners told me that he and Perry found a mine that floated over from Japan, one of the spikey, porcupine kind, beached on the outside of Vancouver Island near Winter Harbour. They took turns shooting it from the bow of *Pride II* with Perry's Marlin. When it went off, Conners said it knocked down a swath of forest a half mile wide and threw boulders out into the ocean."

"That was me, not Conners. And at Langara, not Winter Harbour. We fired a .303, not a Marlin. And it didn't knock down a swath of trees a half-mile wide."

"It don't matter who shot what gun, or where it happened. It just explains what never got explained."

"Maybe the Earth is flat and they sailed over the edge?"

"Never thought of that."

"Sylvia and Conners gave you a pretty good story."

"If it had rolled over, they would have found something. If it had rolled over, there would have been bad weather, and there wasn't any. You know as well as I do that it was the biggest search ever on the whole coast of North America from Alaska all the way down to Mexico and out to Hawaii. Nothing bigger since."

"It's a big ocean."

"Something would have floated even if the boat went straight down. And they would have found it. With the war finished, they mobilized every damn plane and ship and walked every damn beach."

"I'd like to believe you."

"I've got to get Jake his gasket."

Adam untied his rowboat from the stern and pulled it along side.

"I feel like rowing home."

"We should do this another time. Talking's all I need."

He climbed into his rowboat and shoved off. He wet the oars.

"They didn't suffer, Adam."

"I guess it's best to think that way."

"It is."

"Next time I'll buy, and we'll see if talking's all you need."

SEA WITHOUT SHORES

Sitting at her table, where she always toiled, Sylvia persisted with The Book of Corrections, a revision of the Gospels of Mark and Luke in the New Testament. The proliferation of miracles, especially those that had to do with plenty — the miracle of the loaves and fishes (Mark 6.30-44) and the miracle in which Jesus instructs the disciples in their fishing practices (Luke 5.3-11) — had upset her in a dream during the night. In each of these ~~two~~ incomprehsible parables, she vaguely remembers wrestling with the issues of magnanimity and motive. Sylvia took the dream as a sign to concentrate her energies on Corrections 8:14-32, a passage that had brought her journal writing to a halt the previous day.

"As it so happens, the man ~~was~~ was on the shores of Gennesaret visiting his old-

Brad —
Notes · drawings

~ 16 ~

The Unread Word

"Whatever his antecedents he was something wholly other than their sum, nor was there system by which to divide him back into his origins for he would not go."

Blood Meridian, **Cormac McCarthy**

A: WHAT DID you do to your paw?
D: One of Sylvia's bastard cats.
A: We could disinfect that scratch with our finest malt.
D: I prefer to take it internally.
Adam poured a splash into Duende's saucer.
A: What did you learn?
D: She's a writer like you.
A: Indulgent ramblings?
D: Mostly.
Adam gave Duende a jerky.
D: She went on and on about Carver.
A: Who was she talking to?
D: Me.
A: She talks to you?
D: Just a one-way conversation.
A: That's a relief.

D: Maybe she's crazed by loneliness?

A: We all are.

D: A more interesting observation is that she's rewriting the gospels of Luke and Mark. She calls them the *Corrections*.

A: I should have done that long ago.

Scribbler Eleven:

SYLVIA SAT on the steps of her back porch and stared into the slop bucket she had retrieved from Peter's shellfish plant – a blend of oyster cuts, geoduck offal including the briskets, floor sweepings of squashed mussels, seaweed, clams, barnacles, and live, scavenger, shore crabs. In need of distraction, she listened to the crabs tap out a perplexing code against the bucket walls with their serrated pincers and needlepoint legs. She watched their slinky bug eyes scan their waste-world prison, each ocular oddity rotating independently from the other, and each spinning on its own inquisitiveness without the aid of iris or focal competency. The crone had read about the crustaceans in a National Geographic magazine and, realizing that these beings were survivors of the ancient Cretaceous period, she concluded, without further research, or the need for verification, that they had originally marched in from another galaxy with abilities beyond this civilization's comprehension.

She stepped from the porch and waded into a sea of malnourished cats. They yowled and scuffled. Likely Sylvia stepped on a tail. They head-butted her boots and sleazed their furry bodies against her skinny legs. The slithering slatterns, unashamed of their wants, some on hind legs begging like pretend dogs, gave off a cacophony of seductive purrs and mews. A choir of jezebels came running from the woodshed, from under the cabin, down from the trees, rained from the sky, cats not dogs, rivers of orange and black striped cats swirled into the chaos, while the lonely widow upheld the still point of plenitude.

Performing a quick mental count, Sylvia estimated that the

cougar had culled a good number of her pets – at least fifty. She walked further into the garden and stepped on another tail. The cat clawed her boot and bit into her toe. She kicked it away. Unafraid of dipping her hand into the bucket of glop, she sluiced out the bouillabaisse, an apportioning without measure, and the dispersal at thirty-two cardinal points of the compass rose. The felines thickened at these intervals – hackled hair, laidback ears, crouched panther postures, and conductor tail flicks. The earnest business of hissing, spitting, and crunching ensued. Sylvia threw the bucket lid into the tall dew-drenched grasses, and a clutch of cats dashed at the diversion. Sweet sea smells loitered in the morning air. The night had been cool and the *mélange del mar* had not yet ripened.

The felines satiated, she went back inside her cabin to continue her life's work.

SITTING AT her table, where she always toiled, Sylvia persisted with the *Book of Corrections*, a revision of the gospels of Mark and Luke in the New Testament. The proliferation of miracles, especially those that had to do with plenty – the miracle of the loaves and fishes (Mark 6.30-44) and the miracle in which Jesus instructs the disciples in their fishing practices (Luke 5. 3-11) – had upset her in a dream during the night. In each of these incomprehensible parables, she vaguely remembers wrestling with the issues of magnanimity and motive. Sylvia took the dream as a sign to concentrate her energies on *Corrections 8:14-32*, a passage that had brought her journal writing to an abrupt halt the previous day.

As it so happens, the man was on the shores of Gennesaret visiting his old synagogue friends, Simon and Andrew – they had all been precocious students at the temple since the ages of twelve, but recently, his friends had turned from the scriptures to practice the honourable and ancient profession of fishing and, he too, had left the ministry, before them even, to wander the hills labouring in that other ancient profession, shepherding – who begged their friend, the shepherd, to go with them again (the fourth morning in a row) to cast their nets,

Sylvia heard a scuffling on the porch – hissing, then a yipe. She opened the door, and Duende scrambled between her legs. He hid under her writing table. She kicked at five cats and then slammed the door.

"You are the dumbest of dogs!" she exclaimed.

Duende shivered under the table and licked his wounded paw.

"Bother me once and I'll throw you to the lions. Bother me twice… don't even think of it." She sat down at the table and began writing again.

For on each of these previous days, when it seemed there must not be one fish left in the sea, the landlubbing shepherd had said, "Why not try there,

As soon as she wrote, "*Why not try there,*" the widow thought of the newcomer, Carver. She hated that he had become an omen of good luck in her community. She jumped from her chair and paced through the room. "He walks among the people." The New Testament revisionist stopped. "They polish their fishing tackle and sew holes in their dip nets." She circled the room clockwise. "They sharpen their gaffs and blunt their fish clubs." Sylvia opened the back door, and shouted at the cats, "They no longer ask, did you get any? Oh no, guess what, now they ask how many did you get?"

This outburst seemed to clarify her thoughts. She slammed the door, ran back to her writing table, and continued the *Book of Corrections.*

And when they did try in the spot he pointed to, at first, only to humour their friend who hardly knew a fish from a lamb, yet on each of these tries their nets were filled to brimming, so much so, they had to call other fishers of the sea for help,

Sylvia put her pen down and recalled the conversation she had overheard yesterday, when collecting the bucket of slops at the seafarm. Peter's crew, from the Klahoose village in Squirrel Cove, had commented that Carver reminded them of *Tl'umnachm.* Sylvia began circling the room again but noticed Duende sleeping under the table. "*Tl'umnachm*," she shouted at the dog, "Do you know what *Tl'umnachm* means?"

He opened his eyes and looked at her.

"There was only room enough in the canoe for him," she explained.

She pressed both hands to her head and circled the room counterclockwise, but at a quickened pace. "In one of their stories, a young man is lazy, so his father shames him. The shamed one wanders off into the wilderness to train for a full year in seclusion. He gains a special guardian spirit power, and when he returns to his people, they give him the name, *Tl'umnachm*, because he now can catch as many fish as he wants, just like Carver, so many in fact, that there is only room in the boat for him and the fish." She sat down on her chair and quickly added another passage to *Corrections 8:14-32.*

And now on this morning, when he was anxious to return to his flock, to the peace and serenity of the hills (as he had caught up on all the good news he ever wanted to hear), there, at the shore, was another miserable fisher who carried a wrinkled, day-old, sun-struck, dull-eyed carp and he begged the shepherd to come onto his boat and show him where to cast his net, as he had caught but one fish in an entire week, and had a wife and nine children to feed, and on and on the wretched man persisted,

The widow rushed into the kitchen and poured herself a glass of water. She drank it quickly and wiped the perspiration from her brow. She refilled the glass and walked back to her writing table. Duende had woken and now sat in the middle of the room, licking his paw. On seeing him, she said, "You're thirsty, right?"

She walked into the kitchen and came out carrying a bowl of water. She splashed a few drops at her neck, flicked a spray of drops into Duende's face, and then put the water dish down beside his paw. As he lapped the water, she further explained to Duende the source of her unease with Carver.

"See if you can make sense of this. Everyone is busy canning salmon, smoking salmon, turning salmon into lox and jerky, pickling, freezing, drying, and eating salmon prepared from all known recipes, morning, noon and night, until they are sick of it. Fortunately, their dreams compensate with apparitions of greasy pork, beef, lamb, chicken and turtle stew. I have not even mentioned the lingcod, snappers, and rockies that are also loaded into every boat, or the giant halibut that disappeared from our waters decades earlier. Our community, shall we call it his flock, now believes that the threat to the survival of the salmon species on the west coast of British Columbia is a figment of their imagination."

She rushed back to the *Corrections.*

And when this unashamed fisher saw that the good luck shepherd might not be interested in the fishing expedition proposed, he thrust the decaying fish in the man's face saying, "You must help me," and that was the last straw;

"I've reached the last straw with that young buck," she confessed to the hound. "A pattern is developing that goes beyond annoyance. His biased sense of humour really bugs me more than anything else. Last Wednesday, while waiting for the mail plane, Jeremy told one of his slightly off-colour jokes. Everyone in the store thought the joke funny except for Carver. Jeremy told four more jokes, each becoming more lewd, and again everyone laughed, except for Carver. Then Jack Smith, who has no talent for buffoonery, but always tries to be the humourist anyway, related some incident about his identical daughters, Mary and Elizabeth. The so-called punch line went like this, 'The right hand always knows what the left hand does,' and for the first time in a lifetime, Jack had himself an appreciative audience of one, namely the newcomer, who laughed until he couldn't stand. He slapped Jack all over the back, asked for more rib-ticklers from the comedian, and Jack thought he had a friend for life. No one else in the store laughed except for James, whose good heart commanded him to indulge in a few polite chuckles. Now, here's the punch line, Duo; listen up, Carver's deception fetched an invite for dinner, and when he accepted the invitation, zany Jack said, 'I promise it won't be fish,' and they both dissolved into more convulsions. And when the booby, Carver, had recovered enough to speak again, he said, 'Lamb is my favourite.' They both broke down, each with tears streaming from their eyes, and Carver, with the enthusiasm of a well-trained seal, clapped his stupid flippers."

Sylvia noticed that Duende had finished his bowl of water. "Are you still thirsty?" she asked.

She refilled the bowl for the dog, splashed more water on her face and neck, and then said, "Quench the thirst the good Lord has given you," but it seemed he was no longer thirsty, as he had settled under the writing table again.

The sentence, *Lamb is my favourite*, re-entered her mind. Sylvia sat down at the table and persevered.

The shepherd lost control of his emotions, possibly for the first time in his short span of three and twenty years, and he batted the smelly fish from the fisher's hands, where upon it fell to the ground to begin it's own emotional transformation –

She put down her pen and looked under the table. "You're under foot." Duende moved back to the water dish, but didn't drink.

"There's a veneer of high-mindedness that bugs me almost as much as his biased sense of humour. The mail plane had been overdue for two hours even though weather conditions were perfect. As to be expected, Heinrik had become incensed that he had to spend half of every mail day waiting for the plane. His harangue was effective in that Jeremy, and even Laura, supported the content of a petition he had composed earlier for the whole community to sign, complaining directly to the Royal Canada Post about the inadequate service supplied by Coval Air. Heinrik showed around documentation covering the previous six months with dates of deliveries missed, and hours and minutes of deliveries late. However, before the matter could get out of hand, guess who intervened? Carver congratulated Heinrik on his thoroughness, supported the others on their sense of community responsibility and fair play, suggested that one word in the letter be changed, and then another phrase be slightly adjusted. Before long, Jeremy recommended that our newcomer take the letter home for reworking, and the rest of the people in the store concurred. Poor Heinrik had no choice but to surrender his missive. When the plane finally arrived that day, after everyone had given up waiting, except for Carver and me, he volunteered to James to take the outgoing down to the dock and fetch the incoming. I noticed that he spent quite sometime talking with the pilot, Blackie. Thereafter, or at least for a few weeks, deliveries were on schedule, the petition never got sent, and no one knew what the pilot and Carver discussed, except that he led Heinrik to believe that many of his points had been brought up in their discussion. James was happy to have the chronic incident put to bed for a little while, and Heinrik credited himself for The Refuge getting priority when it came to the mail. Carver's reward was another invite to dinner, this time from James. What do you think, Duo?"

It looked as though Duende might not be thinking, but sleeping.

"There's a pattern building, Duo. Wake up doggie! He hates animals, especially you. I think he drowned some of my cats. He throws rocks at seagulls. His eyes don't blink. And he walks into any social situation with confidence. How can a stranger do that? And here's the clincher. Whenever he doesn't want to answer a question, especially about himself, he deflects the probe with another question. Last Monday I asked if his last name was MacLeod or Carver, but before I knew it, I gave my own last name to his inquiry. I blabbed about my origins, my screwed up childhood, and then, without him having to ask, I described the events of my husband's death, including the discovery of the naked bitch passenger, who luckily drowned with him."

Sylvia wiped her nose on her sleeve and resumed writing. The dog had definitely gone to sleep.

first, the eyes clarified, and then the gills pulsated, the large armour plated scales glinted cuprous, bronze, dace bright flickers in the morning light, as if it had been pulled from the sea that very moment; and second, as the resurrected fish smacked its lively tail on the smooth pebbled foreshore, it seemed almost to break in two, and did in fact break in two, however, the two were not separate pieces but two entire new fishes each as big as the original, alive and fresh and flipping: the poor shepherd, surprised as well as enraged, kicked at the wrigglers and they in turn became another two, and he kicked and kicked like a spinning wild dervish from the desert and the fishes multiplied to the glee of the lucky fisherman and the jealously of Simon and Andrew who were now standing waist deep in quivering carp.

The cougar made his decision to prepare for the great changeover. He sat upright and adjusted his front paws so that they achieved perfect symmetry. His knees ~~long~~ touched and all joints stiffened; he arched his long back, and two scapular shoulder blades stuck out like dejected wings. The tail swept across the floor. The black tip flicked twice, quickly, and then came to rest. When his front paws slipped on some blood, he repositioned himself exactly as before. He lay flat, the fur on his back and lay flat his ears. His panting lessened. He groomed his whiskers, one side, then the other, with a long pink tongue. The intensity of the illumination in his eyes grew brighter, and the obedience to fate grew ~~the~~ stronger. He demonstrated no excess of sentiment.

Heinrik loaded a cartridge into the rifle. He heard a gust of wind startle the leaves on the maple tree outside. The cougar heard too, turned his head to the window, and flicked his tail in acknowledgement. A leaf fluttered to the ground. And then

～ 17 ～

This Dream Called Life

"When the stars threw down their spears,
And water'd heaven with their tears,
Did He smile His work to see?
Did He who made the lamb make thee?"

The Tiger, **William Blake**

Scribbler Twelve:

FOR WHATEVER reason the cougar had changed his dietary preferences at summer's end. Perhaps something about Mac-Leod and Sylvia's cats had become distasteful. The impression left was one of an extended halftime before play could resume.

On a Tuesday, The Refuge women gathered on the dock – a feel of fall in the air. Vivian Smith asked if anyone had seen her big Persian, Winifred. No one had seen Winifred.

"The pattern takes a new twist," commented Sylvia.

"The disappearance of Vivian's cat," Nicole said, "doesn't make for a new pattern."

"No, just the beginning of one."

A week later, Jeremy described his loss. "I came out on the porch with Moocho. All I saw was a flash. I whirled – it must have been instinct that made me act so fast. I swung and smashed the cougar's head, but not in time to save my dog. Look at my knuckles."

The Blacks lost Felix-the-Cat from underfoot, while they walked the trail back to the lagoon. "Fuck, it happened quick!" said Liam Black.

"We survived the bear attack, but I don't think we can take much more of this. Sarah won't stop crying," said his wife, Kathleen.

The following day, she confessed to Laura that they were thinking of leaving The Refuge. "Besides, there's lots of salal picking on Cortes, and Sarah needs a real school anyway."

EACH AND every fall, Mutti Pauline and Papa Fredrik arrive with their annual allocation of slivovitz and venison sausage for their son, Heinrik. The parents are octogenarians from a worn, bygone country, who speak halting English though they have lived in Canada for over fifty years.

The venison was supplied by Heinrik from the previous winter's kill, and the filled pig casings prepared by the parents in the ancient, timeless way: an unwritten recipe from the backwaters of Galicia with barely a hint of fatty pork, mountains of ground pepper, and forty other secret herbal ingredients (to be revealed on the death bed between painful rasps of despair and dismay). The sausage recipe, having rebuffed all dubious assaults at innovation, continued to require at least a year for the cylinders to dry, wrinkle, and shrivel, until they exuded the white surface mould foretelling the arrival of a state of perfection, each sausage strung from the basement joist beams in their Vancouver home.

The mash for the slivovitz came from the small orchard of Damson plums on Lulu Island, where the parents hid their 120-litre still – "the happy machine" of copper tubes, broken gauges and stainless vessels – in an abandoned tool shed. In return for these staples, Heinrik took his mother and father fishing each day during their fall visit. They spent their remaining time smoking and canning salmon. The hoarding effort anticipated the dark side of the year, which, in Heinrik's case, led to endless melancholy, as he was most sensitive to winter's withholding of light. In the long, quiet evenings, the reunited family, along with Pemah, watched the single-channel, black and white, newly acquired, twelve-inch/twelve-volt television.

ON A lovely autumnal afternoon, alder and maple leaves sashayed onto the forest floor without a sound. Conifers tolerated the squirrels stealing their cones, and running *ring round the rosy* up and down their trunks. The sea became lazy and forgiving. The family landed three salmon – a late, large Northern Coho and two white Toba Springs – the scales ablaze with intricacies of colour in the slanting, fall sunlight. When Heinrik pulled up to his dock, everyone felt magnificent, as if life had been upgraded beyond the mind's grasp.

The unfortunate combination of slivovitz and old age created balance problems for the parents, as they climbed out of the boat, negotiated the steep ramp, and walked the rickety, narrow boardwalk toward their son's gingerbread cabin. More than once, Heinrik rescued one of his parents from tippling into a patch of salal. Keeping track of his mother, father, and his dog, Pemah, while carrying the three salmon, caused him not to be as alert as he should have been. As they approached his house, Pemah, also relaxed following the bountiful afternoon, seemed unaware, though her job was to be aware, of the potential for danger.

Mutti Pauline and Papa Fredrik struggled through the doorway into the entry hall and on into the main room. The couple sat at either end of a shabby couch; each wore blotchy faces induced by alcohol. Pemah shuffled in next, and with assistance from the parents, jumped up onto the couch. Heinrik entered carrying the three salmon in a plastic tub.

Something – of size – brushed his leg. He staggered and dropped the tub. The three salmon slithered across the floor toward the couch. Slime, blood, and scales garnished the unpainted plywood floor, and a cougar stepped onto the trail of fish.

Heinrik yelled, "Papa! Mein Pemah!"

Papa Fredrik tucked Pemah inside his jacket.

"Heinrik! You drop fish!" said Mutti Pauline.

The voices alarmed the cat. A meter from the couch, the cougar stopped and switched his long tail back and forth, back and forth, like a baffled conductor who couldn't remember the next phrase in his symphony. He appeared gaunt; his tawny fur coat seemed two sizes too large. Rib shadows jutted from his sides, and his tongue lolled. A back paw sunk into a puddle of fish blood. He extended a cluster of claws in order to maintain traction. His front paw nudged the Coho. He raised that paw, sniffed, and shook it, as would someone who abhorred sticky fingers. The cat looked around the room, at the walls and ceiling – a big den perhaps – but when he looked back into the hallway and saw the door, he did not recognize his exit.

Papa Fredrik raised his walking stick in a threatening gesture.

Heinrik retreated to the hallway, slammed the door, slammed the safety bolt, and declared, "Ah ha, we got him!"

The cougar panicked.

He raced round the room spending much of his sojourn running on the walls rather than the floor. He bounced off the ceiling and off the door leading to Heinrik's bedroom. He bounced off the double glazed windows, and thank The Lord they did not shatter. Disorganized bric-a-brac toppled from windowsills and shelves: a raven skull, lustreless ill-formed pearls, a container of eagle feathers, a piece of petrified wood, the shell of a moonsnail, cartridges casings, and other treasures, each of which possessed significance only to their owner.

The inside walls of Heinrik's house had never been sheathed, though pink bats of fiberglass insulation, friction-fit between the studs. Each time the cat's claws connected with the insulation, dusty tufts fell onto the floor. The cougar bit at the tufts, but found them disgusting, much worse that a hairball.

Heinrik opened the door of his gun case on the wall.

As the cougar ran around the room, he repeatedly jumped over the legs of the parents sitting on the couch. When the cat jumped over Mutti Pauline's legs, she waved him off saying,

"Shush kitty," and when the cat jumped over Papa Fredrik's legs, he grabbed for the long lush tail, keeping Pemah tucked safely inside his jacket. The tableau of the three salmon on the floor and the mess of blood, scales, and slime distracted Mutti Pauline. The urge to clean and disinfect, as soon as possible, became steadfast, shutting out all other concerns.

The cougar, exhausted from whirling around the room, collapsed in front of the television in the farthest corner, as if he had finally listened to Mutti Pauline. Heinrik's fingers fumbled in the search to match a correct cartridge to a correct rifle. The parents watched the cat and the cat watched Heinrik.

The cougar made his decision to prepare for the great changeover. He sat upright and adjusted his front paws so that they achieved perfect symmetry. His knees touched and all joints stiffened; he arched his long back, and two scapular shoulder blades stuck out like dejected wings. The tail swept across the floor. The black tip flicked twice, quickly, and then came to rest. When his front paws slipped on salmon slime, he repositioned himself exactly as before. He lay flat the fur on his back and lay flat his ears. His panting lessened. He groomed his whiskers with a long pink tongue, one side then the other. The intensity of the illumination in his eyes grew brighter, and the obedience to fate grew stronger. He demonstrated no excess of sentiment.

Heinrik loaded a cartridge into the rifle. He heard a gust of wind startle the leaves on the maple tree outside. The cougar heard too, turned his head to the window, and flicked his tail in acknowledgement. A leaf fluttered to the ground. And then another. The cat shifted the weight on his haunches. He made another minute adjustment to align his paws. With a hissing inhale, he mirrored the stillness in stone. For all time, the room swirled, as the cougar woke from his dream called life.

because they aren't interesting, but I
make-believe my own stories out of
the pictures that are in the books.
A few pictures are in colour and
they look like paintings. Tara does it
to if she gets bored with his reading.
We put ourselves anywhere into the world
and become one of the persons in the
pictures I was the queen of England.
Tara once pretended to be Annie Oakley
and she shot a bad guy. And once
Sarah came along and she got to be
Bessie Barriscale, who was a movie star
from the days when the movies
didn't have talking. Tara says it's
amazing what you can say if you
don't talk."

"My Name is Sarah.

The wood stove is always full
blast, and he smells like smoke.
Mac'Leod has cookies pretty well
always, but they are storeboughten
and not as good as my Mama's.
He has hairs coming out his
nose and ears, but not much on his
head. My Mama says my dad is going
the same way even though he's
young. There are seventeen long
coils of sticky, red fly paper

~ 18 ~

Girl Talk

"The duende does not come at all unless he sees that death is possible."

In Search of Duende, **Federico Garcia Lorca**

Scribbler Thirteen:

MY NAME is Elizabeth.

MacLeod was a logger and a fisherman, and then he fixed boats. He has a million grey cats. He feeds them canned milk, but the milk's for his ulcers. When he gets too many cats, he kills them . and starts over. If you see a grey cat, it's MacLeod's. The orange and black stripes are Sylvia's. MacLeod told us girls not to name a cat if you're going to kill it. That's so you don't get attached. Our cat is a Persian called Winifred, but she doesn't visit much lately so I guess the cougar got her. Me and my look-a-like sister, Mary, cry silently at night.

Sylvia has more cats than MacLeod. She names everyone. They call her the cat lady, but some people call her the witch lady. She says all living things should have names. And she says that everything is living. Sometimes I wonder about rocks. Whenever there's a new batch of orange kittens, which is quite often, we kids go over to help think up names. But we lose track. Sarah has a name book so it helps. Once Sylvia tried to kill a whole litter all at once, but they scratched out of the plastic bag filled with rocks when she hucked it into the ocean on a dark, rainy night. They swam to the surface and then mewed at her door until she let them in. The mom cat didn't get upset. She just counted to make sure they were all there and then licked them dry. We saw MacLeod's cats washed up with the beach drift in the U one morning when we waited for school to start. He shot them with his over-and-under 4-10 and 2-22. We never heard him shooting, so he must have used the 2-22. It makes a little crack-crack sound. Wade said if he had used the 4-10, there wouldn't be much left. And we would have heard it go off. MacLeod has other ways of doing it like poison and drowning in a barrel. My Mama said, "What a shame," when she saw them floating in the U. I didn't know the dead could float, and got quite upset because his cats died without getting names.

MY NAME is Mary.

MacLeod rows around The Refuge in his rowboat. He calls it the *Ark*. That's funny because the *Ark's* a big boat in the Bible. He stands up when he rows and faces the bow, so he knows where he's going. Most of the old-timers do it that way. Once he lost the *Ark* because he forgot to tie it up. Jeremy found it floating in the channel some days ago, and not hurt at all, with the oars still in the locks and his bailing can floating in the bottom. It could have smashed on the rocks, but didn't. Jeremy copperpaints the *Ark* every year to stop the toredo bugs from chewing through the hull. Then, they have a drink of rye while it dries. MacLeod does the paddles, while Jeremy does the hull. That gives him something to do. Other times MacLeod rides us kids around the bay in his new speed boat, but we have to sit quietly, be still, and always wear a life jacket. He never goes fast with us in the boat. His dog is Son of Mooch, who rides everywhere with his master. Moocho was the father, but the cougar got him. Duo gets to tag along on the rides, but he's nobody's dog. MacLeod says he wants to go to all the old places before he dies. We watch him drive out of The Refuge quite often in his new boat, and when he gets near Hope Point, he guns it. He doesn't have a name for his speedboat, but we call it the *Redonda Rocket.* Redonda is the island we live on. Actually, it's really called West Redonda because there's an East Redonda. He says Desolation Sound is the best place to explore if the tourists aren't there and if you want to see beauty. Which is now. MacLeod rows to the store with Son every Monday, Wednesday, and Friday for mail and supplies, but it takes him all day because he hangs out talking on the docks to anybody who will listen. He wishes the mail came the other days of the week too. He only gets advertising like all the bachelors. He ties up right beside the gas dock even if he doesn't need any, and then walks all the way around the U so it takes more time. He has a cane for walking and uses it to point like a long crooked finger. When we play on the dock, even if it's not a quiet game, like our dancing, which is, except for our feet scuffing on the dock planks, we can hear him coming, even if we don't see him, because he taps the cane really loud. He made the cane from a bush that's twisted and knobby, and it works fine. He whacks Wade's basketball if it gets close. We help carry his stuff back to the *Ark,* because Tara's dad makes us. My twin sister and me don't mind, because we like him.

MY NAME is Charlotte.

Whenever I see MacLeod he has something hidden in his big fists like nickels or butterflies, and once a cricket, which chirped in his hand and then sprang away. And before that a white salamander from under a rock by the generator shed, and then a big piece of fool's gold, which I found out later wasn't worth anything. Sometimes I wrestle with his fist to get what's inside. He lets me win every time. He plays the game for all the kids, but me the most, because I'm the youngest, which is a privilege says my mum. His home is in his machine shop. The shop is falling down and has broken roofs and lots of rooms, which aren't used. It's a good place to play. All of us look for treasure there after school, or build forts on the weekends if we can't think of anything else to do. The bachelors claw through his stuff because they need parts for broken machines. He has everything, or parts that are just as good. Carver lives there too, but in a little cabin right beside the shop. Maybe Carver will work for us on the seafarm soon, if dad gets really busy. MacLeod never even knew he had a nephew. We dance all the time. Me and Tara, and Sarah, and Mary and Elizabeth, who are look-a-likes, spin on the dock whenever we can. Tara and me do it for MacLeod sometimes, if we are visiting him, or I do it in front of my Mama, but most of the time I do it by myself when no one is looking. Tara's brother won't do it. The dance is not like the adult's dance, but a dance we made up ourselves, and the spinning makes our minds go elsewhere. On the other days, that are not mail days, he sits at his table and drinks half and half, which is instant coffee and warm canned milk for his ulcers, but that's in the mornings. He switches to straight tea in the afternoons, which Mama says is bad for his stomach too. He reads his old Books of Knowledge all day long, and they smell like mould and give you a stomachache if you breathe into them. I have allergies. The pages are weak, so they crumble into bits if you don't turn them gently. And the pages fall out because they aren't attached anymore. It is my job to put them back into the right book and the right place in the book, which is not easy. He helps me figure it out. There are twenty-four books, but he lost six. He says there's a big piece of the world that got lost. He gets the books mixed up and spread on the floor, and I have to put them back on the shelf in the correct rearrangement. Tara's dad gives him the magazines that don't sell in the store. They have the covers torn off and will get burned anyway, so it isn't really a gift. He likes the crimes and detectives. I visit him because we live close, and if Tara is over she comes too, but I have to wear a lifejacket in case I fall off the boardwalk built along the shore edge, especially if it's winter. Mama watches me until I get there. Once, I fell, but it was low tide, so I didn't get a soaker, but the rocks cut my leg. We have a game where he pretends he's reading me stories from the Knowledge Books, but it's only stuff about the world. I never listen to the stories because they aren't interesting, but I make-believe my own stories out of the pictures that are in the books. A few pictures are in colour and they look like paintings. Tara does it too, if she gets bored with his reading. We put ourselves anywhere into the world and become one of the persons in the pictures. I was the Queen of England. Tara once pretended to be Annie Oakley and she shot a bad guy. And once Sarah came along and she got to be Bessie Barriscale, who was a movie star from the days when the movies didn't have talking. Tara says it's amazing what you can say, if you don't talk.

MY NAME is Sarah.

The wood stove is always full blast, and he smells like smoke. MacLeod has cookies pretty well always, but they are store-boughten and not as good as my Mama's. He has hairs coming out his nose and ears, but not much on his head. My Mama says my dad is going the same way even though he's young. There are seventeen, long coils of sticky, red flypaper hanging from his ceiling, of which I counted every one, except I kept getting mixed up until I got it straight. He never takes them down and they are loaded with dead flies. The flying carpenter ants come out on the first hot day of every summer. Its funny how you just know, you just stop and feel how hot it is, and then you see clouds of them flying out of old logs and the cracks in things. They lose their wings right away. Our ducks go crazy eating them up. Moths get on his flypaper too. And once a big dragonfly. And once we watched a regular fly fight so hard it stuck its wings by mistake and then torn them off trying to escape. We once pretended the flies were little angels and felt sorry for them. MacLeod's house is full of cobwebs, so I'm careful about not getting near them, because I have an allergy to spiders too, and probably lots of other things that I don't know about yet. We have scribblers and we do drawings, and he has to guess what the drawings are of. He's never right. Another game is where I print down letters in the alphabet, or letters I make up out of my own mind, and then he tries to say the invented words. Because Tara is good at reading, she pronounces them too, and sometimes it sounds like a brand new language. For our game, we buy scribblers at the store from the money Carver gives us. At first I make the words short, then long, then lots and lots of words in really long sentences. I have two scribblers almost full. My printing is big. Tara does writing better than anybody. MacLeod said that he is pretending that I am writing the books he is missing in the Knowledge Books, so I should hurry up. 'fjas oieht fhag mnvuwelmx coiw dfhf' is a sentence for you to figure out. I know myself, because I wrote it. We wrote funny words like that in the HELP bottles. Only Tara got mail back. It makes me and Tara feel important makebelieving we are writing the lost volumes of the world's books. Elizabeth and Mary said you can tell secrets with the made-up words and no one would ever know. So we're all doing it. He got lost in the forest behind his marine ways. Everybody looked for him, but I was the one who found him, because I looked the hardest. He wasn't really lost, because everybody's been there, right where the trail cuts off to Sylvia's. He sat on a stump and had a cut on his head from falling against a rock. His cane fell down on a ledge and I had to scramble down and get it. Son sat beside him and looked worried. I dabbed the cut with his hankie. He was stunned. I took his hand and walked him back to his cabin, and he came without a fuss. His hand was so big I could only hold onto two fingers. It was like I was an adult for him. I got lots of congratulations for what I did. Now the adults check on him most of the time. Carver said he'd check on him too, because he lives right there, but he doesn't.

MY NAME is Tara.

Auntie Alice thinks MacLeod is the shiest man in the world, but none of us girls think so. She loves him. I was going to tell him on a day when I was really brave, just so he knew the truth. I guess it's too bad when two people can't get together, even if they want to more than anything. He gave her a gift once but nothing came of it. It was a bleeding heart. It's my job forever to make sure the weeds and ivy don't get it. When it was really wild the night of the bearbecue, and we ate the bear, and they kept playing Rasputin over and over, my brother, Wade, made me look after Auntie Alice in her wheelchair so he could dance with the rest of them. You had to keep her close to the fire, but not too close, because everybody wanted to be as close as they could get. I didn't mind being in charge. I drove her beside MacLeod on purpose and left her beside him, but still on guard. He danced his walking stick instead of himself, and she looked like she was conducting a big band with her hands keeping the beat. Even in the dark, they must have realized they were beside each other, and it might have been just like the night they danced in the schoolhouse many years ago. They were just like a man and wife that didn't need to look at each other, because they knew the other would always be there. We were playing on the dock, when we saw the *Tom Forge* come in towing MacLeod's new speedboat. We thought he had broken down. MacLeod sat in the stern seat, and when Maddie got close to the dock, it looked like he was asleep. Brad tied up the *Forge* for his aunt and Jim pulled in the towline and tied up MacLeod. We couldn't wake him up. He just kept sleeping. Duende kept sniffing him like sniffing gave him a better idea about what had happened. Dogs are like that. MacLeod had about a twenty-pound salmon lying at his feet, and the lure was still in the mouth. When they carried him out, some of the men slipped on the fish slime. It was a Spring salmon. They are way more slippery than Coho. Nobody thought to turn the motor off until Wade thought of it. My dad said he'd turn the walk-in freezer on, to keep him cold, until the Coast Guard came to pick him up. Aunt Maddie said she saw his boat off *The Point Before The Point Before McGuffey's* going around in circles. She had a hard time getting along side. I was amazed that he looked so calm. When they carried him up to the freezer, they put MacLeod on a sheet of plywood, because some of them didn't want to touch him. The sheet of plywood didn't fit on the ramp up to the store, so they put it on top of the railings and slid it, but he slid too, the other way, and he nearly fell off into the ocean. He bumped his head. They decided just to carry him after that. My dad said he had huge ankles and then he cried. Jeremy cried all the way to the freezer too. My mom told Auntie Alice. When my dad slammed the freezer door, I finally knew what had happened. Like the door would never open again. I really cried, and for a long time after into the nights, and I still do, because I never got to tell MacLeod that Auntie Alice loved him. When the Coast Guard came to take him away, I never watched. No one wanted to eat the salmon, so dad froze it, and it's still there. We've got Son now. Sometimes Son and Angel and Duende sleep together in a big pile behind the wood heater.

centuries more, the kernel of his inventive ~~has~~ brilliance lay shrouded in the aesthetic blindness of his viewers.

Along with the drawings, Leonardo had left behind balsa mock-ups locked inside glass showcases — primitive toys, not sculptures. They resembled weighty bumblebees, confused hummingbirds, elephants with rotating wings for ears, and jumping haystacks unwilling to concede to the will of Galileo. Who could make out what they were? Some ~~said~~ "Ridiculous gizmos." Others, "Aerodynamic impossibilities." Those who said "Aerodynamic," at least knew the direction of his thought. It took five hundred years for the image of the helicopter to ~~flutter~~ incarnate in alloy flesh. Five hundred years for a machine to defy gravity, expose Icarus as a failure, and bring humankind one step closer to freedom.

Nicole had recently taken to sketching. After James and the children went to bed, she sketched. When they went out of the house, she sketched. She hid her work in drawers, under couch cushions, the laundry

~ 19 ~

God Wants It To Stop

"She kept watching him even when she was through cutting the onions and she kept on watching until it was no longer possible for her to see him, because then he was no longer an annoyance in her life but an imaginary dot on the horizon of the sea."

A Very Old Man with Enormous Wings:
A Tale for Children, Gabriel Garcia Marquez

D: HOW'S IT going?

A: Better.

D: Sad about MacLeod.

A: There's more sadness on the way.

D: How do you stop the sadness?

A: I asked Maddie a similar question a week ago.

D: Did she know how?

A: Not a clue.

D: So, you've seen her again.

A: A few times. We drink and talk. She loves to talk.

D: Have you told her about the project?

A: A little bit. I told her I couldn't concentrate on her perfections until the scribblers were done.

D: Did she accept that?

A: She said her perfections were fading fast.

D: That's motivation to get the thing done.

A: She'd like to read the scribblers sometime.

D: She'll be surprised when she sees what goes on in your head.

A: No more surprised than me.

D: The full pile is much higher than the empty pile.

A: Three more scribblers and we're done.

D: You don't think you'll need to buy more?

A: I already bought more. We're getting into the wrap up phase.

D: Let me know when I can help.

Adam threw Duende a piece of jerky, not because the dog had earned it, but simply because he felt generous.

Scribbler Fourteen:

FOR DECADES after his death, Leonardo da Vinci's sketches and mock-up models languished in his studio. The disrespectful voyeurs pried apart bonded pages on his drafting board and revealed the sketches. Other discoveries had been squirreled away in drawers or carelessly intermingled with heaps of rubbish. Three very fine specimens were found as over-drawings on supply lists for the studio, as if he had no notion that his every mark would some day become eternal.

An abnormality emerged. These histories of his thought process, each new tingle of invention, became superbly distorted by the bleaching effect of light. One must also give credit to ubiquitous moisture stains, growth of mould, nibbles by mice, burrows and tunnels of insects, and even the fecal remains of spiders. These accidents (what else could they be, blemishes, disfigurements?) with their persistence seemed coordinated by the incessant strokes of Time. And these accretions from year to year amplified Leonardo's contributions to Time, as if his creative moments had been merely starting points, insignificant ideas, which Time could blend into delicacies for future generations. Gossipers, and those with blasphemous intentions, dared to say that his unique genius became secondary to that immortal force. In a sense, the detractors were correct, though their unkindness erupted from jealousy. Now we are left to think that in his death, the "apprentice" entered into collaboration with the greater Master.

When learned, Post-Renaissance men discovered these drawings, they deliberated over the work, and as the images appeared beyond anything they could envision – in fact, gross departures from the newly emerging goal in art of reflecting what *is* – they decided that his intention had been aesthetic, definitely not functional, and perhaps from an earlier period in the creator's life. Some even thought these cast-offs nothing more than doodles from a precocious youth, not the imaginings of a prodigy. They asked questions such as: "Is this art?" or, "Is there purpose here?" It seemed that the brain of its day was unprepared to accelerate into the future.

Time passed. The smell of mould continued to infect the storage lockers. A sad beauty radiated from the ongoing decay. His precise lines altogether lost the fine edges from the scratchings of his sharp quill. His dyslexic notations in the margins deteriorated such that his unique backward ciphers could no longer be read, even though mirrors had become common devices for understanding his images and thought processes. For generations and centuries more, the kernel of his inventive brilliance lay shrouded in the aesthetic blindness of his viewers.

Along with the drawings, Leonardo had left behind balsa mockups locked inside glass showcases – primitive toys, not sculptures. They resembled weighty bumblebees, confused hummingbirds, elephants with rotating wings for ears, and jumping haystacks unwilling to concede to the will of Galileo. Who could make out what they were? Some said, "Ridiculous gizmos." Others, "Aerodynamic impossibilities." Those who said "Aerodynamic," at least knew the direction of his thought. It took five hundred years for the image of the helicopter to incarnate in alloy flesh. Five hundred years for a machine to defy gravity, expose Icarus as a failure, and bring humankind one-step closer to freedom.

NICOLE HAD recently taken to sketching. After James and the children went to bed, she sketched. When they went out of the house, she sketched. She hid her work in drawers, under couch cushions, the laundry hamper, and in the sauerkraut crock jar, which had not seen duty in years. Whatever caught her eye, she trapped in her sketchbook: a cup, a saucer, the grain in a log, a chimney pipe, the kettle, the designs on the tiles over the sink, pictures in magazines, Angel behind the heater, Son behind the heater, and Duende behind the heater – ordinary things.

She made no drawings of the outside world. She would never look out the window and gather in the landscape. Or draw a boat at the gas dock, as Wade had often done. Never would she go outside and draw a flower, a tree, a rock, an insect, or a bird. And never, from memory, would she dash off a wildflower, as she had done for James many years ago, when she lived in Victoria and yearned to be at The Refuge.

Recently Nicole had explained her unhappiness to Alice, who perhaps understood her point of view. Her complaints to the old woman had been confused in the beginning, but lately had crystallized into an indestructible thought: "Dreams must be respected."

To the statement, Alice had said, "You modern women have an advantage over us...possibilities can become probabilities. You can think thoughts we could not."

Nicole was rendering an empty beer bottle when she heard a tap-tap-tapping on the door. She hid her drawing under the tablecloth and then opened the door.

"Good to see you, Seb," she said.

Sebastian wore a necklace of eagle beaks, which clacked when he entered. He carried De Gaulle in his arms. Nicole, anticipating the need, made a resting place on the bear rug. The dog wore burlap coveralls pincushioned with downy eagle feathers.

Duende, Son, and Angel got up from behind the heater and sniffed De Gaulle.

Nicole asked, "Is De Gaulle ill?" She bent over and petted the dog's head but jumped at the touch.

"He's dead!"

Sebastian wagged a scolding talon. He covered De Gaulle with Angel's blanket.

Nicole ran to the living room window and stared outside. After a time, she turned off CBC's *This Country in the Morning*. She sat down at the dining table and motioned for Sebastian to join her. He left his dog, but adjusted the blanket first. The other dogs wandered back to their warm spot behind the heater.

Seb and Nicole sat quietly and looked through the window onto The Refuge. A watery blue day. James fuelled the *Tom Forge* and talked with Maddie. A large flock of goldeneyes fed on a band of blue mussels bysalled to the shoreline of tiny Oyster Isle. With their moss covering, the bluffs on Centre Island had achieved a quiet harmony now that the fall fogs had saturated the air. A boat worked the longlines at the seafarm. Lewis Channel was empty of boat traffic. A silent sky-writer from Comox Air Base left a feathery trail high above Cortes Island.

Nicole asked, "Seb, why won't you talk?" Again, he wagged a scolding talon.

"We all worry about you."

He removed a crumpled piece of paper from his jacket pocket – a letter written when his head had ached more than ever before, so much so that he had passed out during the writing. He flattened the sheet on the table with the backs of his knuckles and pushed it toward Nicole. He turned back to gaze out the window.

After some minutes, Nicole looked up. "Your writing is too hard to make out, Seb, but I do understand some of it."

Her hands shook. She pointed at words and phrases in the letter. "This word is 'black' and that one is 'children'…is that right, Seb?"

He continued to look out the window.

"God wants it to stop…does it say that here?" She had her finger on the line and turned the letter to face him.

"Help me Seb, until I get the hang of it."

His body began to shake.

Nicole reached over to comfort him, and when she touched his arm, Sebastian whirled, as if seared by a firebrand. He knocked his chair over and screeched. The piercing sound made the frightened woman cover her ears.

He held his arm to his side, much like a bird with an injured wing, and hurried over to gather up De Gaulle.

"Seb. I'll rewrite the letter for you...is that what you want...did you want to send it somewhere?"

For a moment, he seemed to gain composure, but then wagged another scolding talon. In his arms now, De Gaulle moulted feathers onto the bear rug. Nicole, down on her knees, plucked at the feathers, saying, "Please help me, Seb, please let me help."

Sebastian ran out the door and down the trail to the docks. Nicole followed in the wake of the barking dogs. She heard screeching in the forest.

At the top of the ramp, she watched Sebastian race out of The Refuge in the *Oystercatcher*. In one hand, Nicole clutched the crumpled letter, and in the other, she held a fist full of feathers. He disappeared around Hope Point heading towards Desolation Sound. Maddie and James watched from the fuel dock.

WITH ENHANCED vision, from the stern of his boat, Sebastian saw a spiralling path appointed years before. On the most northerly islet of Prideaux Haven, where Desolation Sound and Homfray Channel intersect, an abandoned nest was wedged into the crotch of a double-leader fir snag. The nest of sticks, twigs, bark, deer bones, weeds, grasses, mosses, a length of blue polypropylene rope, and a green plastic garbage bag, measured twenty feet in depth and weighed two tons. He watched a transformed essence on the perimeter of the high structure stretch its immense wings.

His outboards screamed, and the boat raced toward the islet. The painful step-by-step meander to this pinhead of sticks was now nearly complete. He felt the old habits fall away. A fundamental disgorging of the old world had been accomplished even without the blessing of fully functional wings. The air rushed across his face, and his headache vanished with the wind.

The eagle man had done all that he could do. The decision to go to Nicole – an instinctual command from an archaic impulse to deliver words, knowing full well they would be received without reverence and without understanding – confirmed that her worry was counterfeit. Her scorching touch on his wing proved her devotion to a violent reality.

As he steered at the helm, his disembodied thoughts tumbled over the sea ahead of the skiff, barely detectable beyond the bow. The speed of the boat could hardly keep pace. The skiff rushed forward, and his thoughts tumbled, bouncing from ring to ring on the surface of the sea – crystalline structures, multi-faceted, refracting embryos of truth. Gradually, they smoothed their edges against the abrasive sea. Happily, the friction of the sea spurred them to life, and much as would playful dolphins, they scrubbed in his bow wake. They smiled, squawked, and piloted him to the steep mountains rising from the sea, the cold crags, and his waiting friends.

When he arrived at the islet, Sebastian didn't bother to anchor his skiff. He lifted out De Gaulle and two wooden crates. The boat drifted from shore, and his disembodied thoughts frolicked nearby. He planned to swoop and grasp the more interesting ones later. One crate contained ropes, climbing spurs, and a climbing belt. He emptied the contents and put De Gaulle into the crate. He tucked a blanket around the dog, attached lines to the other crate, and fastened the ends to his belt loops. He clamped the spurs to his caulk boots and flipped the climbing belt around the trunk. The snag leaned slightly, and he used the advantage – no need to run up the tree, as he might have done during his earlier, high-rigging days.

On the nest platform, he threw his climbing gear over the side. He pulled up De Gaulle and then the larger crate. Eagle shadows, venturing from the blue sky, passed over the nest. Across Desolation Sound to the southwest, a boat skirted the far shore of West Redonda Island and droned like a fastidious bee. Another boat entered the Sound between Sarah Point and Kinghorn Island and sniffed that shoreline.

Sebastian stripped naked and threw his clothes over the side.

From the large box, he removed a sleeveless shirt sewn from the same burlap material that De Gaulle still wore. Eagle feathers were woven into the shirt. He had devised a tedious method of interlocking the contour feathers to the fabric by drilling pinholes through the quills, and then tying them with a lightweight fish leader. The mottled grey feathers were intricately lapped, meticulously preened, progressively sized, shoulder to waist: the effect – tidy, dense, and birdlike. Eagle-like. The feather sweater over his naked torso immediately bulked out and warmed his gaunt figure. He had manufactured a similar construction of burlap trousers, feathers fastened in front and back. Before putting them on, Sebastian secured bracelets of eagle talons to each of his ankles.

He experimented – gripping nesting materials with his toes – and discovered a new dexterity. He put on swimmer's goggles, the glass painted yellow around the perimeter. When he looked at the sun, his new nictitating membrane shunned the glare.

The birdman checked the progress of the two boats entering the Sound and realized his sight had improved. He saw a salmon nose the surface a mile away; the water riffled and then lay quiet again. He pulled on a balaclava helmet sheathed with smaller white feathers. Each addition of birdware charged him with energy, so much so that he screeched his delight. He fastened a marsupial pouch to his chest before attaching the immense wings.

Seb had made the skeletal wing structure from long, glued, balsa strips, tightly stretched over with a burlap skin. He had feathered three sections: shoulder to elbow, elbow to wrist, and sockets for gloved fingers. Leather straps interlocked the wings to his arms and hands.

Before securing the primary fingertips, he tucked De Gaulle into the pouch and tied the drawstring. He secured the primaries, and stretched and tested the wings. Overhead, eagles glided high on warm thermals, specks in the blue air. As Sebastian's congregation ascended higher, the gyres they traced widened. At ease in the wind, the birds floated by the cold crags of the steep mountains jutting from the sea. He looked away from the birds and the mountains to the ocean below. Reflections of inverted snowy pinnacles on the calm, glazed waters of Homfray Channel appeared magnified. He considered stepping from the nest – a short hop over the sea – onto the highest peak. But that was the old way.

His aluminum skiff turned in a tide eddy. Though at least a mile away, he saw with his enhanced binocular vision, James, Nicole, and Heinrik in MacLeod's runabout, and Peter in the *Gigas,* with Carver and the Klahoose crew. Maddie, Brad and Jim, and Duende followed in the *Tom Forge.* The three boats converged on Prideaux Haven.

The time had approached when his emergent voice would add to the celestial chorus. Like any fledgling, he felt nervous at this penultimate moment. He called to those who knew him, "Kleek-kik-ik-ik-ik-ik," and once again looked to his brothers and sisters cruising in the sky – how he ached to sail in the immaculate air. He extended his wings beyond the edge of the nest. The substantial updrafts rustled and swirled. His plumage protested until the meshed barbs in each feather vane loosened, and the air gushed through. Fortunately, he didn't lose balance and fall, which had happened to many fledglings when they first considered flight. Sebastian wiggled his stiff primaries, finger-like. Satisfied, he tucked the wings against his sides.

Metamorphosis now complete, he had arrived at the final reality. The novitiate watched the mentor eagles rush toward him from the high cold crags, slicing through the dense air. The birdman launched. On his way to where the universe sings, he thrummed his wings, while De Gaulle slept. As he had imagined, the textured air felt generous, and the stir of flight exotic. Briefly, even though everything had been planned perfectly, he worried. In the free-fall of excitement, as the cold air hastened by, he worried over temporal matters – the young ones – but very quickly put those thoughts aside. Instead, he worried about how long it would take to perfect the sky-dance, the talon grapple, and the very difficult snicker call.

Each morning Heinrik backpacked Pemah up the mountain path behind his house along with materials for his antenna farm. Perched on the highest rock bluff, overlooking the Sea without Shores, with Vancouver Island far to the west, and the alien cities of Vancouver and Seattle far to the south, he had constructed his aluminum forest. Without planning and without foresight, Heinrik had become the founder, designer, general contractor, and manager of the Refuge Cove Pirate Cablevision Network, although his subscriber base was small.

In the beginning, the plan had been no more ambitious than to buy a 12-volt ~~battery television~~ television and live with the limitations of rabbit ears.

~ 20 ~

TV

"Lord, how simple it is to be happy!"

Maidenhair, **Mikhail Shiskin**

ADAM AND Duende watched The Refuge from the kitchen nook. The white raven landed in the arbutus tree next to Adam's cabin.

D: There's the raven again.

A: He creeps me out.

D: Likewise.

A: He never hung out at MacLeod's, and look what happened.

D: The same for Sebastian.

A: I thought he'd be too busy to visit us.

D: Busy at what?

A: Ferrying souls to other realms.

D: MacLeod's soul would be easy, but Sebastian's could be a challenge.

A: Elaborate.

D: Sebastian was unable to bring truth to the surface.

A: But he tried.

D: A valiant effort. He'll get stuck between realms.

Adam sipped on his scotch and Duende lapped at his dish. They watched the raven fly off, heading for Sylvia's.

D: I see the Blacks have moved to Cortes.

A: I saw their boat loaded down, but didn't know where they were headed.

D: They wanted to send Sarah to a bigger school.

A: And I see that the Smith's have taken the twins to Campbell River.

D: How did you learn that?

A: Wade dropped over with mail and supplies. He said they could get better jobs in the River.

D: And I see that Jeremy has given up on log salvaging. Now he works on a dry-land-sort, south of Powell River.

A: Remember how I predicted a micro-Apocalypse?

D: Some time ago.

A: The rest of us will hunker down and make the best of it.

D: I don't see much of the dancing girls these days.

A: Wade's basketball is quiet too.

D: Soon it'll just be you and me.

A: What a destiny.

D: A man and his dog living in the wilderness.

A: Not such a bad thought.

D: We'd have to depend on each other, more than ever.

A: I'd definitely count on your olfactory prowess.

D: And I'd count on your persistence.

A: In the wilderness, the team concept is a guarantee for success.

D: My saucer's empty.

Scribbler Fifteen:

EACH MORNING Heinrik backpacked Pemah up the mountain path behind his house along with materials for his antenna farm. Perched on the highest rock bluff, overlooking the *Sea without Shores,* with Vancouver Island far to the west, and the alien cities of Vancouver and Seattle far to the south, he had constructed his aluminum forest. Without planning and without foresight, Heinrik had become the founder, designer, general contractor, and manager of The Refuge Cove Pirate Cablevision

Network. His subscriber base was small.

In the beginning, the plan had been no more ambitious that to buy a 12-volt television and live with the limitations of rabbit ears. But the signal had been poor, disrupted by static, haze, and intermittent silence. His parents had complained about the reception all through their holiday.

He worked secretly and burned the midnight oil. He renewed his passion for knowledge, but the hells of desolation would not lessen. MacLeod was gone. Sebastian was gone.

Instead of purchasing a multi-purpose antenna on his next trip to Campbell River, Heinrik searched in his scientific journals for subjects pertaining to the theory, construction, installation, and operation of receiving antennae. His resources didn't fetch much, but the quest for knowledge sharpened his brain. He began with a meditation on the electromagnetic spectrum, then ruminated on the singularity rule, celestial causative agency, gravitational redshifts, centrifugal confusion, and event horizons; he deliberated for some time on recession velocities, the phenomenon of energized black light, the stretching and bending of time, not to mention space, and the origins of one way time, and two and three way spaces via wormhole travel to multi-parallel universes. He enjoyed learning more about chaos theory. Finally, he descended to the doldrums and ground swells of wave theory, and soon his thoughts meandered to the task at hand – identification of the exact locations of transmitters on the west coast, boosters and receivers that could be invented or adapted, calculations of line loss, equations, interference variables, inverters, converters, diagrams, more equations, interfaces, regulators, and any number of considerations, which brought him eventually to the point at which he could pirate television signals arriving from throughout the Province of British Columbia and the State of Washington.

In mid October, the remaining cloistered folks began to wonder about Heinrik, the recluse. He worked feverishly, up and down the mountain path with Pemah on his back, carrying bits of aluminum rod, guywires, reflector shields, and tools. He whistled an atonal tune while he worked. His goal was to bring in perfect reception for Channels 2, 4, 5, 6, 8, 9, 11, 12 and 13.

He couldn't keep the triumph from the community though. He had to invite people over to witness the creation. Partly he felt proud and simultaneously anxious to reconnect with his friends. For the most part, the people were amazed at the clarity, the number of channels, and the excellent sound. When Alice heard the rumour of improved reception, she immediately summoned Heinrik to her parlour for an estimate of costs. The visits to Alice and the visits from his peers prompted the second phase of the project during which 12-volt televisions were purchased. Heinrik and enthusiastic volunteers strung miles and miles of antenna wire throughout the forest, over the bluffs and along the shorelines of The Refuge, so that every resident would at last be connected to the outer world. Sylvia remained the single holdout. Now everyone's loss could be mitigated by the flow of a ghostly blue light during the dark nights of winter.

Heinrik tried to exercise dominion over the programming. He had particular disdain for game shows and soap operas. He coaxed, and at times, demanded that people not watch these programs. He encouraged observance of the Canadian content rule. After a time though, lacking the requisite censorship authority, the project, like his lending library, like creation itself, had become compromised in the implementation phase.

He took solace, however, in the fact that people were distracted from the harshness of life. Everyone appreciated the diversion. Almost everyone.

(Corrections 3 – 12-28)

> Dusk fell and another cold night under the open sky of God's majesty unfolded; the gibbous moon ascending obediently, just as the creator had intended, and the shepherd's flock settled indiscriminately, but instinctively close, one to the other, on the brow of a lush hill: there and

then, from the contented ruminantia emerged a cloud of warm air hovering above the flock, distillations of breath, dissolving and inhaling, and like any god, as if the man had wrapped himself in the silken cocoon of a comforting dream, the way each of these his evenings began, the purpose of his journey always the same, to choose like any potent Arabian prince might, one, probably two, subjects from his harem of thousands for an evening of carnal pleasure – the ladies giggled and jiggled, bleated and baaed, some moaned, hoping to draw attention to their beatitudes and pulchritudes veiled beneath uncarded white, brown and black fleeces, whereas others pouted their thick black lips and fluttered butterfly eyelashes, "pick me, pick me," they all said without words, but baleful glances as he walked slowly and silently, cherishing the choice, prolonging the choice, anticipating a covetous congress the creator had not foreseen, and mimicking the distant creator too, with his own tumescent promise of teasing and flickering warmth – he checked often with the crook of his staff for purposes of practicality whether ewe or ram, doe or buck, and treasured a nostalgic moment when he fondled with his gentle fingers one maiden's remote regions and she whimpered, "Sir, I haven't been chosen for two whole months," but he went by her on this eve to await the precious state of estrus of a future night, knowing also that continued abstinence would inflate her desire further, possibly allow her to recapture the friskiness of first blossoming youth for one last time, which he now mourned was quickly passing her by.

Alice put her binoculars down. A white raven had landed on the roof of the stove. Lately he had been there every day watching her. Tara and Charlotte, who were visiting, also watched the bird.

"That bird keeps hanging around," Charlotte said.

"I've read," said Alice, "That they're the most intelligent of all birds."

"Do they know The future, Auntie Alice?" Charlotte asked.

"They're not That intelligent."

"How come it's white?" asked Tara

"They're special" explained Alice.

"I brought poppy seed cake," said Tara.

"It's called Bundt cake. Please Thank your mother."

The girls took The cake, already cut into wedges, into The kitchen

~ 20 ~

I Cannot Stay for the Light of Day

"Though my senses were sinking into oblivion, they seemed to expand ere they reached it. They perceived the magic song of nightingales, and the odour of invisible hay, and stars piercing the fading sky."

The Other Side of the Hedge, **E. M. Forester**

A: IT'S MORE difficult now.

D: Your voice trembles. Your eyes are dark and troubled…an unpleasant sight to say the least.

A: As I mentioned previously, we have a sad project before us.

D: You knew that from the start.

A: Knowing is different than experiencing.

D: Your comment reminds me of the time when you claimed the present was simply a way station. You thought that *waiting*, in and of itself, didn't carry an emotional punch.

A: Pride prevented me from seeing the energy in the *now*.

D: We learn at our own pace.

A: I have a request, Duende. Would you do the next little bit? Duende paused for a considerable time before he answered.

D: I'll tell you what. You continue to lay bare the story, but I'll stand by. Take our project as far as you can.

A: Make sure you're close at all times.

D: I am, though you don't always realize it.

Adam poured himself another scotch and then picked up Parker. Barely able to keep the pen on the page and barely able to keep the ink between the lines, he wrote, "NICOLE MET the mail…"

Duende slept on the cushion beside him.

Scribbler Sixteen:

NICOLE MET the mail plane. Blackie gave her a grey, plastic canister containing MacLeod's ashes. The pilot hugged Nicole and said, "MacLeod was a gentle man."

Nicole delivered a single, incoming mailbag to James in the store, and then went home carrying the ashes. She placed the urn on the kitchen table and made herself a pot of tea. Angel and Duende slept on the bear rug.

As the water heated, she thought, It looks like a cookie jar.

She opened the screw-top lid and pulled out the liner bag filled with MacLeod's remains. It's not dust, it's grit, she thought. She opened the bag and extracted a fragment, which looked like a shard of bleached coral. Nicole broke a piece. "This is too hard to support life," she said to the dogs.

NICOLE KNOCKED on Alice's door and let herself in. Alice slept in her chair. Nicole hit the kill switch on the generator. The absence of vibration woke her friend.

"I brought the ashes," said Nicole.

Alice put her teeth in. "Thank you dear. Put him on the TV."

"Is that a good place?"

"I will see him when I watch my favourite programs," said Alice.

"Would you like to have a ceremony? Should we cast his ashes to the sea?"

"Not right now dear."

"Would you like me to warm your coffee?"

"Not right now dear. My programs are on."

Nicole pushed the remote switch for the generator, and it started up.

That night she dreamed that MacLeod's ashes fell off the television due to the generator vibration.

ALICE PUT her binoculars down. A white raven had landed on the roof of the store. Lately, he had been there every day watching her. Tara and Charlotte, who were visiting, also watched the bird.

"That bird keeps hanging around," Charlotte said.

"I've read," said Alice, "that they're the most intelligent of all birds."

"Do they know the future, Auntie Alice?" Charlotte asked.

"They're not that intelligent."

"How come it's white?" asked Tara.

"They're special," explained Alice.

"I brought poppy seed cake," said Tara.

"Its called Bundt cake. Please thank your mother."

The girls took the cake, already cut into wedges, into the kitchen, and brought back three pieces wrapped in paper towels. Alice motioned for her piece to be placed on the side table.

With the sound off, they watched a pride of lions on the savannahs of East Africa. Four cubs frolicked in the foreground. Mt. Kilimanjaro loomed behind, snow-capped.

"Imagine, snow on the equator," Alice said.

"We have TV too," Charlotte replied.

Alice said, "Everybody does now."

"I've seen Heinrik's antenna farm," said Charlotte.

"It must be wonderful." Alice looked in the direction of Heinrik's home.

"Sylvia doesn't have TV," Tara said.

"She's entitled to her idiosyncrasies."

"Ours isn't colour," said Charlotte.

"None of us have colour," commented Alice.

Now the cubs suckled their mother. The girls ate their cake. The male lion gnawed on the haunch of a gazelle. Beads of perspiration formed along Alice's brow and upper lip. She wore her caftan – a glossy, green, synthetic print that didn't show sweat marks. She had decided not to dress today. Her slippers looked as though they might be two sizes too small.

"My Mom says Macleod could fall off the TV," Tara said.

Alice turned to the urn. "I think he's fine where he is."

"When they do Sebastian and DeGaulle," Charlotte asked, "will they go in the same jar?"

"I believe so. Nicole will suggest that to the memorial people."

A ballet began, an adaptation of West Side Story. Alice clicked off the blab-off and said, "This is a vast improvement over what we had before. Heinrik needs to be congratulated."

A modern dancer, Maria, still in belief of her innocence, streaked across the screen. Lesser dancers followed.

"Remember when I told you to always improve yourselves. These are the shows you should be watching."

The girls nodded their heads.

A gust of wind slashed at the hummingbird feeder outside Alice's bay window, and the empty container clattered against the windowpane.

"We should refill the feeder," said Alice.

"The hummingbirds won't come back 'til spring," said Tara.

"I forgot."

Now the whole ballet troupe danced. Maria rushed between the arms of her suitors. The forces, that moved her from one side of the stage to the other, seemed to be pulled on invisible strings.

"This program will make us feel better," Alice said.

Charlotte jumped from the couch, and quickly executed a few pirouettes. She sat down and giggled onto Tara's shoulder, because she had been so funny. Then Alice imitated Maria by flapping her own arms – slow and unoiled hinges, executing a jerky performance. She tried to back splay her fingers and palms, but the arthritis wouldn't allow it. She hoped that her red nail polish suggested the vibrancy called for in the scene.

Once again, taking Alice's mood as a signal, Charlotte jumped off the couch, threw off her jacket, and twirled in the middle of the parlour.

Alice forgot the imperfections in her life: fungus growing

on her shower walls, the incessant smell of creosote, the stink of ashtrays, and the vibrations from her generator. She forgot her battles for fairness in every negotiation, and her years of solitude, even when Reg was alive. She forgot the long line of friends, who had gone before, and her – *what if he had not been so shy* – daydreams.

Forgetfulness felt delightful. She saw her own hand waving at Tara, to get up off the couch and join the dance.

The two girls spun in her parlour, and Alice saw herself dancing with them. She had kept herself alive for this precious moment. Her shoes were red. The girls' shoes were red. Charlotte and Tara raced to her like tornadoes, and Alice became the tornado. The floor quaked under her chair, and the room flung apart. Her chair never stopped spinning.

When Nicole came in later, the girls sat huddled on the couch, watching a new program, Conversational French. Alice had slouched in her chair.

"Charlotte thinks she's asleep," said Tara.

(Corrections: 4. 2-9)

> And she was left alone; and a being wrestled with her until dawn; And when the being saw that he couldn't defeat Alice, he struck her on the hip socket, and Alice's hip wrenched out of joint and she breathed the first before the last fire. And she still would not let go. And he said unto her, "Let me go: a new dawn comes for the only fear I know is light." And she said, "I will not let you go until you bless me with the name of another." And he said, "I cannot stay for the light of day." She was quiet with her steely grip and he could not leave. And as the sun breached the horizon, he relented and said, "What is your name?" And she said, "Alice." And he said, "Your name will no longer be Alice, Queen-of-

the-Meadow, thine dried leaves shall no longer be sedative, nor thine number five, nor colour green, nor stone agate, nor element silver, nor sign Gemini, but forever and a day shall ye be, *She Who Has Struggled with a God,* because you have struggled with a god and you have won. Thus thy new name I honour." And she let go.

Nicole discovered two enormous cedar
carvings under the pile of cedar
shakes — a head and a hand. The
head — 6 ft tall, similar to an
Easter Island stone image, huge brow,
large nose and ears, & a sad but knowing
face with ~~eyes~~ long, hair-like strips
of cedar bark, the braids & twisted,
crinkled and dangling   — gave
her an inspirational idea. Nicole
saw in her mind's eye, the head
as a sentinel guarding the entrance
to the Refuge. She wrote: "Install
head carving on centre Island
visible to all ~~boat~~ traffic." she knew
just the spot. James helped her
~~drag~~ the head to the foright shed
and ~~asked~~ ~~asked~~ asked —

~ 21 ~

In The Dim Coming Times

*"Because, if we are honest with ourselves, we must admit
that, with a little care, a touch more foresight and some
proper circumspection, we could have prevented the
tragedy, couldn't we? Consider that this defenseless
creature, she who we might rightly regard now as God's
little outcast, this little lamb, was liable to all kinds of
danger, prey to any tramp or passer-by – to anything
and everything my friends, being out all night, soaked
through to the bone in that heavy rain, out in the wild
wind, easy prey to all the elements… and, through our
blind thoughtlessness, our unforgivable wicked thoughtlessness, she was left wandering round like a stray dog,
here in our vicinity, practically in our midst, driven here
and there by all kinds of forces while never straying too
far from us."*

Satantango, Laszlo Krasznahorkai

A STEADY rain fell on The Refuge, and low clouds shrouded the
hills. Adam flipped the calendar to November and re-pasted the
Forge on a Remembrance Day scene – RCMP, cenotaph, pop-
pies. In the November 11 square, he wrote, *row on row.*

He sipped from his tumbler, and Duende lapped the remaining

drops on his dish. The final scribbler lay open before them; Adam had been unable to write a single word during the last two weeks.

D: I see you've almost filled the final scribbler.

A: Not with words.

D: I counted fourteen pages of doodles. A new record for you.

A: Between inebriations, I realize that I might stray from the truth. That's why Parker has become so obstinate.

Duende's earlier recommendation, that Adam give permission to Parker to take charge of the project, had worked for a time; in fact, he was willing to credit his pen with the GIRL TALK scribbler. On giving himself up to the whims of his fountain pen, it seemed that the liquid voices had flowed easily. Adam had watched his pen perform without a hand to hold it, and watched his same hand pour multiple glasses of malt even while Parker beckoned the voices. But today, and for the previous fourteen days, his pen behaved like a bloodless vessel, though he had filled it with Indiga's juices, though he had threatened to return it to the Parker Pen Company for imagined defects.

D: You've been digging into your library.

A: Old favourites, mostly introspective titles.

D: More like distractions.

A: On the contrary, I'm developing a new paradigm: the universe is sentient.

D: You mean the rocks see you.

A: Exactly. And the sea hears you.

D: And the sky touches you.

A: And the flowers smell you.

D: Animacy strives within the stillness.

A: Correct.

D: Nature bears witness.

A: Correct again.

D: Humankind and Nature speed to reconciliation.

A: And atonement completes.

D: Dogs know these things. We don't need to read Nature's footnotes.

Adam extracted a book from the pile on his table, *Letters on*

Cezanne by Rainer Maria Rilke, and entered a quotation into his journal: *This testing by the real exceeded his capacities, that he failed, even though in his mind he was so convinced of the need for this testing that he instinctively sought it out until it embraced him and clung to him and never left him again.*

D: You're at the end of your tether.

A: Yes, although Maddie gives me hope.

D: In what sense?

A: We talk about watching the sunrise together.

D: Does that mean you will move with her to Seaford?

A: We could live a past that was once scripted, then discarded.

D: A big commitment.

A: Tentatively, we plan to watch the sunrise above Desolation Sound on Winter Solstice. The view from her little house is spectacular.

D: A new direction might be easier now that your fantasies aren't so full of expectation.

A: Both of us could accept the consequences of time.

D: Your fantasy sounds wonderful, but what of the project?

A: Paralysis has set in.

D: Then you need to invoke the gods.

A: I don't care a wit for the gods. I'm asking you to keep your promise.

D: Are you saying if we don't heed the signs, we'll have a *happily ever-after* ending?

A: If it is left to me.

This request the dog accepted with some trepidation, as time had manufactured a change, whether they wished it or not. Adam recharged his tumbler and the dog's dish. Together, they grew solemn, realizing the project was ending, and also realizing that their friendship must move beyond the terminal phase. Adam saw how he could map out a new life, but only after they had finished the last scribbler. He now understood why atonement depended on a creative act.

As for Duende, he would miss his interesting friend, but the dog also knew that new alliances waited; he heard their howls reverberating throughout the universe, saw their inept dancing on echoless stages, and smelled their frustration corrupting the air.

D: How should we proceed?

A: Since wielding Parker is not your forte, I suggest that you dictate and I scribble.

D: You must promise that your role will be strictly as scribe.

A: I promise.

D: You must write every word exactly as I speak them.

A: I promise.

D: If I pick up the threads and weave the tapestry to conclusion, my overriding thought will be to find an ending that lasts forever.

A: My only request is that you strive for simplicity.

D: I'll try.

A: Feel free to ask for as much jerky and malt as you require.

D: Thank you.

Scribbler Seventeen:

IF A PHANTOM observer were to make a closer inspection of The Refuge, with an ear poking through an outside wall, it would hear in every home the noise of talk shows and game shows during the mornings. In early afternoons, if its long nose were extended, the apparition would smell the greases and burnt flesh of cooking programs, and later, as the dying light flickered all around, upon looking through the walls with X-ray eyes, it might see lethargic bodies and vacant stares that could not turn their eyes from cartoons and soap operas. Nightly, if the supposed essence were an especially diligent type, it would return to the same homes, with the same extended organs of surveillance, and listen to the drone of news broadcasts, the shouts and applause at football games, and much later, as the evenings tediously wore to a conclusion, the melee of car chases, loud explosions, machine gun chatter, and sirens in search of the wounded. Our spectre would be struck by the oddity that the distant world had become the source of all inside light and sound.

Whereas outside, this phantom would affirm the putter of generators, the rumbling of bearings and rings, the rattle of exhaust pipes, loose nuts and bolts, which, by day, had interfered with the backdrop chirps of small songbirds, and by night, the intermittent hoots of owls. The essence would testify to the smells ' of spent hydrocarbons. It would attest to antenna wires strung in confusion and profusion from the trees, over the bluffs, and along the shoreline. Our witness would be offended, but what could it do? (*Adam, even though he had promised not to interfere, now offers a sort of answer to the above question, and simply suggests that "the essence could still take comfort in the burnished brilliancy of the stars, the rise of the new moon, and the slow accumulation of fog ethers along the shores of Centre Island." My good friend additionally insists that "the witness might notice the one person immune to the noble, neon gas tainting the natural light." An excellent suggestion!*)

IN EARLY November, Nicole walked down to the airplane dock carrying an out-going mailbag. Blackie landed the Beaver off Hope Point and taxied into the harbour. When the seaplane came alongside, she fended off the pontoon and snapped the quick tie.

"Looks like one bag, both ways," said the pilot.

"Hardly worth the stop," replied Nicole.

Blackie opened the cargo door, grabbed the single incoming bag, and then took the outgoing bag from Nicole. "I've got something else," he said.

"Another cookie jar?"

"Two more."

The pilot gave Nicole a grey canister and said, "This is Sebastian."

"De Gaulle's in there too. I told the memorial people to put them together."

Trying to strike a positive note to the morning, Blackie said, "Finally, the dog and man were able to fly."

"Briefly," she replied.

He reached into the cargo-hold again and brought out another canister. "Here's Alice."

Nicole put the first canister on the dock and clung to the second one. Ever so sweetly, Blackie gave her a hug and said, "I knew her for many years, a wonderful old bird."

"We'll be having a memorial ceremony. I hope you'll come."

"For Alice?"

"MacLeod and Sebastian too. And the dog. I'll let you know the date."

"Make it a mail day."

"Okay," said Nicole.

Nicole walked back to the store. She had self-imposed the responsibility of arranging a farewell to the cast of fallen angels, because, as she had concluded, no one else possessed the energy, or foresight, to even consider the solemn task.

She gave James the mailbag and locked the ashes of Sebastian and De Gaulle in the store's safe, commingled as instructed.

"What did you put in there?" asked James.

"Seb and the dog."

"Together?"

"Of course. Can you turn that TV off?"

"I wanted to hear the noon news." He turned the store's television off.

Nicole picked up an empty carton and lined it with a sheet of newspaper. She unscrewed Alice's canister lid and carefully emptied the contents into the box. A small dust cloud hovered above her hands.

Startled, James asked, "What are you doing?"

"I gave instructions to the memorial people to leave her rings on."

"You told me they were willed to a niece."

"I didn't want them to cut her finger off."

"They would've cut the rings, not her finger."

"I didn't want to send cut up rings."

Nicole began pawing through the ashes. She found the engage-ment and wedding rings melted and fused, the small diamonds captured inside the precious metal. She ladled the ashes back into the canister and dropped in the symbols of betrothal.

"Christ, Nicole, what will you tell the niece?"

"I already wrote her a letter."

"And?"

"I said the crematorium screwed up."

"You think she'll buy that?"

"James, she's rich and could care less."

Nicole screwed the lid back on and left the store with the container, slamming the door behind her. A row of cigarettes fell off the shelf behind the cash register. Without considering another alternative, she had decided that the ocean would be the final resting place for everyone. She expected no objections, could care less if there were any, and intended no consultations with her somnambulistic neighbours. She entertained no thought that a minister might conduct a memorial service, and would have objected if such a suggestion were made. Nicole entered Alice's house and placed Alice alongside MacLeod on top of the unplugged TV. Together at last, she thought.

That night, while her family watched the Saskatchewan Rough Riders play the Hamilton Tiger Cats on a field of snow, Nicole decided to shelve her sorrow. The distraught woman had too much to do. She climbed the stairs to the loft, put on her pajamas, and quickly fell asleep.

When James yelled out, "unbelievable catch," she woke, and was able to grab a remnant of her dream: *Ceremonies must have fire.* She switched her flashlight on, and wrote in a memo pad on the night table, "fire bigger than bearbecue's." She now kept the notebook within easy reach, as her mind had recently been releasing thoughts in avalanches. She turned off her light and tried to sleep. She turned on her light again and wrote, "Mementos."

Rowing over to the marine ways next morning, Nicole saw Carver carrying a battery down to MacLeod's rowboat. As she tied up at the wharf, he shoved off, saying, "Need juice for the TV, ketch you later."

As he paddled off, she shouted, "I'll need tons of fish for the wake."

"Just tell me when," replied Carver.

On entering MacLeod's home, Nicole smelled musk, mildew, and mould. The sink overflowed with unwashed plates and utensils. She found piles of coverless crime and mystery magazines. Nicole hoped to discover a keepsake, a telling letter hidden in a shoe, an old photo of MacLeod running a steam donkey, or a handcrafted object brought on by lethargy. She had imagined finding a sculpture constructed from rusted gears and pistons, or a delicately carved spoon from arbutus wood. She boxed up his Books of Knowledge and took his walking stick. At least, she had a few mementos. She wrote another note, "Get congregation to recall their best memories."

Nicole thumbed to the back of the memo pad and crossed "Cats" off her worry list. MacLeods's remaining grey cats had scattered throughout The Refuge, since Carver had refused to feed them. Now, most of the felines lived on the outskirts of Sylvia's cabin and seemed to have signed a non-aggression pact with her orange and black stripes.

On leaving the marine ways, in the corner of a covered porch, she noticed a bulky table lamp with a square, ceramic base, crudely constructed, and without a lampshade. The plug and cord were wrapped around a cheap, brass, light receptacle, which leaned to the side, as if it were either broken, or had never been installed. No light bulb. Nicole wondered why MacLeod would have an electric lamp, since he had no generator.

She examined nature scenes on the four walls of the lamp base, textured with thick daubs of clay, and applied by inexperienced hands. The crafts-person had used a primitive tool, perhaps a sharp stick to render the swirls into the images of bushes, trees, and rocks. The lamp had never been kiln fired, but left to bake in the sun. The colours looked drab: beige, dark brown, dull green, and black for the ocean, most probably from MacLeod's old paint tins.

She suspected that he had made this object and now realized his attempt to capture the scene of The Refuge: seashore, ocean, trees, hills, sky, and a bird flying beside a dark cloud, perhaps an eagle. As she turned the lamp, she recognized his little house and clutch of sheds near the marine ways, and on the opposite side-wall, Alice's house. Smoke spirals swirled from both chimneys, found each other in the open sky, and intermingled. Involuntarily, a tear rolled down her cheek. She included the treasure with the books and walking stick, and while rowing home, decided to keep the lamp.

LIFE NUMBER two – not an easy assignment.

A few days later, Nicole rowed Wade and Tara over to Charlotte's home for lessons. Laura had shut down the little school since the small subsidy from the Campbell River School District had been discontinued now that Sarah, and the twins, Mary and Elizabeth, lived elsewhere.

Feeling guilty, Nicole said to Laura, "We can take turns doing lessons when I'm not so busy."

"No big deal, I know that the wake is time consuming," answered Laura.

"Thanks."

"We've been watching Sesame Street each morning."

"I haven't watched it yet, but I hear that it's educational."

"Charlotte loves Kermit."

Nicole rowed across the bay to Sebastian's floathouse on the seafarm. Between longlines, she passed Peter hauling out oysters for the morning's shucking.

"I'm going to check Sebastian's place," she said.

"I'd love to get it out of here," replied Peter.

"If you drag it over to the dock, I'll dung it out."

"That's a big job, Nicole."

"It needs to be done."

"The tide's high this evening. As soon as I get these oysters up, I'll prep to tow it over."

Rowing home, Nicole realized that the farewell presented her with an opportunity for a truly creative act – the first since coming to The Refuge. The wake planner concluded that once the sea had taken its due, she would drop the curtain on the vestiges of her community, and go with or without James, but with Wade and Tara to the city. Death and failure had pushed her to this decision, a decision not yet discussed with her husband.

Next morning, when she looked down on The Refuge from her kitchen window, she saw Sebastian's floathouse tied alongside the dock in front of the freight shed. What a sorry sight, she thought.

"Take the kids to Laura this morning," Nicole told James, "I'm too busy."

Nicole walked down the trail to the store, and then down the ramp to the seaplane dock, where Brad and Jim had tied their little houseboat. She knocked on the door and yelled, "I need help from you guys."

Jim answered, "We good at helpin."

"I need both of you."

Bradley came to the door. "To do what?"

"We have to deal with Seb's stuff."

"We'll have tea first."

While she waited for the Jenzen brothers, Nicole entered Seb's house for the first time. The rumours were true – trails, more like steep, narrow canyons of junk. And the smell of dead things. Nicole decided to deal with the heavy non-burnables first. When the brothers showed up, she said, "Let's pile everything along the tie-up rails. I'm sure everybody will need some of his things," and as an after thought, she said, "and make a separate pile for yourselves."

"We just want pa's stuff," commented Jim.

"You'll be surprised, Jim. Seb has lot's of treasures."

From Seb's life, they lined the edge of the dock with: electric motors, electric windings, electric tubes, pistons, rings, drive shafts, gears, sprockets, radiophone parts, stove parts, tins of nuts and bolts and screws, coils of wire, outboard parts, outboards, rock chisels, bent propellers, glass insulators, glass canning jars, cracked plates, bearings, tins of grease, four copper hot water tanks – all leakers; copper piping and bushings, a valve collection, a froe blade, two maple wood mallets, oyster knives, grinding wheels, seized blocks and pulleys; broken jacks, axe heads, hammer heads, rusted tools, fishing gear, boom chains with broken links, a kerosene fridge, 12 volt batteries with fused cells and low liquid levels; and freezer plates, acetylene tanks, propane tanks, plate steel of various dimension, balls of string, four boxes of rubber boots and rubber gloves, bolts of burlap, three sinks, a toilet, and three stoves – none of the above in working condition. Whenever she came across an item that Jim or Brad might want, she would say, "How about some lures?" or, "Bet you guys could use the grinding wheel," or, "The nuts and bolts will come in handy."

"We want pa's stuff," replied Jim.

As the pile grew along the edges of the dock, Nicole thought she needed a sign. She walked up the ramp to the store, found a piece of cardboard, and painted the words, "Help Yourself."

At the end of the second day of dunging out, no one had expressed interest in Sebastian's estate. Calvin, whom she hadn't seen in weeks, had walked by, made a quick survey, and headed home. When Sylvia had arrived to collect her mail, wearing her witch's uniform – black hat, black coat, black trousers, and black pocked boots – Nicole said, "You need boots. What about Seb's boots?"

"My boots are fine," Sylvia had answered, and continued on to the store.

Nicole remembered that, not long ago, her community would have coveted this dispersal of inventory.

On the third morning, she sent Brad in his rowboat to get Carver from MacLeod's marine ways. When they arrived back at the government dock, she told them to transport the junk to Squirrel Cove with the *Oystercatcher*. They made seven trips, while Nicole and Jim spent the afternoon dunging out the rest of Seb's floathouse.

"Okay Jim, if I say 'saltchuck,' you throw the thing I give you into the saltchuck. And if I say 'freight shed,' you put the thing in the freight shed."

"O K," said Jim.

"And if you want anything for yourself, make your own pile."

"I want pa's stuff."

"Let's start with the moonsnails. Saltchuck. Use this box because Seb had tons."

"We got a snail box too," said Jim.

Jim filled nine box loads and dumped them into the ocean.

Next she started on body parts, including skulls and femurs of birds, rodents, and fish skeletons – mostly red snappers. "Saltchuck." He dumped eleven box loads. She found his zither. "Freight shed." She found an old tape deck and tapes with his renditions of favourite songs: *Freight Train, Some Enchanted Evening, Gaudeamus igitur, Blue, Old Blue, You Good Dog You, You are Young and Beautiful,* and so on. The batteries still had a charge, so Nicole played the recordings as they worked. On her memo pad, she wrote, "Seb's tapes for music." She found his handicrafts. Seashell earrings and salt crystal sculptures created through his evaporation, non-patented-saltwater-drip method. To Nicole, the saline sculptures looked like contorted and fused bodies, in some cases not human, more like bizarre, rutting beasts. "Freight shed." Often the memory of Sebastian and De Gaulle splattered on the rocks at the entrance to Homfray Channel hindered her focus. She had never before seen a bird's wings and feathers detach in free fall. Another memory disturbed her too: the five eagles that had descended from the sky, presumably to arrest Sebastian's flight. "Earrings and sculptures," she wrote on the memento list.

The birdman had stored oodles of feathers in cardboard boxes, not just eagle feathers. She thought back to Charlotte, holding vigil with Sebastian near the gas dock, telling the summer boaters, "If he holds the feather, he can't lie." Nicole kept the more outstanding feathers. "Freight shed." She planned to encourage everyone to take one and recall their memories. She wrote, "Speak with feathers."

They discovered an entire corner piled with used cedar shakes. "We'll use these for the final conflagration, Jim."

By his look, she knew that he didn't understand the meaning

of "conflagration."

"Fire, Jim. Fire. The shakes will be kindling."

"Like fire lots," replied Jim.

Under the pile of cedar shakes Jim and Nicole discovered two enormous cedar carvings– a head and a hand. She thought the head – six feet tall, similar to an Easter Island stone image, with huge brow, large nose and ears, a sad but knowing face with long hair-like strips of cedar bark, the braids twisted, crinkled and dangling – would make a perfect sentinel guarding the entrance to The Refuge. Now excited, she wrote, "Install head carving on Centre Island visible to all boat traffic." She knew just the spot on the shelving rocks near the outer tip of the island. The hand, cut off just below the elbow, featured bulging veins, fingers with inlaid shell fingernails, finely carved fingerprints and palm lines. She visualized the hand struggling out of the earth beside the head. (*Adam just interrupted again, "No, not struggling, but pushing triumphantly through solid rock."*)

Nicole considered the effect nature would have on the sculptures. Mosses and lichen would grow on the carvings, wind would weather the features smooth, the sun would bleach the dark skin, and sea spray slowly pickle his creations.

"We'll leave the carvings here for now. Not saltchuck and not freight shed. Okay, Jim?"

"O K."

A few begonia and fuchsia plants showed signs of life. She couldn't tell if they were "rains" or "run-offs." Nicole had no hope they would ever bloom. She wrote, "alter, begonias."

James walked by on his way to the gas dock.

"Get rid of the *Redonda Rocket* and the *Ark*. Same for the *Oystercatcher*. I don't care who gets the money."

"What ever you say," replied James.

Jim found a journal, and came running from Seb's house to show Nicole. "I foun tori book."

She took the journal and said, "I don't think it's a story book, Jim…but you never know."

"Like pa's tori book." He pulled his father's logbook from his back pocket to show Nicole.

That evening, Nicole took Sebastian's journal home, and while the children and James watched the television, she sat at the dinner table and thumbed through the pages discovering the interests and complexities of Seb's mind. The text grew less comprehensible as the years had passed. The very existence of the journal had come as a surprise. For a bookmark, she used the impenetrable letter Seb had given her the day he tried to fly. She had reread the letter many times since he attempted flight, and still couldn't make sense of it. She had hoped that by studying the patterns and peculiarities of his word-making in the journal, then she might unlock the mysteries in the letter. Her main conclusion, though preliminary, was that he intended the message (if that's what it was) for the community, not her alone. Maybe the world?

LIFE NUMBER three.

The following afternoon, Nicole turned her attention to Alice. She thought Alice's house would take the longest, but it didn't. Perhaps she felt exhausted and wanted the wake to be over and done with. She decided no one would get the TV, fantasizing that all televisions in the world should be detonated. She wrote, "Destroy TV after wake." Then she wrote, "James – generator – get rid of." She found a case of liquorice allsorts and wrote "allsorts" under the food column for the menu plans. She found old picture albums for people to thumb through during the service and wrote, "photo albums." Nicole took two pictures as keepsakes – Alice in her younger years reeling in a salmon and Alice in later years sinking into her chair. Remembering Tara's affection for the old woman, Nicole dug up the bleeding heart and transplanted it into a pot. Following dinner, she gave the gift to her daughter. Tara sobbed a moment and then went back to the television.

That night Nicole dreamed that Sebastian and Alice's homes were tied together and anchored off Centre Island, ablaze. She now envisioned the fire as a grand inferno lighting up the entire northern section of the Strait of Georgia.

Remembering that Jeremy had left behind a cedar log float, which he had promised to remove and hadn't, Nicole instructed James: "Organize Heinrik, Peter, Calvin, Carver, and Brad and Jim. I don't care how many it takes, just cut back the ivy, kick out the support timbers, lower the house at a high tide, and drag it onto Jeremy's float."

"We'll have to ask Jeremy."

"James, he'll never come back for that worm-eaten float."

"That's a big job."

"Just do it."

"What will you do with the house?"

"We'll burn both houses in the middle of the bay."

"You'll need a permit."

"We want a *huge* fire. I'll get the permit," she said.

James and the others tore into Alice's house next day. At the high tide, Peter positioned the log float in front of her home and tied it to shore. Jim and Brad used James' wrecking bars to remove the boardwalk attached to the shore side of house. Calvin cut away the ivy. James and Carver brought over the old haul-out winch from MacLeod's marine ways. Calvin monkeyed with the Lister diesel and managed to get it to fire after only ten minutes of hand cranking. They slid three skid logs under the house and used Gilchrest jacks to lower it onto the logs. At the highest tide in the series, the winch pulled the building onto the raft. Peter towed it around to the government dock and tied the two structures together. The crew made quick work of the non-burnables, loading them into two boats, and soon Cortes Island had more treasures to fight over.

From the porch of her home on the cliff above the store, Nicole looked down on the derelict domiciles of the dead and the inhabited buildings around The Refuge, all in a similar condition. She saw rotting boardwalks and broken handrails, the government dock piled with clutter, and a motley assortment of boats tied with pieces of string. The rat-infested freight shed's roof sagged at the peak, and Wade's basketball hoop hung askew. Everywhere, she saw peeling paint, private docks sinking, and their ramps to the shore unattached, projects unfinished, skeletons of buildings, skeletons of boats, piles of lumber creeping back into the forest, firewood left to the rain, and any catchall a graveyard for motors, cables, and rusted barrels. Her tunnel vision overlooked the grandeur of the trees and the splendour of the sea. Nicole remembered that when she had first arrived at The Refuge, she felt a huge urge to tidy the entire place, but as the years had worn away, the tidying no longer seemed like a priority.

She made an effort to understand her unhappiness. Since moving to The Refuge, Nicole had put others first, suppressing her creative self to the extent that now Nature tied her in knots. Every patch of moss and every sunset intimidated her.

Nicole remembered the City of Victoria, her parent's home of manicured garden beds and weedless lawns, and the heritage houses on her street. She recalled the clean avenues, always a parking space, whole streets in bloom with ornamental cherry trees, shrubs in a blaze of colour even in January, piles of leaves lining the boulevards in the fall, fallen chestnuts on the sidewalks, transplanted British heritage, the wax museum, teas at the Empress Hotel, second-hand accents, lawn bowling, and horses clip-clopping tourists in carriages around the Parliament Buildings and along the quay of the inner harbour. *(Adam desires to include the following statement: "Never was the need for a spiritual Renaissance greater.")*

THE MEMORIAL day arrived, November 30, 1975. A nor'wester blew. The early fog lifted and the sky cleared. Already making last minute arrangements on the dock, Nicole noticed eagles soaring and boats arriving with friends of the deceased. The Rutabaga Family from Galley Bay came in their pirate ship and brought turnips for the potluck. The *Tom Forge* came from Lewis Channel with a crowd of loggers, Maddie, and Jake. Most loggers carried a hip flask of rye, and Maddie carried a large platter of leftover pancakes, turned into jelly and peanut butter sandwiches. Nicole pointed, and said, "Maddie, the potluck table is over there." Nicole thought Jake looked pissed off. The *L.O. Larson* unhitched a tow of logs behind Kinghorn Island and then moored at the gas dock. The crew fed the dogs wieners while they waited for the festivities to begin. A Forestry vessel arrived. Peter, under their supervision, had been charged with the burning of the buildings. The remaining children in The Refuge, Wade, Tara, and Charlotte, boarded the vessel to visit with the captain, who let them play with his pet monkey. Oyster farmers came from Malaspina, Theodosia, and Okeover carrying buckets of oysters. Clam diggers came from Lund and Savary Island with sacks of clams slung over their shoulders. The coast guard crew from the *Racer* motored into the bay and tied alongside the *L.O. Larson*. The crews knew each other, sat on the gunnels, and quietly visited. Friends arrived from Cortes Island with kale salads and a fresh side of venison. Peter's gang from the Klahoose village brought chum salmon, smoked and cooked in the traditional way on open fires. Jeremy motored up from Powell River in his *Storm Chaser*. Nicole told him that they had commandeered his log float. "It's a piece of shit," he said, "don't worry about it." He did not seem his exuberant self, and Nicole attributed his aloofness to his loss of friends. The Smith's, with the twins, Mary and Elizabeth, boated over from Campbell River, and on the way, had picked up the Black's, with Sarah, from their new home on Cortes Island. When Nicole greeted Jack Smith, she expected to hear one of his tasteless, off-colour jokes, but he greeted her with a warm hug. She encouraged the girls to visit with Tara and Charlotte, "Go see your friends," but they stuck close to their parents.

Blackie landed the seaplane, and Nicole instructed James, "Go help Blackie tie up." The locals showed, one by one, in the country potluck fashion carrying food and beverages: mushrooms from Sylvia, scallops from Peter, homemade sake from Calvin, and two cases of cream soda from Brad and Jim. Nicole had specified that Carver supply snappers and lingcod only, and in his dependable way, delivered a boatload. While the guests arrived, the newcomer set up a cleaning table and filleted the snappers and cod, cutting the fillets into sections and taking extra care to remove the small bones with tweezers. Heinrik brought his commercial deep fryer down from the Burger Palace as well as four buckets of peeled potatoes sliced into French fry portions for the grand feast of fish and chips, planned for later in the afternoon.

Nicole had mentally rehearsed the ceremony program many times during the past weeks. The wake would begin on the dock and end on the dock. She had gathered props, assigned actors, and written a script with stage directions. The diligent woman supplied chairs and boxes for seating, tables for food and beverages, and plates, glasses, and cutlery. She has planned an informal inspection of the structures, where Sylvia has set up alters for the ashes. Nicole has provided a separate table for memorabilia and would invite people to take away mementos. She had asked Wade to take charge of Seb's tape recorder, and now heard, *You are Young and Beautiful,* playing softly in the background.

Nicole has double-checked that all vessels for transporting guests had adequate lifejackets aboard. Peter and James would tow the structures to the middle of the bay and anchor them. Then they would move on to Centre Island and install Sebastian's head and hand carvings. Nicole intended to pour the ashes into the sea at Hope Point, where she would invite people to remember the deceased with fond memories and humourous anecdotes. She would give everyone a feather and a Book of Knowledge, if there were enough to go around. They would have a final toast to the deceased with Heinrik's parent's happy juice.

After the speeches by mourners, she would read Sebastian's letter. She had worked out a translation, and thought it close to being accurate. His slide over the years into incomprehension had not opened doors to a meaningful understanding, although she had noticed a pattern, if you will, a trail for interpretation. During her spare moments, over the past weeks, she had frequently studied the journal and letter, in particular, the last line in the letter, "wat kds pr kdlss y lwt haepn nt grrntd wat is 2 kdsss." The mangled word, "kds," with its variants of plurals, "kdlss" and "kdlsss," appeared to mean "children." The word, "wat" meant "what," and "haepn" meant "happened," and "y" meant "why," and "pr" meant "poor." She was still unsure about "grrntd." She had puzzled over "nt," at first thinking it meant, "not," but in his frightful scribbles the "n" could have been a "c." In any case, as she had suspected from the start, his letter appeared to present an ecological message, which would set the tone for the day, situate the event into a greater context, and put a positive spin where there had been none before. Nicole felt certain that Sebastian had worried over the welfare of future generations, in fact all of humankind, especially children.

At the end of the service, as Nicole has planned, they would return to the government dock to watch the conflagration light the skies for another wild night at The Refuge. They would feast on food and drink, and, as tongues loosened, share more memories. At that point, she would step into the background and let the event become whatever it wanted – a wake in the traditional sense. It could go on for days for all she cared. She might even have her own fling at the mystifying emotions of sorrow and grief. And then, at the end of the end, some would head off for new lives and new destinations, while others might stay. As far as Nicole was concerned, the land and sea could reclaim its past. *(Adam interjects once again and I will let his exuberance shine, "Shouts, drums, dance, dance, dance, dance!")*

None of this happened.

NICOLE SIGNALLED Wade, standing under the basketball hoop with Carver. "Music please sweetie...softly." Sebastian's rendition of *Gaudeamus igitur* started up. She rejoiced when she saw flocks of seagulls, crows, ducks, herons, and ravens flying helter-skelter above the bay, as though they had received an invitation too. The solitary white raven perched on the peak of Alice's house.

From the ramp to the store, Nicole looked over the scene and had the impression that everything looked perfect. As she prepared to call the assembly to order, the mourners turned in the direction of Hope Point where they heard the throaty engines of a vessel throttle down. *Persistence* from Campbell River dropped off her plane and sunk to the Plimsoll line. Her aggressive wake crashed against the rocky bluffs. Nicole overheard Jeremy, "Fuck, those guys are going to hit us with a Jesus, big, sternwake."

The vessel slowed and motored into the harbour. Pleased that they had come, Nicole said to everyone, "We'll wait for the RCMP before starting." She hurried down to the freight shed docking area, the only berthing spot available.

The Smith's caught the tie-up lines. Two officers secured the vessel and the other four officers immediately circulated through the crowd. Nicole approached two of them and said, "I'm so glad you came," but they brushed by her.

Carver stood alone under the basketball hoop. Two officers approached the newcomer and asked, "Is your name, Robert Clavell?"

"I am he," said Robert. They began reading him his rights, while Sebastian's tape deck played his zither rendition, *Old Blue, You Good Dog You.*

Robert ran for the ramp to the store, but Heinrik and Sylvia tripped him, and together they kneeled on his chest and stomach as the officers arrived. They handcuffed Robert and led him back to the *Persistence.* Angel and Pemah chewed on Robert Clavell's boot and tore at his pant cuffs. The officers didn't seem to mind. Jim pounded on his back, repeating over and over, "him bad man."

Two officers approached James and asked if they could meet somewhere in private. The officer in charge, Captain Williams, said, "We want the Baxters, Masons, Blacks, and the Smiths to attend the meeting." James decided Sebastian's floathouse would be the best place. They stepped aboard the abandoned aerie. The remaining mourners on the dock were left to circulate rumours among themselves.

Inside Sebastian's floathouse, Captain Williams said, "We

apologize for disturbing your wake and promise not to stay long. We'll return for further interviews and evidence once we have the prisoner in lock-up." He then read from a prepared statement, "Mr. Robert Clavell has been on our wanted list for sometime. He is a known sex offender with many aliases, whose whereabouts was unknown until this past week."

James put his arm around Nicole, but she brushed it away.

"Mr. and Mrs. Liam and Kathleen Black of Campbell River, recently came forward with complaints about the alleged sex offender, but were unwilling to lay charges. At the time, they were unaware that more children than their nine-year-old daughter, Sarah Black, were involved. Our duty today is not only to arrest and charge Mr. Clavell, but to verify the handwriting of Tara Mason in the packet of letters we have brought with us."

An assistant officer produced a bundle of letters, held together with a large elastic band, from Tara Mason addressed to Mr. Bruce Harris on Savary Island. The officer approached Nicole and asked, "Mrs. Mason would you please confirm that your daughter, Tara, wrote these letters?"

Captain Williams intervened, "Mr. Harris forwarded these letters when he became alarmed at their content. It seems that the earlier letters are a friendly correspondence; whereas the last letter in particular, which Mr. Harris received a week ago, included references to all the girls in Refuge Cove. Mrs. Mason, your daughter has written specific details."

He handed Nicole the top letter from the packet and said, "We only need you to verify the handwriting as belonging to your daughter."

Nicole quickly looked at the letter and handed it back to the officer. "That's my daughter's handwriting."

He took back the letter, and she said, "I want to see the last letter."

"Mrs. Mason, we only require that you verify the handwriting."

"Well, I require that you give me the last fucking letter."

Nicole slapped the bundle of letters, and they fell to the floor. Nicole quickly extracted the last letter from the bottom of the pile and began reading. She bit her knuckle to contain the pain. James read over Nicole's shoulder, the straight forward and honest account in the handwriting of his daughter, describing events, which, at some remote depth within his being, he now felt he had already known, yet had never been able to bring that knowledge to light. While he read, he reflected bitterly and shamefully that it took his child, and all the children, to put an end to the blindness of the adults.

Words raced by Nicole and James like bats spooked from a cave.

"He did the twins together."

"He put quarters in us for pay."

"He wouldn't let us tell the mothers and fathers."

"The touching was everywhere."

"He said we must never tell." *(Here Adam wishes that we not dwell on the graphics.)*

The Baxters wept. The Blacks wept.

Laura volunteered that she knew Tara's handwriting too, as she was her teacher. Laura and Peter read the last letter and together they shared the agony of revelation. In retrospect, they also realized that the truth had always been there, as now the shape of inconsistencies surprisingly took a form.

The Captain consoled the parents by saying that, for the time being, it was only necessary to confirm the handwriting. Statements and more evidence would be collected later.

Thoughts raced through Nicole's mind: Dreams are blinding… Alice did not understand…Sebastian understood…MacLeod did not understand. Finally, the mother wondered, Who else knew?

Captain Williams said, "Later, we can provide counselling services."

Nicole said, "Later! There will never be later, only now and now and now!" James tried to comfort her, but she refused to allow it.

She crumpled Sebastian's letter and threw it at the officer. "Here's more evidence."

A silent crowd of mourners watched *Persistence* motor out of the bay. Billows of steam rose from her stern exhausts. The newcomer to The Refuge embarked on his new journey. Words rippled through the crowd, and mourners returned to their homes by water and some over land.

(Corrections: 17. 6 – 10)

> And the guilt of James was great for he had a dream that he offered up his daughter, who had not known a man, and he had invited the man of Sodom, to do with her as he pleased, but only that he should leave his heavenly guests alone, and he did have the audacity in his dream to beg him not to act so wickedly. He, who begged him not to act so wickedly, who envisioned a trade of one choir of angel for another, who had spake in a dream without thought, now he wisheth, for even while he wakes, the guilt is with him, that he could trade that one guilt for another, that he could indulge that other second guilt though it be fictitious, whatever it might be, and he would be willing to endure the second guilt much longer, and even give this lesser guilt over to future generations, yes, be willing to trade and upgrade the second guilt, accept multiplications of the lesser guilt, live for all time with that guilt, guilt, no matter how increaseth it, never would it compare to the original guilt where he did offer to sacrifice his daughter. All these promises to avoid a remembrance of the thoughtless dream, yet the Lord of Lords would not let this negotiation come to pass, and instead, James carried the one guilt for it would always be the greater. He thought and felt these things, though but from a dream.

Acknowledgements

Firstly, a debt of gratitude to Rex Weyler, my good friend, unflinching activist, Go partner, "scribbler guy," and meticulous editor.

To Carol Tidler, wholehearted thanks for your scrupulous and insightful observations on every draft.

To my manuscript readers, Ian Ross, Christian Gronau, Aileen Douglas, and Marne Andrews, for your thoughtful comments and encouragement.

To Priya Huffman, Rex Weyler and Ruth Ozeki for your testiment to the merits in this novel.

To Filipe Figueira for your masterful interior and cover design.

To Lisa Gibbons, my wonderful daughter, for your stellar artwork.

Lastly, my endless love to Denise.

Note on Sources

1. Chapter One – Subterfuge: "I have always been of an inferior race." From **Arthur Rimbaud,** *A Season in Hell and The Drunken Boat,* translation by Louise Varese, New Directions, 1961. Page 9.

2. Chapter Seven – Devotees to a Scripted Life: Title from the poem *Geese* in the collection, *The Territory Home* by **Priya Huffman,** RiverstoneArtsPress, 2014. Page 36.

3. Chapter Seven – Devotees to a Scripted Life: White raven references taken from, *Two Wolves at the Dawn of Time,* Kingcome Inlet Pictographs, 1893-1998 by **Judith Williams,** New Star Books, 2001. Page 147.

4. Chapter Seven – Devotees to a Scripted Life: Technical information regarding death by drowning from **Sebastian Junger,** *The Perfect Storm,* W.W. Norton & Co. 1997.

5. Chapter Thirteen – Hot Tub: Technical information regarding rock pots from **Dorothy Kennedy** and **Randy Bouchard,** *Sliammon Life, Sliammon Lands,* Talon Books, 1983.

6. Chapter Sixteen – The Unread Word: The story of *Tl'umnachm* from **Dorothy Kennedy** and **Randy Bouchard,** *Sliammon Life, Sliammon Lands,* Talon Books, 1983.

7. Chapter Twenty-Two– In the Dim Coming Times: Chapter title from **William Butler Yeats,** *To Ireland in the Coming Times.*

8. Chapter Twenty-Two – In the Dim Coming Times: "This testing by the real exceeded his capacities, that he failed, even though in his mind he was so convinced of the need for this testing that he instinctively sought it out until it embraced him and clung to him and never left him again." From **Rainer Maria Rilke,** *Letters on Cezanne,* Douglas & McIntyre Ltd., 2002. Page 60.

9. Chapter Twenty-Two – In the Dim Coming Times: "…as the dying light flickered all around," Adapted from the lyrics of *Fallen Warriors,* CD album, **Rex Weyler,** *Catch the Light.*

ABOUT THE AUTHOR

Photo by Darshan Stevens

NORM GIBBONS has lived in the Desolation Sound region for the past forty-five years. He has a background in social work, shellfish aquaculture and business. He studied Creative Writing at the University of Victoria, British Columbia. Presently he is retired and lives on Cortes Island, where he continues to write the *Edge of Desolation* trilogy.